DANGEROUS PLAYTHINGS

"Then it must figure," Lisa pointed out, "that the people of Earth and the people of Tirol *did* have a common ancestry."

"I no longer believe that to be so," said Exedore. "A coincidence, I'm afraid."

Rick's eyebrows went up. "A coincidence?! But Exedore, the odds on that have to be nothing less than . . . ah—"

"Astronomical," Lisa finished.

Gloval snorted. "And the odds against our co-existing together? . . . They may be even greater."

"So the truth is," Exedore concluded, "that although our races are similar, they are not identical. My race, the Zentraedi, was Protoculturally devoid of everything save the biogenetically-engineered desire to fight. We were nothing but *toys* to our creators—*toys of destruction.*"

The ROBOTECH™ Series
Published by Ballantine Books:

GENESIS #1

BATTLE CRY #2

HOMECOMING #3

BATTLEHYMN #4

FORCE OF ARMS #5

DOOMSDAY #6

ROBOTECH™ #6:

DOOMSDAY

Jack McKinney

A Del Rey Book

BALLANTINE BOOKS • NEW YORK

A Del Rey Book
Published by Ballantine Books

 Published in the United States of America by Ballantine Books, a division of Random House, Inc., New York, and simultaneously in Canada by Random House of Canada Limited, Toronto.

Library of Congress Catalog Card Number: 86-92038

ISBN 0-345-34139-2

Manufactured in the United States of America

First Edition: June 1987

Cover Art by David Schleinkofer

FOR SHOJI KAWAMORI AND THE '80s GANG AT STUDIO NUE; HARUHIKO MIKIMOTO; IPPEI KURI AND KENJI YOSHIDA OF TATSUNOKO: ROBOTECH MASTERS THE LOT OF THEM—ALTHOUGH THEY DIDN'T REALIZE IT AT THE TIME.

CHAPTER ONE

Had the Robotech Masters the power to travel as freely through time as they did space, perhaps they would have understood the inevitabilities *they were up against: Zor's tampering with the Invid Flower was a crime akin to Adam's acceptance of the apple. Once released, Protoculture had its own destiny to fulfill. Protoculture was a different—and in some ways* antithetical—*order of life.*

Professor Lazlo Zand, as quoted in *History of the Second Robotech War*, Vol. CXXII

THE DIMENSION OF MIND... THE RAPTURE TO BE *found at that singular interface between object and essence ... the power to reshape and reconfigure:* to transform...

Six hands—the sensor extensions of slendor atrophied arms—were pressed reverently to the surface of the mushroomlike Protoculture cap, the Masters' material interface. Long slender fingers with no nails to impede receptivity. Three minds... *joined as one.*

Until the terminator's entry disturbed their conversation.

Offering salute to the Masters, it announced:

—Our routine scan of the Fourth Quadrant indicates a large discharge of Protoculture mass in the region where Zor's dimensional fortress defolded.

The three Masters broke off their contact with the Elders and turned to the source of the intrusion, liquid eyes peering out from ancient, ax-keen faces. Continual contact with Protoculture had eliminated physical differences, so all three appeared to have the same features: the same hawkish nose, the flaring eyebrows, shoulder-length blue-gray hair, and muttonchop sideburns.

—So!—responded the red-cowled Master, though his lips did not move—Two possibilities present themselves: Either the Zentraedi have liberated the hidden Protoculture matrix from Zor's disciples and commenced a new offensive against the Invid, or these Earthlings have beaten us to the prize and now control the production of the Protoculture.

There was something monkish about them, an image enhanced by those long gray robes, the cowls of which resembled nothing so much as outsize petals of the Invid Flower of Life. Each monkish head seemed to have grown stamenlike from the Protoculture flower itself.

—I believe that is highly unlikely—the green-cowled Master countered telepathically—All logic circuits based on available recon reports suggest that the Invid have no knowledge of the whereabouts of Zor's dimensional fortress.

—So! Then we must assume that the Zentraedi have indeed found the Protoculture matrix, ensuring a future for our Robotechnology.

—But only if they were able to capture the ship intact...

The organic systems of the Masters' deep-space fortress began to mirror their sudden concern; energy fluctuations commenced within the Protoculture cap, throwing patterned colors against all but breathing bulkheads and supports. What would have been the bridge of an ordinary ship was here gven over to the unharnessed urgings of Protoculture, so that it approximated a living neural plexus of ganglia, axons, and dendrites.

Unlike the Zentraedi dreadnoughts, these spadelike Robotech fortresses the size of planetoids were designed for a different campaign: the conquest of inner space, which, it was revealed, had its own worlds and star systems, black holes and white light, beauty and terrors. Protoculture had secured an entry, but the Masters' map of that realm was far from complete.

—My only fear is that Zor's disciples may have mastered the inner secrets of Robotechnology and were then able to defeat Dolza's vast armada.

—One ship against four million? Most unlikely—nearly impossible!

—Unless they managed to invert the Robotech defensive barrier system and penetrate Dolza's command center...

—In order to accomplish that, Zor's disciples would have to know as much about that Robotech ship as he himself knew!

—In any event, a display of such magnitude would certainly have registered on our sensors. We must admit, the destruction of four million Robotech vessels doesn't happen every day.

—Not without our knowing it.

The terminator, which had waited patiently to deliver the rest of its message, now added:

—That is quite true, Master. Nevertheless, our sensors *do* indicate a disturbance of that magnitude.

The interior of the Protoculture cap, the size of a small bush on its three-legged pedestal base, took on an angry light, summoning back the hands of the Masters.

—System alert: prepare at once for a hyperspace-fold!

—We acknowledge the Elders' request, but our supply of Protoculture is extremely low. We may not be able to use the fold generators!

—The order has been given—obey without question. We will fold immediately.

High in those cathedrals of arcing axon and dendrite-like cables, free-floating amorphous globules of Protoculture mass began to realign themselves along the ship's neural highways, permitting synaptic action where none had existed moments before. Energy rippled through the fortress, focusing on the columnar drives of massive reflex engines.

The great Robotech vessel gave a shudder and jumped.

Their homeworld was called Tirol, the primary moon of the giant planet Fantoma, itself one of seven lifeless wanderers in an otherwise undistinguished yellow-star system of the Fourth Quadrant, some twenty light-years out from the galactic core. Prior to the First Robotech War, Terran astronomers would have located Tirol in that sector of space then referred to as the Southern Cross. But they had learned since that that was merely *their* way of looking at things. By the end of the second millennium they had abandoned the last vestiges of geocentric thinking, and by A.D. 2012 had come to understand that their beloved planet was little more than a minor player in constellations entirely unknown to them.

Little was known of the early history of Tirol, save that its inhabitants were a humanoid species—bold, inquisitive, daring—and, in the final analysis, aggressive, acquisitive, and self-destructive. Coincidental with the abolition of warfare among their own kind and the redirecting of their goals toward the exploration of local space, there was born into their midst a being who would alter the destiny of that planet and to some extent affect the fate of the galaxy itself.

His name was Zor.

And the planet that would become the coconspirator in that fateful unfolding of events was known to the techno-voyagers of Tirol as Optera. For it was there that Zor would witness the evolutionary rites of the planet's indigenous life form, the Invid; there that the visionary scientist would seduce the Invid Regis to learn the secrets of the strange tripetaled flower that they ingested for physical as well as spiritual nourishment; there that the galactic feud between Optera and Tirol would have its roots.

There that Protoculture and Robotechnology were born.

Through experimentation, Zor discovered that a curious form of organic energy could be derived from the flower when its gestating seed was contained in a matrix that prevented maturation. The bio-energy resulting from this organic fusion was powerful enough to induce a semblance of bio-will, or *animation*, in essentially inorganic systems. Machines could be made to alter their very shape and structure in response to the prompting of an artificial intelligence or a human operator—to transform and reconfigure themselves. Applied to the areas of eugenics and cybernetics, the effects were even more astounding: Zor found that the shape-changing properties of Protoculture could act on organic life as well—living tissue and physiological systems could be rendered malleable. Robotechnology, as he came to call this science, could be used to fashion a race of humanoid clones, massive enough to withstand Fantoma's enormous gravitational forces and to mine the ores there. When these ores were converted to fuel and used in conjunction with Protoculture drives (by then called reflex drives), Tirol's techno-voyagers would be able to undertake hyperspace jumps to remote areas of the galaxy. *Protoculture effectively reshaped the very fabric of the continuum!*

Zor had begun to envision a new order, not only for his own race but for all those sentient life forms centuries of voyaging had revealed. He envisioned a true mating of mind and matter, an era of *clean* energy and unprecedented peace, a reshaped universe of limitless possibilities.

But the instincts that govern aggression die a slow death, and those same leaders who had brought peace to Tirol soon embarked on a course that ultimately brought warfare to the stars. Co-opted, Robotechnology and Protoculture fueled the megalomaniacal militaristic dreams of its new masters, whose first act was to decree that *all* of Optera's fertile seedpods be gathered and transported to Tirol.

The order was then issued that Optera be defoliated.

The bio-genetically created giants who mined Fantoma's wastes were to become the most fearful race of warriors the quadrant had ever known—the *Zentraedi.*

Engrammed with a false past (replete with artificial racial memories and an equally counterfeit history), programmed to accept Tirol's word as law, and equipped with an armada of gargantuan warships the likes of which only Robotechnology could provide, they were set loose to conquer and destroy, *to fulfill their imperative:* to forge and secure an intergalactic empire ruled by a governing body of barbarians who were calling themselves the Robotech Masters.

Zor, however, had commenced a subtle rebellion; though forced to do the bidding of his misguided Masters, he had been careful to keep the secrets of the Protoculture process to himself. He acted the part of the servile deferential pawn the Masters perceived him to be, all the while manipulating them into allowing him to fashion a starship of his own design—for further galactic exploration, to be sure—a sleek transformable craft, a super dimensional fortress that would embody the science of Robotechnology much as the Zentraedi's organic battlewagons embodied the lusts of war.

Unbeknown to the Masters, concealed among the reflex furnaces that powered its hyperspace drives, the fortress would also contain the very essence of Robotechnology—a veritable Protoculture factory, the only one of its kind in the known universe, capable of seducing from the Invid Flower of Life a harnessable bioenergy.

By galactic standards it wasn't long before some of the horrors the Masters' greed had spawned came home to roost. War with the divested Invid was soon a reality, and there were incidents of open rebellion among the ranks of the Zentraedi, that pathetic race of beings deprived by the Masters of the very essence of sentient life—the ability to feel, to grow, to experience beauty and love.

Nevertheless, Zor ventured forth in the hopes of redressing some of the injustices his own discoveries had fostered. Under the watchful gaze of Dolza, commander in chief of the Zentraedi, the dimensional fortress embarked on a mission to discover new worlds ripe for conquest.

So the Masters were led to believe.

What Zor actually had in mind was the seeding of planets with the Invid flower. Dolza and his lieutenants, Breetai and the rest, easily duped into believing that he was carrying out orders from the Masters themselves, were along as much to secure Zor's safety as to ensure the Master's investment. The inability to comprehend or effect repairs on any Robotech device and to stand in awe of those who could was programmed into the Zentraedi as a handicap to guard against a possible grand-scale warrior rebellion. The Zentraedi had about as much understanding of the workings of Robotechnology as they did of their humanoid hearts.

So, on Spheris, Garuda, Haydon IV, Peryton, and numerous other planets, Zor worked with unprecedented urgency to fulfill *his* imperative. The Invid were always one step behind him, their sensor nebulae alert to even minute traces of Protoculture, their Inorganics left behind on those very same worlds to conquer, occupy, and destroy. But no matter: In each instance the seedlings failed to take root.

It was at some point during this voyage that Zor himself began to use the Flowers of Life in a new way, ingesting them as he had seen the Invid do so long ago on Optera. And it was during this time that he began to experience the vision that was to direct him along a new course of action. It seemed inevitable that the Invid would catch up with him long before suitable planets could be sought out and seeded, but his visions had revealed to him a world far removed from that warring sector of the universe where Robotech Masters, Zentraedi, and Invid vied for control. A world of beings intelligent enough to recognize the full potential of his discovery—*a blue-white world, infinitely beautiful, blessed with the treasure that was life . . . at the crux of transcendent events, the crossroads and deciding place of a conflict that would rage across the galaxies.*

A world he was destined to visit.

Well aware of the danger the Invid presented, Zor programmed the continuum coordinates of this planet into the astrogational computers of the dimensional fortress. He likewise programmed some of the ship's Robotech devices to play a part in leading the new trustees of his discovery to a special warning message his own likeness would deliver to them. Further, he enlisted the aid of several Zentraedi (whose heartless conditioning he managed to override by exposing them to music) to carry out the mission.

The Invid caught up with Zor.

But not before the dimensional fortress had been successfully launched and sent on its way.

To Earth.

Subsequent events—notably the Zentraedi pursuit of the fortress—were as much a part of Earth's history as they were of Tirol's, but there were chapters yet to unfold, transformations and reconfigurations, repercussions impossible to predict, events that would have surprised Zor himself . . . had he lived.

"*Farewell, Zor,*" Dolza had said when the lifeless body of the scientist was sent on its way to Tirol. "*May you serve the Masters better in death than you did in life.*"

And indeed, the Robotech Masters had labored to make that so, having their way with Zor's remains, extracting from his still-functional neural reservoir an image of the blue-white world he had selected to inherit Robotechnology. But beyond that Zor's mind had proved as impenetrable in death as it had been in life. So while Dolza's Zentraedi scoured the quadrant in search of this "Earth," the Masters had little to do but hold fast to the mushroom-shaped sensor units that had come to represent their link to the real world. Desperately, they tried to knit together the unraveling threads of their once-great empire.

For ten long years by Earth reckoning they waited for some encouraging news from Dolza. It was the blink of an eye to the massive Zentraedi, but for the Robotech Masters, who were essentially human in spite of their psychically evolved state, time moved with sometimes agonizing leadenness. Those ten years saw the further decline of their civilization, weakened as it was by internal decadence, the continual attacks by the Protoculture-hungry Invid, a growing rebellion at the fringes of their empire, and heightened disaffection among the ranks of the Zentraedi, who were beginning to recognize the Masters for the fallible beings they were.

Robotechnology's inheritors had been located—"Zor's descendants," as they were being called—but two more years would pass before Dolza's armada made a decisive move to recapture the dimensional fortress and its much-needed Protoculture matrix. There was growing concern, especially among the Elder Masters, that Dolza could no longer be trusted. From the start he seemed to harbor some plan of his own, reluctant to return Zor's body twelve years ago and now incommunicado while he moved against the possessors of Zor's fortress. With his armada of more than four million Robotech ships, the Zentraedi commander in chief stood to gain the most by securing the Protoculture matrix for himself.

There was added reason for concern when it was learned that "Zor's descendants" were humanoid like the Masters themselves. The warrior race literally looked down on anything smaller than itself and had come to think of normally proportioned humanoids as "Micronians"—ironic, given the fact that the Masters could have "sized" the Zentraedi to any dimension they wished. Their present size was in fact an illusion of sorts: Beating inside those goliath frames were hearts made from the same genetic stuff as the so-called Micronians they so despised. Because of that basic genetic similarity, the Robotech Masters had been careful to write warnings into the Zentraedi's pseudo-historical records to avoid prolonged contact with any Micronian societies. Rightly so: It was feared that such exposure to emotive life might very well rekindle real memories of the Zentraedi's bio-genetic past and the true stuff of their existence.

According to reports received from Commander Reno (who had overseen the return of Zor's body to Tirol and whose fleet still patrolled the central region of the empire), some of the elements under Breetai's command had mutinied. Dolza, if Reno's report was to be believed, had subsequently elected to fold the entire armada to Earthspace, with designs to annihilate the planet before emotive contagion was spread to the remainder of the fleet.

The Zentraedi might learn to emote, but were they capable of learning to utilize the full powers of Robotechnology?

This was the question the Robotech Masters had put to themselves.

It was soon, however, to become a moot point.

Hyperspace sensor probes attached to a Robotech fortress some seventy-five light-years away from Tirol had detected a massive release of Protoculture matrix in the Fourth Quadrant—an amount capable of empowering over four million ships.

CHAPTER TWO

Throughout the territories we traveled (the southwest portion of what was once the United States of America) one would encounter the holed hulks of Zentraedi warships, rising up like monolithic towers from the irradiated and ravaged wastelands . . . At the base of one such apocalyptic reminder sits the cross-legged skeleton of a Zentraedi shock trooper, almost in a pose of tranquil meditation, still clad in his armor and bandoliers, a Minmei doll insignificant in his huge metalshod hand.

Dr. Lazlo Zand, *On Earth As It Is In Hell: Recollections of the Robotech War*

"THEREFORE, IT IS OUR CONCLUSION, BASED upon the available information, that human and Zentraedi are descended from very nearly the same ancestors!"

Exedore leaned back in the chamber's straight-backed chair to cast a look around the circular table as the weight of his pronouncement sank in. Continued exposure to Earth's sun these past two years had brought out strong mauve tones in his skin and turned his hair an ochre red.

To his immediate right was the somewhat dour-looking Professor Zand, a shadowy figure who had emerged from Lang's Robotech elite; to Zand's right were two Zentraedi, micronized like Exedore and sporting the same blue and white Robotech Defense Forces uniforms. Clockwise around the table to Exedore's left were Claudia Grant, the SDF-2's First Officer—a handsome and intelligent representative of Earth's black race—Commanders Lisa Hayes and Rick Hunter (*Made for each other,* Exedore often said to himself), and Admiral Gloval, serious as ever.

The rich golden warmth of Earth's sun poured into the fortress through two banks of skylights set opposite each other in the conference room's cathedral ceiling.

Exedore had been working side by side with Dr. Emil Lang and several other Earth scientists, deciphering some of the numerous documents Zor had thought to place aboard the SDF-1 over a decade ago. But his announcement of Terran and Zentraedi similarity came as the result of an extensive series of medical tests and evaluations. The distinction *Human* or Zentraedi no longer applied; indeed, it was beginning to look as though there existed—lost somewhere in time—an ancestor race common to both.

Exedore had noticed that the Terrans accepted this with less enthusiasm than might otherwise be expected. Perhaps, he speculated, it was due to the fact that they continued to reproduce in the *natural* way, whereas the Zentraedi had long ago abandoned that unsure method for the certainty of genetic manipulation. In Earthspeak the word was "clone"; the Zentraedi equivalent approximated the English term "being."

New discoveries awaited them in the documents, especially in the latest batch of trans-vids uncovered. Exedore had yet to view these, but there were indications that they would provide answers to questions concerning the historical origins of the Zentraedi race, answers that might shed light on the origins of the Terrans as well. All evidence pointed to an extraterrestrial origin, an issue hotly debated by Earth scientists, most of whom believed that the Human race *evolved* from a tree-dwelling primate species that had roamed the planet millions of years ago.

But if all these protohistorical answers were coming fast, the whereabouts of the Protoculture matrix Zor had built into the ship remained a mystery. Hardly a place had been left uninvestigated by Exedore, Breetai, Lang, and the others; and Zand had even suggested that the Protoculture was *in hiding*!

Responses to Exedore's announcement proved varied: The misshapen, gnomish Zentraedi heard Claudia's sharp intake of breath and Lisa Hayes's "Ah-hah," voiced in a fashion that suggested she had expected no less. Commander Hunter, on the other hand, sat with eyes wide in a kind of fear—the personification of a certain xenophobic mentality that permeated Terran cultures.

Gloval was nodding his head, saying little. His white commander's cap was pulled low on his forehead, so Exedore couldn't read his eyes.

"So, Admiral," Exedore continued, leaning into the table. "There is little doubt—our genetic makeup points directly at a common point of origin."

"That's incredible!" Gloval now exclaimed.

"Isn't it? While examining the data, we noticed many common traits, including a penchant on the part of both races to indulge in warfare."

This brought startled reactions around the Terran side of the table.

"Yes," Exedore said flatly, as if to forestall any arguments before they had a chance to flare up. "Both races seem to *enjoy* making war."

Rick Hunter held his breath, counting to ten. How could the Zentraedi believe his own words, he asked himself, when it was *love* and not war that had doomed the Zentraedi to defeat? The Zentraedi race had started the entire conflict, and Rick nursed a suspicion that this pronouncement of Exedore's was his way of letting himself off the hook.

Exedore seemed to be enjoying his so-called micronized state, and Rick further suspected that this had more to do with a new sense of power the small man had gained than it did with exploring the ship for this Protoculture factory that had yet to turn up. Exedore couldn't bear to admit to himself that his commanders had waged a war for something that didn't even exist; they had nearly brought destruction to both races, chasing after some goose that was supposed to lay golden eggs. Truly, this was the saga that would go down in their history as legend: the pursuit of a ship that supposedly held the secrets of eternal youth, the capture of one hollow to the core.

Rick looked hard into Exedore's lidless pinpoint-pupiled eyes. He didn't like the idea of Exedore poking into every nook and cranny in the fortress, acting as if it was more his property than Earth's. Only a moment ago the Zentraedi had seemed to be sizing him up, well aware of the effect of his words. Rick wasn't about to disappoint him.

"Well, with all due respect," he began acidly, "I disagree. We don't fight because we *like* to—we fight to *defend* ourselves from our enemies. So, under the circumstances we have no choice in the matter. Do you understand?"

Rick's hand was balled up into a fist. Lisa and Claudia looked at him in surprise.

"That's nonsense, Commander," said Professor Zand, who had Dr. Lang's marblelike eyes. He stood up, palms flat on the table, to press his point. "There have always been wars in progress somewhere on Earth, even before the invasion from space. I think this clearly indicates the warlike nature of Humans."

Another Zentraedi sympathizer, thought Rick. And talking like an alien to boot. He began to stammer a response, always feeling outgunned when up against academics, but Zand interrupted him.

"A perfect example: Look what happened on Earth when the *peacemakers* tried their best to prevail. They formed the League of Nations and the United Nations, *both* of which *failed*!"

Rick got to his feet confrontationally. What did all this have to do with Humans *enjoying* war? The best he would allow was that *some* humans enjoyed war but most didn't. Most enjoyed . . . love.

"I can't believe you'd simplify the facts like that," Rick shouted. "You're practically rewriting history!"

"Facts, sir, do not lie," said Zand.

Rick was about to jump over the table and convince the man, but Exedore beat him to the punch, fixing Zand with that unearthly gaze of his and saying:

"We're merely telling you the results of our best data analysis. Please don't interject your opinions."

So when we have something to say, it's an opinion, and when they have something to say, it's a fact, Rick thought, restraining himself.

Gloval cleared his throat meaningfully.

"Fascinating... So we're all descended from the same race, are we? And who can say in what direction all of us are headed. We may never know..."

Rick dropped back into his seat, staring off into space. Whatever happens, he told himself, we mustn't ever allow ourselves to become like the Zentraedi, devoid of emotions—no better than robots. *Never*!

The conference room, scene of Exedore's briefing, was located on level 34 of the new fortress, the so-called SDF-2, which had been under construction for almost as long as the city of New Macross itself. The spacc fortress was a virtual copy of the SDF-1 and currently sat back to back with it, linked to its parent by hundreds of transfer and service corridors, in the center of the circular human-madc lake known now as Gloval, in honor of the admiral. The arid, high plateaus of northwestern North America seemed ideally suited to the reconstruction of the city that had once grown up inside the original super dimensional fortress: The area was cool compared to the background radiation of the devastated coastal corridors, untainted water was plentiful enough, the climate was temperate, and there was no shortage of space. As a result the city had risen swiftly, prospered, and spread out from the lake, a burgeoning forest of skyscrapers, high rises, and prefab suburban dwellings. In the two years since its founding, the population of New Macross had increased tenfold, and its was considered (though not officially recognized as) the Earth's capital city.

New Macross had its share of Zentraedis, though not nearly as many as the cities that had grown up at alien crashpoints throughout the continent—New Detroit and nearby Monument City chief among them. The Zentraedi enjoyed less freedom than the Humans, but this was conceived of as a temporary measure to allow for gradual readjustment and acculturation. Most Zentraedi had opted for micronization, but many retained their original size. However, control of the Protoculture sizing chambers fell under the jurisdiction of the military government, the Robotech Defense Force, alternatively known as the Earth Forces Government. Micronization was encouraged, but the return to full size of a previously micronized Zentraedi was rarely if ever permitted. This had given rise to a separatist movement, spearheaded by Monument City, which advocated the creation of autonomous Zentraedi free states. Critics of these proposals pointed to increasing incidents of Zentraedi uprising as justification for maintaining the status quo. The innate blood lust that had earned the Zentraedi their reputation as fearsome warriors was not always so easily overcome and controlled.

At factories in the industrial sector of New Macross City, humans and aliens worked together toward the forging of a united future. The Zentraedi were fond of work, having had no previous experience with it during their long history of enslavement to war. Manual labor or assembly line, it made no difference to them. Giants hauled enormous cargos of wood and raw materials in from the wastelands, while their micronized brethren worked at benches completing electronic components, adding Protoculture chips to Robotech circuit panels—chips that had been salvaged from the ruined ships that dotted the landscape.

But there was tension in the air on this particular day. Unused to a life without war, some of the aliens were beginning to question the new life they had chosen for themselves.

Utema was one of these. A massively built red-haired Goliath who had served under Breetai, he had worked in New Macross for eighteen months, first assembling steel towers in the Micronian population center, then here, scouring the countryside for usable materials. But on one of these forays, he had stumbled upon an encampment of former warriors who had abandoned the Micronian ways, and ever since he had harbored an anger he could not articulate. An urge to . . . *destroy* something—*anything*!

His eyes had seized on one of the factory trucks parked in the fenced-in yard, a harmless tanker truck used for the transport of fuels. He approached it now and booted it, experiencing a long-lost thrill as the toy vehicle exploded and burst into flames.

Laborers at their work stations inside the factory heard Utema bellow:

"I quit! I can't stand it! I quit! This is stupid!"

The explosion had rekindled his rage. He stood with his fists clenched, looking for something else to demolish, ignoring the protests of his giant coworker. The two had faced off.

"It's worse than stupid—it's degrading!" Utema roared. "I've had enough!"

Violently, he side-kicked a stack of dressed logs, a guttural cry punctuating his swift move.

"Shut up and don't interfere," he warned his companion. "I'm leaving!"

The second giant made no move to stop Utema as he stepped over the chain-link fence and headed off toward the wasteland. Two others had arrived on the scene, but they too let him walk.

"But where are you going?" one of them called out. "Utema—come back! You won't survive out there!"

"It's *you* that won't survive!" Utema shouted back, pointing his finger. "*War!* War is the only thing that will save us!"

At a supper club in Monument City, Minmei, wearing a gauzy blue dress that hung off one shoulder, stood in the spotlight, accepting the applause. It was nowhere near a full house, and, disappointed by the turnout, she hadn't put on her best show. Nevertheless, those few who had been able to afford tickets applauded her wildly, out of respect or politeness, she couldn't be sure. Perhaps because most of her fans rarely knew when her performance was off—she was her own most demanding critic.

The light was a warm, comfortable curtain she was reluctant to leave.

Kyle was waiting for her backstage in the large and virtually unfurnished dressing room, leaning against the wall, arms crossed, looking sullen and angry. He was dressed in jeans and a narrow-waisted jacket with tails. She could tell he'd been drinking and wondered when he would go into his Jekyll and Hyde number again. No doubt he'd caught all her off notes, tempo changes, and missed words.

"Hi," she greeted him apologetically.

"That was terrible," Kyle snapped at her, no beating around the bush tonight. It was going to be a bad evening, perhaps as bad as the night he had kicked a bottle at her.

"Sorry," she told him mechanically, heading straight for the dressing table, seating herself on one of the velour stools, and wiping off makeup.

Kyle remained at the wall.

"I'm worried about that charity concert tomorrow—if it goes like this."

"I'll be okay," she promised him, looking over her shoulder. "There were so few people tonight that I was really taken by surprise. Don't worry, I'll be all right tomorrow."

"This is a high-class club," Kyle persisted. "We let our patrons down."

She sighed. He wasn't going to let go of it. She couldn't do anything right anymore. He was constantly lecturing her and trying to change her behavior.

"I know," she said meekly, sincerely depressed—not for disappointing Kyle but for giving anything less than her all to the audience.

"Well, there's nothing we can do about it now—the damage is done."

She began applying crème to her face. "You could have reduced the admission price a bit, right?"

"Y' get what you can," Kyle said defensively, shaking his fist at her or the world, she didn't know which. He approached her. "And then, don't you forget, my pet—we'll be sharing the dough we earn with all the *poor* people, *right*?"

His scolding voice was full of sarcasm and anger, hinting that she was somehow to blame for his actions: He *had* to charge a lot for the tickets because *she* was the one who insisted on splitting all the profits with the needy. Little did Kyle know that she would gladly have worked for no profit. It just didn't seem right anymore to work for money with so much need, so much sadness and misery, in what was left of everyone's world.

"Then why don't we give *all* the money to charity?" she asked, meeting his glare. "We have enough."

Kyle was down on one knee beside her now, anger still in his eyes but a new tone of conciliation and patience in his voice. He put his hands on her shoulders and looked into her face.

"We have, but not enough to make our dreams come true. You certainly ought to be able to understand *that*!"

"Yeah, but—"

"We promised ourselves we'd build a great concert hall some day and do all our work *there*—right?"

She wanted to remind him that they had made that promise years ago, when such things were possible. A great concert hall now—in the middle of this wasteland, with things just beginning to rebuild and isolated groups of people working the land who never strayed five miles from home? But she just didn't have the energy to argue with him. She could imagine the accusatory tone in his voice: You're *the one who ought to understand about dreams—you had so many*. . .

"Now, get cleaned up," Kyle ordered her, getting to his feet. "After you get dressed, I'll take you out for a good dinner, okay?"

"I'm not very hungry, Kyle," she told him.

He turned on her and exploded.

"We're going to eat anyway! I'll get the car."

The door slammed. She promised herself she wouldn't cry and went to work removing the rest of her makeup, hoping he would mellow somewhat by the time she met him at the stage door. But that didn't happen.

"Come on, get in," he ordered her, throwing open the sports car's passenger door.

She frowned and slid into the leather seat. Kyle accelerated even before she had the door closed, burning out as they left the club. He knew that she hated that almost as much as she hated the car itself—a sleek, dual front-axled all-terrain sports car, always hungry for fuel and symbolizing all that she detested in the old world as much as the new: the idea of privilege, status, the haves and have-nots.

"Where would you like to eat?" Kyle said unpleasantly, throwing the vehicle through the gears.

"Your dad's restaurant. We haven't been there in a long time."

"I don't want to go there."

"Then why do you bother asking me where I want to eat, Kyle? Just let me off and I'll go there myself!"

"Oh?" Kyle started to say, but swallowed the rest when he realized that Minmei had thrown open the door. An oncoming van veered off, narrowly missing them, as Kyle threw the steering wheel hard to the left to fling her back into the vehicle. But he overcorrected coming out of the resultant fishtail and ended up in a swerve that brought him into oncoming traffic. The car went through several more slides before he could safely brake and bring them to a stop on the shoulder. Afterward he leaned onto the steering wheel and exhaled loudly. When he spoke, all of the anger and sarcasm had left him.

"Minmei . . . we could have been killed . . ."

Minmei was not nearly as shaken by the incident, having achieved some purpose.

"I *am* sorry, Kyle. But I'm really going there, even if I have to walk." She opened the door again and started to exit. "Good-bye."

"No, wait." he stopped her. "Get back in the car."

"Why should I?"

"I'll . . . I'll drive you as far as the city line."

She reseated herself and said, "Thank you so much, Kyle."

The doors of the rebuilt White Dragon slid open as Minmei approached just short of closing time. Still the center of the city as it had been on Macross Island and later in the SDF-1, the restaurant was packed even at this late hour.

"Hi! I'm here," she called, cheerful again, the argument with Kyle long behind her now.

Aunt Lena was cleaning up. Tommy Luan, the barrel-chested mayor of Macross, and his fusty wife, Loretta, were having tea.

"Oooh, you're back!" said Lena, a warm smile spreading across her face, the mother Minmei had lost.

"Heyyy!" called the mayor, equally happy to see his long-lost creation.

She greeted Lena with an embrace.

"Welcome back, darling! But shouldn't you be rehearsing for your concert?" Minmei was the daughter Lena had never had as well as a replacement for the son she seemed to have lost.

"Uh huh," Minmei told her and let it drop. "Mr. Mayor, how are you?"

"I'm just fine, Minmei."

"Good seeing you, dear," said his stiff wife. A head taller than her husband, she had a long, almost emaciated face underscored by a prominent chin. She wore her wavy auburn hair pulled back into an unattractive bun and kept the collar of her blouse tightly fastened at the neck by a large blue brooch.

Loretta and Tommy were almost as unlikely a couple as lithesome Lena and squat Max, who was just stepping from the kitchen now, his cooking whites and chef's hat still in place.

"Heyyy, Minmei," he drawled.

"Uncle! . . . Would it be okay with you if I stayed here tonight?"

"Of course it'd be okay! M' girl, you can even have your old room back again."

"Oh, thanks, Uncle Max," Minmei said, suddenly overcome with a feeling of love for all of them, happy to be back in the fold, away from the lights, crowds, attention . . . *Kyle*.

"Isn't that great?" the mayor crowed. "She hasn't changed a bit, even after becoming famous!"

Three male customers had left their table to surround her, wondering what she was doing there, taking advantage of the casual nature of her visit to ask for autographs.

"Success hasn't spoiled our Minmei."

"She's still our little girl," said Max.

Which is just what she wanted to feel like at the moment: to be the one taken care of instead of the one who always had to keep things going. But she said, laughing:

"Oh, no! That makes me sound like a little child who hasn't grown up at all!"

"Oh, I didn't mean it that way!" Max recanted, joining the laughter.

After signing autographs and having something to eat —Lena refused to take no for an answer—Minmei excused herself and went upstairs to her room. There were no questions about Kyle; it was as if he were no longer part of the family.

Lena and Max hadn't changed a thing even after the relocation of the restaurant from the hold of the dimensional fortress; they must have put everything back where it had been—even the whimsical pink rabit's head bearing her name that she had tacked to the door.

Once inside, a flood of memories began to overwhelm her:

Her first night in this very room when she'd arrived on Macross Island from Yokohama—the balcony view from these very windows of the reconstructed SDF-1; the Launching Day celebration and the madness that had ensued; the years in space, and the strange twists of fate that had brought her fame... And through it all she saw Rick journeying along with her, accompanying her, though not always by her side.

She looked up at the corner of the room damaged by Rick's Battloid on the day fate had thrown him a curve. The cornice of the room had been repaired, but the place never seemed to hold paint for very long, as though the spot had decided to memorialize itself.

Minmei crossed over to her bureau, opened one of the drawers, and retrieved the gift Rick had given her more than three years ago on her sixteenth birthday. The titanium Medal of Honor he had received after the battle of Mars. She recalled how he had appeared beneath her balcony only minutes before midnight and tossed the gift to her. "It says what I can't say to you," Rick had told her then.

The memory warmed her heart, thawing some of the sadness lodged there. But suddenly she felt far away from the joy and love of those earlier times; something inside her was in danger of dying. She sobbed, holding the medal close to her breast:

"Oh, Rick, what have I done?"

CHAPTER THREE

What do I remember about those days in New Macross?... Anger, strident conversations, despair—it almost seemed as if Protoculture's shape-shifting capabilities had taken hold of fate itself, changing and reworking individual destiny, transforming and reconfiguring lives...

Lisa Hayes, *Recollections*

THE SUN ROSE INTO CIRRUS SKIES ABOVE NEW MACROSS City, autumn's first crisp and clear day. The stratospheric dust and debris that for two years now had led to blue moons, sullen sunsets, and perpetual winters was at last dissipating, and there was every indication that Earth was truly on the mend.

Minmei, dressed in a white summer-weight skirt and red sweater, stepped out of the White Dragon and took a deep breath of the cool morning air. She felt more rested than she had in months; the comfort of her own room and the company of her family were warm in her memory. A newsboy, brown baseball cap askew on his head, rushed by and dropped off the morning edition; she greeted him cheerfully and started off down the street, unaware that he had turned startled in his tracks, recognizing the singing star instantly and somewhat disappointed when she hadn't stopped to talk with him for a moment.

She had a lot on her mind, but for a change she felt

that there was all the time in the world to see to everything. The band would be expecting her for rehearsal, but that was still hours off, and she wanted nothing more than to walk the streets and say hello to the city in her own way. *That's no EVE projection up there,* she had to remind herself, unaccustomed to sunny skies. She had been a creature of the night for too long, victimized by her own needs as much as she was by Kyle's grandiose plans for the future.

Last night's argument seemed far removed from this new optimism coursing through her. If Kyle could only be made to understand, if he would only stop drinking and return himself to the disciplines that made him unique in her eyes . . . Sometimes he appeared to be as displaced as the Zentraedi themselves, yearning for new battles to wage, new fronts to open. He detested the presence of the military and continued to blame them for the nearly total destruction of the planet. Minmei pitied him for that. The military had at least managed to salvage a place for new growth. And as for their presence, the threat of a follow-up attack was a real one—not manufactured, as Kyle claimed, to keep the civilians in line. The Earth had been ravaged once, and it could happen again.

But these were dark thoughts to have on such a glorious day, and she decided to put them from her mind. There was beauty and renewed life everywhere she looked. Skyscrapers rose like silver towers above the rooftops, and Lake Gloval looked as though it had been sprinkled with gems. . . .

In the outskirts of New Macross Rick had already commenced his morning run, in full sweats today, a beige outfit Lisa had given him for his birthday. The city was still asleep, taking advantage of the chill to spend a few extra moments cuddled under blankets, and there was no traffic to fight; so he jogged without any set course in mind, along the lakefront, then into the grid of city streets. Flat-bottomed cargo crafts ferried supplies to and from the supercarriers still attached to the SDF-1, while launches carried night-shift work crews away from the SDF-2, back to back with its mother ship and rapidly nearing completion.

Breathe in the good, breathe out the bad, he chanted to himself as he ran—and there was a great deal of the latter he needed to get rid of. If asked what he was so angry about, he probably wouldn't have been able to offer a clear explanation. Only this: He was tense. Whether it had something to do with his situation with Lisa, or Minmei's situation with Kyle, or Earth's with the Zentraedi, he couldn't be sure. Probably it was a combination of everything, coupled with an underlying sense of purposelessness that had given rise to this unnatural cynicism and despair.

"Both races seem to enjoy *fighting,"* Exedore had said. He regretted now that he had turned the briefing into a debate—he would have felt differently had he been able to make his point—but was still certain of his feelings: that the Zentraedi, for all their genetic similarities to humans, were no better than programmed androids. All one needed to do was look around to see that he was right: The Zentraedi were hungry for war—*biologically* hungry. They were deserting their positions, sometimes violently—the recent incident in New Portland was a case in point—to take up with their fellow malcontents in makeshift compounds in the wasteland, off limits to humans, who would not be able to withstand the lingering radiation. Perhaps a mistake had been made in attempting to band together despite the gains to New Macross thanks to the literary *larger* labor force? But Rick was certain it was only a matter of time before all the Zentraedi followed suit and returned to war.

He exhaled harshly and increased his pace.

Just down the street from the White Dragon, only a few blocks from Rick's present course, a delivery van pulled to a stop in front of a two-storied building with a red and white striped awning and a rainbow-shaped sign that read CLEANING. At the wheel was Konda, one of the three former Zentraedi spies.

"Rico! Gimme a hand with this!" Bron called out from the sidewalk, a full basket of laundry in his brawny arms.

The door to the shop opened, and the founder of the Minmei cult stepped out, affecting oversized and unnecessary eyeglasses, convinced that they enhanced his appearance. Rico had also let his hair grow and was dressed in a short-waisted blue and white uniform that fit him like a leisure suit.

The three former secret agents had secured jobs with the cleaning service several months ago, their fascination for clothing as strong now as it had been when they first experienced Micronian life in the holds of the SDF-1.

"Hey, guess what happened?" Konda said, leaning out of the van.

Rico was quick to respond, leaving Bron (a good fifteen pounds lighter than he'd been two years ago) to fend for himself. "What happened?" he asked excitedly.

"Guess."

"What?" Rico repeated, enjoying the game but still vague about the rules.

"Minmei's back in town—she stayed at the restaurant last night!"

"No kidding!"

"I got it straight from his honor the mayor himself."

Rico made a puzzled gesture. "But I saw in the paper that Minmei's got a concert in Stone City today." He wanted to believe Konda, but still . . .

"Well, if she leaves early enough today, she can still make it," Konda offered as an explanation.

Rico snapped his fingers. "Rats! If I had known, I would have gone to the restaurant last night to eat." He dug into his pants pocket and produced a small notebook, which he immediately began to leaf through. It was possible he'd been mistaken about the Stone City concert. "Hmmm . . . let's see . . . It looks like I've forgotten her concert schedule in my other notebook." If Konda's information was correct, then perhaps Minmei would be spending another night at the White Dragon.

Rico reveled in the idea of "having a mission." He and his sidekicks had had their share of dull evenings lately. Things didn't seem to be working out too well between the three of them and Kim, Vanessa, and Sammie. He was at a loss to explain the reasons for this but reasoned that it had something to do with *procreation*, that mystery of mysteries so important to Micronian females. Not everyone could be as fortunate as Miriya Parino and her mate . . .

Just then Bron appeared behind him, a neatly folded stack of sheets in his arms.

"Hey! We're supposed to be dry cleaners, not gossipmongers." Bron took his job very seriously, judging it to be one of the most important things a Micronian could attend to—next to cooking, of course. The care and maintenance of uniforms especially. "Now, either you ship up or shape out or I'm gonna just have to—huh?"

Bron shouldered Rico aside and advanced a few steps along the sidewalk, staring at a woman pedestrian headed their way.

"Hey . . . Am I dreaming?" he said. Then: "It is!"

"Huh?" said Rico, tempted to remove his glasses.

Konda leaned from the van. "Is that . . ."

"*Minmei!*" the three of them said together, unable to believe their luck.

"Hi." She smiled, raising her hand. She hadn't seen any of them in months—since her last open-air concert in New Macross, where they had had front-row seats and carried artificial flowers.

Rico and Bron ran to her, Konda quick to bring up the rear.

"Minmei, would you . . . well, would you like to autograph this?" Bron said, offering her his pile of pressed linen.

"Hey, Bron, that belongs to a customer," Rico pointed out, confident that his knowledge of Micronian protocol would impress Minmei.

But Bron ignored him. "So what! I'll buy the customer a new one!"

This found favor with Rico and Konda, both of whom reached for the sheets simultaneously, touching off an instant tug-of-war for what hadn't already fallen to the sidewalk.

Minmei backed up, worried about how this battle might escalate; but finally she laughed and dug into her purse for a pen.

* * *

Elsewhere in the city a more violent battle was under way.

Mayor Tommy Luan had been attending to his morning ritual (putting on a tie, then taking it off), when he saw something fly past his second-floor bedroom window —something large and red that had about as much business being in the air as a tie had around his neck. He moved to the window in time to see a compact car crash to the street and explode. Pedestrians were screaming and fleeing the scene. *Some idiot's driven off the roof of the parking garage,* Luan told himself as he made for the stairway.

By the time he reached street level, flames and thick smoke had engulfed what was left of the car. But he had scarcely stepped from the building when a second explosion filled the air, more ground-shaking than the first. Luan saw a second black cloud rise over the rooftops from somewhere nearby and ran toward the direction of the smoke, revising his earlier hypothesis. Was this a sneak attack or some new terrorist group at work?

As he approached the intersection, an airborne girder took out a streetlamp, sending up a fountain of sparks and stopping him in his tracks. From around the corner came two Zentraedi giants, one brandishing a long pipe and carrying a large sack stuffed with who knew what. Luan had begun a slow retreat down his street, but the two saw him and began to pursue him. Spent after a block, the mayor stopped, collapsing to his knees in front of his home.

The Zentraedi stood over him, threatening him with the pipe.

"I beg you—h-have pity."

"I'll spare you if you give me everything you've got!" growled the pipe wielder instinctively, with no real purpose other than intimidation in mind.

"T-that's easier said than done," Luan answered him, trying to figure out just what he might possess that would appeal to a sixty-foot warrior.

Inside the house, Luan's wife, Loretta, having

glimpsed the terrifying street scene from the living room window, had already raised the base on the phone. The clenched fist of one of the aliens filled the plate window behind her.

"Right . . . right," she was saying, growing panic in her voice. "They've suddenly become very violent and extremely dangerous. They're trying to take our food and our possessions and everything we—"

Something took hold of her, cutting off her breath.

Now she was being lifted off the floor and carried through the front door, her narrow shoulders and fragile neck pinched in the grip of giant fingers. The warrior, who had gone down on both knees to fish her from her home, held her ten feet above the sidewalk, choking the life from her while he roared into her face.

"Whaddaya think you're up to? Sit down!" he said gruffly, slamming her to the concrete. This knocked the wind out of her and dislocated her back. Through the pain she recognized that she was sitting in a most unladylike position, her pleated blue skirt up around her thighs, but there was nothing she could do about it. Then suddenly Tommy was beside her, holding her and spitting at the aliens:

"You monster! You've hurt her." Luan wrapped his beefy arms around his wife. "Be strong, darling. We're going to get you to a hospital as soon as we—"

"You're not going anywhere!" the two Zentraedi bellowed, moving in to cast a grim shadow over both of them. . . .

Rick was breathing hard, pushing himself into a sprint, when he heard his name called. He forced himself to stop, doubled over with hands on his knees, panting for a moment, before he turned around. *Lisa!* He had purposely avoided his usual route for fear of bumping into her, and now here she was not ten feet away, shapely in her blue skirt and orange V-neck sweater. There had been some awkward moments between them these past few weeks. She had stopped coming by his quarters—even (in a roundabout fashion) returned the key he had given her. She thought he was seeing Minmei again, but he wasn't. Not *really.*

"What are you doing up so early?" he asked as she approached.

She stammered, "Um . . . well, I wasn't sleeping too well."

"Why not?" Rick said, feeling a sudden concern.

"Something's wrong."

"Wrong? Whaddaya mean?"

Lisa stared at him. Was he ever going to be able to *talk* to her? "I don't know," she told him. "I'm not really sure . . ."

"Well, working on patrol has made me pretty sensitive to what's going on—there's some tension, but we can handle it."

Was he talking about tension between the two of them, or did he mean tension among the Zentraedi? Lisa asked herself. Patrol was making him sensitive . . . to what? She wanted to believe that this was Rick's way of apologizing.

"I'd better be reporting in," he said, motioning toward the SDF-1. "It's breakfast time."

Lisa smiled to herself. It was like pulling teeth . . . but she wasn't going to give up on him. Not yet.

"Mind if I walk with you? I don't feel like going back to the barracks by myself, okay?"

"Come to think of it," Rick said as they started off, "you may be right about there being trouble."

It was as prescient a comment as Rick had uttered in quite some time—although subsequent events would erase it from his memory—because Minmei happened to be walking up the very street Rick and Lisa had entered when they rounded the corner scarcely ten paces ahead of her.

Minmei froze, sucking in her breath, as those haunting memories she had experienced in her room last evening returned. Seeing him now, practically arm in arm with this other woman, only strengthened her earlier longings and, worse still, reinforced her worse fears. *What had she done?*

"Oh, listen," she heard Rick tell Lisa. "I forgot to tell you—I put your picture in my album."

"You did? That was sweet."

Rick turned to Lisa and started to say, "I hope you don't mind, but I—"

Then he saw her standing there.

The moment was full of real-life drama, but Minmei held the edge. She stood still long enough for him to hear her sob and see the tears; then she turned and ran.

Her performance wasn't lost on Lisa. But Rick was fully taken in, already chasing after her, calling for her to wait.

Why? Lisa yelled at herself. *Why does she have to manipulate him, and why does he fall right into it, and why am I chasing him now when he's chasing her?*

Rick and Lisa were right behind Minmei when she turned the corner, but all at once she was nowhere in sight.

"How could she have disappeared so quickly?" Rick said, looking around.

Lisa was out of breath. She had figured—correctly, in fact—that Minmei was hiding in one of the storefronts up ahead.

She was about to suggest they try a different direction, when a thunderous bass voice suddenly yelled: "I said shut up!"

Rick and Lisa turned. Towering above the building situated diagonally across the intersection from them, two Zentraedi workers were faced off in an argument. The red-haired one stepped forward and threw a sucker punch, catching the second across the jaw and dropping him to the street with a ground-shaking crash.

"Come on!" Rick said, hurrying toward the fracas.

By the time Rick and Lisa arrived on the scene, the red-haired Zentraedi was straddling his opponent, pummeling the other's face. A third Zentraedi, obviously allied with the winner, stood smiling off to one side. Tommy Luan was cowering on the sidewalk nearby.

Rick braced himself and stepped forward. "Stop that fighting right now!" he yelled. "Stop it, I said!"

The mayor, supporting his injured wife, ran to Rick's side from across the street.

"Commander! Thank goodness you're here!"

"What's this all about, sir?" Rick asked him.

"They were threatening to kill us! Then this one showed up, and they started arguing—"

"I can't live here anymore!" bellowed the red-haired Zentraedi, pinning his opponent to the street.

Luan, encouraged by Rick's presence, stepped forward to address the giant. "I told you—I understand your problem, but you have to be reasonable about—"

"Be quiet, fatso!" the former warrior said, getting to his feet. "I'll squash you, got it?!"

Luan and his wife hid behind Rick.

"Tell him not to get angry about it, Commander."

Just then the streets began shaking with a recognizable thunder. Civil defcnse sirens blared as four Excalibur MK VIs took up positions on either side of the Zentraedi, their twin-cannon arms raised. Bipedally designed relatives of the MAC II cannon, the mecha bristled with gatlings and were capable of delivering devastating volleys of firepower.

Rick wasn't sure what he was going to say next, but the sudden arrival of Robotech mecha on the scene was a booster shot to his confidence.

"The authorities are here. *Now* will you stop fighting?"

The upper gun turret of the lead Excalibur slid forward, and the mecha's commander elevated himself into view.

"Zentraedi!" his small but amplified voice rang out. "Stop! We've got you surrounded!'

The giant who moments before had been flat on his back got up and stepped out of harm's way, leaving the red-haired one and his cohort center stage. Rick, recognizing the voice of the mecha commander, cupped his hands to his mouth and shouted: "Dan! Hold it!"

Dan looked down from his cockpit seat, surprised to find Rick in the middle of this. "Commander! What happened here?"

"Let me handle this," Rick told him.

Dan gave a verbal aye-aye, and Rick moved in angrily to confront the giants.

"Now, you listen to me, and listen good! I know life

with us is hard for you, but the authorities *want* to help you with your problems—*if* you'll give them the chance."

The red-haired Zentraedi, clutching his sackful of valuables once again, went down on one knee to answer Rick, equally confident and angered.

"Wait a minute!" he growled. "If your government is so worried about us and so concerned about our welfare, why don't they let us go out and be with our own people where we *belong*?"

"Uh, well, that's—"

"*I* am a warrior, *understand*?"

"Well, what about it?" asked the second Zentraedi threateningly. "Bagzent wants to fight—can you help him?"

"I'm good with my fists, and I can handle practically any weapon," continued the one called Bagzent. "So what do you say? Can you help? Speak up, I can't hear you . . . Well? . . . Are you gonna help me or *not*?"

The scene was turning ugly again. Mayor Luan, his wife, and Lisa sensed it and began to back away. The CD mecha shifted slightly, their guns traversing somewhat.

At the corner, unseen, Minmei gasped.

"Well," Rick began, "we have no firm guarantee you won't band together and attack us again. If you want to—"

"Huh!" Bagzent grunted, tiring of the game. "If you can't help me solve my problem, then what's the point in saying that you or your government will talk about it?" All at once his right hand had moved forward. "Micronian!" he uttered in disgust, flicking his forefinger.

Rick took the full force of the movement. The Zentraedi's log-sized forefinger caught him full body, from knees to chin, lifting him off his feet and tossing him a good ten feet through the air. Dazed and bloodied, he landed solidly on his rump at the clawlike foot of one of the Excaliburs.

Startled gasps went up from the humans pressed together on the street corner, but those were not as bothersome to the Zentraedi as the sounds of weapons being leveled against them.

"On my signal," said Dan. "Blast 'em!"

The two Zentraedi backed away, suddenly afraid. Gatlings were ranged in.

"Wait," one of them pleaded. "Don't shoot."

Rick shook the pain from his body, struggled to his feet, and raced back to the center of the arena. He raised up his arms and shouted to Dan again, "Hold your fire!" Then he held his face up to Bagzent, blood running from the corner of his mouth.

Bagzent snarled. "Listen to me, Micronian," he started to say.

"No! *You* listen to me," Rick interrupted him. "We've given you sanctuary and *this* is how you repay us?!"

The corners of Bagzent's mouth turned down. "I'm sorry," he grumbled—not apologetically, but as if to say: *I'm sorry it has to be this way.*

Bagzent and his companion turned and began to walk off, but the third Zentraedi stepped forward now, calling to them.

"Come back! You'll regret this! When we first came here, you thought their culture was a great thing—you were so impressed by Minmei's songs."

The Zentraedis stopped for a moment as if considering this, then continued their heavy-footed retreat.

"Stay and give it one more try!" the third was shouting. "It's worth the effort, isn't it? We've come so far, we can't give up now!"

When he realized his words were having no effect, he added: "Stupid cowards! Come back!"

Concealed from Lisa and the Luans, Minmei brought her hand to her mouth to stifle her sadness and terror. When she could no longer contain herself, she fled.

Lisa was at Rick's side now, watching the Zentraedis move stiffly away.

"They're getting more and more dissatisfied," said Rick, spitting blood. "We're gonna have to do something."

"I wonder . . . what'll they do after they leave here?"

"I know one thing," the mayor interjected. "Whether

they survive out in that wasteland or not . . . *we're* responsible."

Rick spun around, angry and confused to find yet another sympathizer in his midst. But the mayor stared him down.

"That's right, Rick," Luan said knowingly. "We haven't heard the last of this."

CHAPTER FOUR

The mythologies of numerous Earth cultures identified north and the arctic regions with evil and death. I don't believe it was convenience or coincidence that led the militaristic heads of the Earth council to construct their ill-fated Grand Cannon there; nor do I think that Khyron just happened *to land his ship there. As water seeks its own level, so does evil seek its own place.*

Rawlins, Zentraedi Triumvirate:
Dolza, Breetai, Khyron

THE MILE-LONG ALIEN CRUISER LAY BURIED UNDER ice and snow, with only its igloolike gun turrets visible above the frozen, howling surface. No squad of Air Force personnel would come to investigate this one, nor would any human-chain prophylactic magic circle be formed to contain its evil intent. It was too late to watch the skies...

In the observation bubble inside the ship, Khyron, his burgundy uniform and forest-green campaign cloak looking none the worse for wear through two long years, leaped from the command chair as Gerao delivered his latest report.

"Are you absolutely sure of this, Gerao?"

"I'm certain of it, m'lord," said Gerao, thrice lucky for having lived through the explosion of the reflex furnaces on Mars, the holing of his ship during a *Daedalus* Maneuver, and now the holocaust itself. He brought his fist to his breast insignia in salute.

"Our spies have reported that thousands of dissatisfied Zentraedi are leaving town after town. They are estimated to be around ten thousand, sir."

"Ah, splendid," said Khyron, clenching his right hand, the devilish eyes of his handsome face peering from beneath blue bangs. "A most interesting occurrence—well worth the two-year wait in this terrible place!"

Khyron, through either an act of prescient will or cowardice unheard of among the Zentraedi, had absented his ship and crew from the battle that had all but destroyed the last of his race. It certainly wasn't Khyron's plan to bring Breetai and Dolza into confrontation, so why allow the Botoru Battalion to get caught up in High Command's madness? All along Khyron had maintained that the best way to handle Zor's ship was to destroy it. Anyone should have been able to see that from the beginning. But instead the fools had attempted to capture the fortress, unaware of the Micronian malignancy spreading fast through the fleet. The existence of the Protoculture matrix Zor's fortress was thought to contain was not, however, so easily dismissed. Indeed, Khyron had saved himself for this greater purpose; but the fact remained that his warship's precious fuel and weapons supply were all but depleted.

He had hidden on the far side of the Earth during the catastrophic explosion that had wiped out Dolza's four-million-ship armada—the armada that had once made his race the most feared throughout the Fourth Quadrant. Surely the Micronians had the traitors Breetai and Exedore to thank for their success, although how those two had gained any knowledge of the barrier shield's inversion capacity was beyond him. In all likelihood it was a stroke of luck—and the judgment of fate for the Zentraedi.

Khyron had chosen to put down in the frozen wasteland of the half-dead planet in the hopes of salvaging something from the Micronian's reflex weapon, the so-called Grand Cannon. But nothing remained of it.

He was aware, however, that his elite group did not represent the last of the Zentraedi; somewhere in the quadrant between Earth and Tirol, there was Commandor Reno's ship, along with the automated Robotech factory, still fabricating battle mecha for a handful of warriors. There were also the contaminated Zentraedi from Breetai's fleet who had elected to stand shoulder to shoulder with the Micronians. Khyron's own spies were at work infiltrating this latter group, in addition to the renegade bands of Zentraedi who had already abandoned the Earth population centers to inhabit the wastes; and Khyron knew that someday soon they would prove to be his allies. Then, Reno and Khyron would rebuild the Zentraedi war machine with the help of the Masters themselves. And once the Earth was incinerated, they would scour the quadrant for new worlds to conquer.

But first he needed to get his ship spaceworthy once again.

And now the word he'd been waiting for had finally come.

He turned to the one who had stood beside him through the long wait, in defiance of the old ways, a symbol of the new order of things.

"Our faith is vindicated, my dear Azonia."

"Indeed," The former commander of the Quadrono Battalion smiled. She was dressed like her lord, save that her cloak was blue. Her arms were folded, and she wore an arrogant grin. When her own ship had been holed by fire from Dolza's armada, it was Khyron who had come to her aid, convincing her to abandon Breetai's forces and join him. *"Let them battle it out together,"* he had said. *"We will live to see the rebirth of the Zentraedi!"*

"Their taste for the Micronian life-style was only temporary," Khyron was saying. "I knew that after a little while they'd grow tired of it. And you see I was right!"

Two years under the ice and snow had brought a strange new closeness between Azonia and her commander—a closeness that had more to do with life than death: the stimulation of the senses, *pleasure*. Azonia believed it had something to do with the planet itself—this Earth. But she kept these thoughts to herself. If pleasure was the cause of the warriors' desertion, she couldn't blame them—Miriya included, although it remained a puzzle why she would bother to take a Micronian mate over a Zentraedi.

"Yes, Khyron," said the fourth Zentraedi in the command center—Grel, who had been Khyron's trusted lieutenant through many long campaigns.

Azonia shook her fist, mimicking Khyron's gesture of determination. "Now, look," she announced. "If things keep going as planned, we can put together a battalion that I guarantee will *take* them!"

Khyron smiled to himself. It was only right that his underlings echo his sentiments, but Azonia had a lot to learn. What could *she* guarantee, save that *Khyron* would be victorious in the end? That *Khyron* would take them!

Nevertheless, he humored her without seeming patronizing.

"Yes, of course we shall."

The Backstabber moved to the comlink of the cruiser's command bubble to address his troops, who had gathered in the astrogational hold below.

"Now, listen, everyone," he began. "You needn't hide yourselves any longer! You are Zentraedi warriors! I want you to see to it that our former comrades are led here. Those who have established camps for themselves in the wastelands and those who have yet to leave the Micronian population centers. And I want you to tell all the micronized Zentraedi that if they join us, I will return them to their original size so that they too may walk tall and proud once again!"

The soldiers began to cheer their lord and savior with cries of "Long live the Zentraedi, long live Khyron!"

Khyron's lips became a thin line as he took in the collective outpourings of his troops.

Yes, he promised himself, he would return the Zentraedi to their original size—their rightful place in the universe. And the destruction of this planet would be his first step in that direction, including the destruction of that secret weapon the Micronians had used so effectively against his race, that weapon the deserters had learned to embrace: that *Minmei*!

Kyle gave another look at his wristwatch: seven forty-eight and she still hadn't arrived.

He glanced out from the wings of the stage. It was a

small crowd who had gathered in Stone City's open-air amphitheater (half a dozen giant Zentraedi in the far tiers, mesas and monoliths in the distance, a pink and blue sunset sky) but a vocal one nonetheless, clapping and shouting now, eager to bring Minmei on stage. The warm-up group was well into their second set, but the audience had already tired of them halfway through the first.

Kyle cursed himself for letting her out of his sight, especially after last night's fight and that crazy stunt she had pulled on the Macross Highway.

"Hey, Kyle!" said someone behind him. There was an unconcealed note of anger in the voice, and Kyle swung around ready for action, happy to vent his own frustration and rage if the opportunity presented itself. Vance Hasslewood, Minmei's booking agent, was striding down the corridor toward him.

"What's the idea? Where the devil is Minmei?" Hasslewood demanded.

Hasslewood was wearing his customary aviator specs, a sweater-vested white suit and tie, and a scowl on his clean-shaven face.

"Minmei'll be here," Kyle told him tiredly.

"But showtime's in just ten more minutes—you realize that?"

"She'll show," Kyle said more strongly. "Minmei is not the kind of singer who ignores her obligations. You oughta know that by now, Hasslewood."

"I *do* know that. But just the same, Kyle, I want her here at least half an hour before showtime."

"She'll be here!" Kyle repeated, his patience fading fast. He gestured to the audience. "You know, you put on a pretty good *act* as a promoter, Hasslewood—attracting an audience that size."

Hasslewood's nostrils flared. He was getting sick and tired of having to answer to Kyle's demands and criticisms and was of half a mind to turn his back on the whole deal. But he couldn't bear the thought of leaving Minmei in the care of a hothead like Kyle. A drunk and degenerate—

"Hey, she's here!" a stagehand called out.

As Hasslewood turned around, one of the band members ran up to him.

"Minmei's here. She's in her dressing room," he told them, feeling it necessary to point the way.

Kyle snorted and shouldered his way past Hasslewood. He didn't bother to knock at the dressing room door, merely threw it open and demanded:

"Where have you been?"

Minmei was putting on her face. She was wearing the same off-the-shoulder ruffled blue dress she had worn at the supper club last night.

"Sorry I'm late," she answered without turning around.

"I don't know why we're even bothering to do this gig—there's hardly anyone out there. This is the pits."

"I don't care that much about the size of the audience," she said into the mirror. "I'm through worrying about all this, Kyle. I'm just going to sing for my fans, just the way I always have."

"What's with you?" he said, standing over her now.

Minmei shot to her feet and faced him. "*You* worry about our *take,* Kyle! I'm just singing for myself, do you understand me? Just for myself!"

She pushed past him and left the room.

Her anger had taken him by surprise. *Minmei just singing for herself?* he asked himself, then turned to the door with a sullen look.

He'd see about that.

Back in New Macross, Rick, Lisa, and Max and Miriya Sterling were summoned to a briefing in Admiral Gloval's quarters aboard the SDF-1. Hunter and Hayes had spent most of the day filling out reports concerning that morning's incident with the Zentraedi malcontents. Rick was sore head to foot from Bagzent's finger flick. Max and Miriya were *sans* Dana, their child, for a change but joined at the hip nonetheless.

Gloval looked plain tired. Perhaps, as a former Earth hero had once remarked, "it wasn't the years, it was the miles." He'd been spending more and more of his time in the old ship, and on those rare occasions when he did put in an appearance elsewhere, he seemed impatient and troubled. Gone was the tolerant, accepting paternal figure who shared the sense of fear and purpose that united the rest of them. In his place was a man of secret purpose, bearing the weight of the world on his narrow shoulders. Exedore, who in a sense had become his right-hand man, was also in attendance.

"What I'm about to tell you is strictly confidential," Gloval told the four RDF commanders. "Not a word of this is to leave this room. If it were to get out, the damage would be catastrophic."

The old man was seated at his desk; behind him the clear starry night poured in through the fortress's massive permaglass window.

The commanders responded with a crisp, "Yes, sir."

Exedore stepped forward to address them now, the whites of his eyes practically glowing in the dim room.

"Yesterday, we finally spotted the Zentraedi automated Robotech factory satellite. Space cruisers large enough to destroy the Earth with a single blast are being constructed within the satellite." He caught their gasps of surprise and hastened to add, "Yes, it is a terrible thing."

"Listen carefully," said Gloval, more harshly than was necessary. He was standing now, palms flat against the desk. "I want you people to survey that system and bring me additional data on the satellite."

The four commanders exchanged puzzled looks. There was something the old man wasn't telling them—aside from answering how it was they were supposed to get offworld—unless of course he was planning to recommission the SDF-1 itself.

"Commander Breetai will fill you in on the details," Gloval explained after a moment. "We have no way of knowing if and when the remaining Zentraedi will attack us again, but for our own defense we have to have as many space cruisers as we can lay our hands on." He turned to them now to emphasize the point, "You understand that."

"Yes," Exedore said softly. His eyes were closed, his brow furrowed, and one could almost believe that he felt a twinge of pain at the thought of bringing warships to bear against his own kind once again.

Rick and the others voiced their assent: It not only

meant that they would be leaving the planet again, it meant that they would be relying on the Zentraedi as well. And yet Gloval was right: *It was for their own defense.*

Minmei stepped onto the stage and grasped the microphone. Colored spots played across the plank floor, until at last a single rose-toned beam of light found and encompassed her in its warm glow. Her face was sad, blue eyes wide and full of loss. The crowd was chanting, "We love Minmei, we love Minmei," but all she could think about was Rick, Kyle, those giant Zentraedi who had fought in the streets of New Macross only hours ago.

She felt as though she had failed everyone.

She had decided to scrap the first upbeat tune of the set and go immediately into "Touch and Go," a laid-back number that started with a simple piano and string riff and bass slide but grew somber and melancholy at the F-sharp minor/C-sharp 7 bridge, with a sort of crying guitar distortion punctuation backed by a stiff snare beat.

I always think of you,
Dream of you late at night.
What do you do,
When I turn out the light?
No matter who I touch,
It is you I still see.
I can't believe
What has happened to me.

Tears began to form in her eyes as she sang. The audience was mesmerized by her performance. She sensed this and began to experience an extraordinary sense of nostalgia and yearning, entering the tune's bridge now:

It is you I miss.
It's you who's on my mind,
It's you I cannot leave
behind.

If the connection could always be this strong, she said to herself. If only she had the strength to *will* things right, and good, and peaceful. If only she had the power to become that symbol once again, that perfect chord everyone would vibrate to . . .

It's me who's lost—
The me who lost her heart—
To you who tore my heart
apart.

But *loss* was the world's new theme; loss and betrayal, anger and regret. And what could she hope to achieve against such malignant power? She had tried and failed, and the day would come soon when song itself was but a memory.

If you still think of me
How did we come to this?
Wish that I knew
It is me that you miss
Wish that I knew
It is me that you miss . . .

CHAPTER FIVE

[The joint Terran/Zentraedi exploration of the SDF-1] was the only occasion when Breetai allowed himself to undergo the micronization process [prior to the SDF-3 Expeditionary Mission to Tirol]. As soon as it became obvious that Zor's prize [i.e., the Protoculture matrix] was likely to remain hidden for some time longer, Breetai immediately had himself returned to full stature. He had little of the curiosity for Micronian customs that Exedore had; nor did he share the same fascination for Minmei that was responsible for so many other deviations from the Zentraedi way. Breetai enjoyed being looked up to . . .

Rawlins, *Zentraedi Triumvirate: Dolza, Breetai, Khyron*

GROUND FOG LAY LIKE SPUN SUGAR ACROSS LAKE Gloval and swirled through the early morning streets of New Macross like autumn ghosts. In the shadow of the gargantuan dimensional fortress—like some techno-Neptune protector—a three-stage rocket added its LOX exhaust to the mist. An RDF shuttle (the same that had carried Lisa Hayes from the SDF-1 to Alaska Base two years ago) was affixed to the rocket's main booster pack.

In another part of the field, nine Veritechs were also holding in preflight status. Each ship was outfitted with deep-space augmentation pods and positioned atop individual blast shield transports.

The *Shiva* was fully primed for launch; gantries and attendance vehicles had already been pulled back, and the sound of the countdown Klaxons lent an eerie sound track to the scene.

In the control tower, techs ran last-minute crucial

checks on the shuttle's propulsion and guidance systems. Readouts flashed across myriad monitor screens too quickly for the untrained eye to make sense of, and two dozen voices talked at once but never at cross-purposes. Robotechnology had simplified things substantially since the pioneering days of space travel, but certain traditions and routines had been maintained.

"Calculations for orbital fluctuations have been received," one of the shuttle crew said through the comlink. "We have lock and signal, control."

"Shuttle escort," a male controller directed toward one of the Veritechs, "we are at T minus fifty and counting. Your lift-off is at T three."

A second Veritech pilot was being questioned by a female tech: "Escort V-oh-one-one-two, your gravitational tracking status is *what*? Please clarify."

"Tower control," the pilot responded. "Uh, sorry about that. Little snafu with the guidance switch, if you know what I mean..."

"Watch it next time, mister," the tech scolded him.

On the field Max and Miriya, strapped into their respective blue and red Veritechs, went through final systems checks. Max flashed his wife a thumbs-up from the cockpit as he lowered the tinted faceshield of his helmet.

Evacuation warnings were being broadcast through the field PA: "All ground support vehicles evacuate launch area immediately... All Veritechs complete final systems check... We are go for lift-off. Repeat—we are go for lift-off... Countdown commencing—T minus thirty seconds..."

In Skull One, Rick surveyed the field as the transport's massive hydraulic jacks lifted the Veritech to a seventy-two-degree launch angle. Simultaneously a thick blast shield was elevated into position behind the Veritech's aft rockets. Thinking about the importance of the mission, he was overcome by a wave of nostalgia, a curious sense of *homesickness* for space. He realized suddenly how disappointed he would have been had the admiral left him out of this one...

"You are going to rendezvous with the Zentraedi flagship," Gloval had explained at the briefing. *"Only at that*

time will you receive your final instructions. I have put Commander Breetai in charge of this mission for reasons that will become clear to you later."

Rick glanced over his shoulder at the *Shiva*, the shuttle piggyback on its gleaming hull. It was amazing, he decided: going off to rendezvous with Breetai, the Zentraedi who had once torn his Vermilion Veritech limb from limb. He wondered if Lisa was remembering that time, that kiss...

"Shuttle to tower control... all systems on-line and awaiting green light."

"Roger, shuttle," the controller radioed to the crew. "Stand by..."

Inside the shuttle, Lisa leaned toward the permaglass porthole closest to her seat. It was not an easy maneuver, but she hoped to catch a glimpse of Rick's lift-off. One by one the Veritechs were being nosed up now... Max's, Miriya's... Rick's... She pulled herself away from the view and sighed, loud enough for Claudia and Exedore to hear her and inquire if she was all right. It was a strange mixture of emotions that tugged at her thoughts: memories of the time she'd spent in Breetai's ship and recent events that continued to confuse her feelings. In some ways this return to the stars was less like a mission than a vacation.

"Shuttle escort launch at signal zero—*now*!"

The Veritechs lifted off, the sound of their blasts like a volley of thunderclaps echoing around the lake. Then, with a more continuous roar, the *Shiva* rose from its pad, a fiery morning star in the scudded skies over New Macross.

Breetai's ship, one-time nemesis and subsequent ally of the SDF-1, was holding at a Lagrange point inside the lunar orbit. More than ten kilometers in length, armored and bristling with guns like some nightmare leviathan, the vessel had never put down on Earth. But teams of Lang's Robotechs, working side by side with Zentraedi giants, had retrofitted the ship to accommodate human crews. Elevators and air locks had been incorporated into the hull; holds had been partitioned off into human-size work spaces and quarters; automated walkways were installed; and the astrogation hold now contained control consoles and the latest innovations from Lang's projects-development labs. All this had been child's play for the Earth techs—many of the same men and women who had overseen the original conversion of the SDF-1, had later fabricated a city for 60,000 inside the fortress itself, and were currently involved in the construction of the SDF-2—but it had struck the Zentraedi (who had no understanding of the Robotechnology bequeathed to them by the Masters) as near miraculous.

Now, while the shuttle craft carrying Exedore, Lisa, and Claudia entered one of the flagship's docking bays, the nine Veritechs under Rick's command were reconfiguring to Guardian mode and putting down in formation on an external elevator. In the bay a human voice announced the shuttle's arrival in English.

"All personnel in docking zones D-twenty-four and D-twenty-five—attention: Micronian shuttlecraft now commencing final docking procedures in upper landing bay."

The use of the term "Micronian" was no longer considered to be pejorative, in spite of its derivation; it had simply come to mean "human-size" as opposed to "microbelike." So Lisa and Claudia were not fazed; nor was Rick, topside, when a shock trooper welcomed the Veritechs aboard likewise.

The Zentraedi shock trooper stood a good sixty feet tall, but the fact that he was wearing armor and a helmet suggested that he might be one of the inferior class of warriors incapable of withstanding the vacuum perils of deep space unless properly outfitted.

"Uh, thanks," Rick told him through the com net. "It's good to be here." The trooper flashed him a grin and thumbs-up. "If you're ready, let's bring her down," Rick added.

The giant proudly displayed a device in his gloved hand. He tapped in a simple code, and the elevator began to drop into the ship.

Elsewhere, Lisa, Claudia, and Exedore exited the shuttle's circular doorway and descended the stairway to the hold floor. Breetai was waiting for them there, his blue uniform and brown tunic looking brand-new.

"My Micronian friends—welcome," his voice boomed.

Lisa looked up at him standing there with arms akimbo and found herself smiling. These past two years had worked a subtle magic on the commander. It was well known that he refused to micronize himself, but merely working with humans had been enough to change him somehow, soften him, Lisa thought. The gleaming plate that covered one side of his face seemed more an adornment now than anything else.

Meanwhile Exedore had stepped forward and offered a stiff human salute.

"Greetings and salutations, your Lordship. We are at your service."

Breetai bent down, a look of affection contorting his face. "It's good seeing you, Exedore... It's nice to have you back on the ship."

Exedore must have noticed the change also, because he seemed genuinely *moved*. "Why, uh, *thank you*, sir," he stammered.

Breetai turned to Claudia and Lisa, their upturned faces betraying gentle amusement. "And I especially wish to extend a welcome to *you*," he told them, making a gallant gesture with his hand. "I am deeply honored to have you under my command."

Lisa, versed in Zentraedi protocol, returned: "It's a great honor, sir, to have this opportunity."

Breetai came down on one knee to thank her. "As you know, my people are unaccustomed to contact with beauty such as yours," he said flatteringly. "So don't be offended by any strange reactions you may encounter."

Lisa and Claudia turned to each other and laughed openly as Breetai drew himself up to full height again.

"Now then... if you'll permit, I'll show you to your quarters."

In the hangar space below the docking elevator, Max stood beneath Miriya's scarlet Guardian. He called up to the open-canopied cockpit, "Okay, that's it," signaling her with a wave of his hand. "Now bring the cradle pod down."

Miriya activated the device only recently installed in her Veritech.

"Here it comes," she told him.

Servomotors whined, and a royal-blue cylindrical pod —which could have passed for a turn-of-the-century bomb—began to drop from the rear seat, riding a telescoping shaft down beneath the legs of the fighter.

A Robotech delivery, Max said to himself as he approached the pod. He went to work disengaging fasteners, and in a minute the pod's blunt nose swung open. Max peered inside the heavily padded interior, smiled, and said, "There . . ."

He reached in and pulled Dana into his arms, a tiny wiggling astronaut in a white helmet with tinted faceshield and a pink and white suit that fit her like Dr. Dentons. Dana cooed, and Max hugged her to himself.

Miriya saw him step from beneath the Veritech with Dana cradled in his arms. Max assisted Dana in a wave; Miriya smiled and felt her heart skip a beat.

Breetai paced the observation bubble deck anxiously. Terran techs had effected changes here as well. The bubble shield had been dismantled and an openwork semicircular flattopped walkway installed in its place; humansize consoles occupied a flyout platform at the center of the arc. In addition, the circular monitor screen Max Sterling had once piloted a Veritech through was back in one piece.

"Any fluctuations from the satellite factory?" Breetai inquired into one of the binocularlike microphones.

"Negative," answered a synthesized voice. "Maintaining solar stasis."

"Notify me immediately of any change," he ordered.

"Yes, sir," the computer responded.

Breetai assumed the command chair and steepled his fingers. "Think, Breetai—think of a plan," he said aloud, as demanding of himself as he was of his troops. "If we are able to convince Reno that we have the Protoculture, we will have little difficulty in securing his complete cooperation . . . Otherwise, we will have quite a fight on our hands. Our forces will be vastly outnumbered."

Claudia turned from her console and monitor station on the walkway. "But we don't possess any Protoculture," she saw fit to remind him, her console mike carrying her words to the commander. "How do we convince him that we do . . . uuhh," clearing her throat here, her eyes going wide for an instant, "assuming we're given the chance?"

Breetai grinned. "We'll have our chance," he said certainly. "But for now, entering hyperspace is our immediate concern, wouldn't you say?"

Claudia traded looks with Lisa, seated at the adjacent station. It was obvious now that Breetai's musings were not really meant for their ears at all. Whatever the plan, it seemed likely they would be the last to know.

Max and Rick stood together on one of the moving walkways, marveling at the changes the ship had undergone and reveling in memories that time had rendered less severe.

"Hey, remember the last time we were on this ship?" asked Max.

"Heh! Being a prisoner wasn't much fun, was it?" said Rick, turning the tables on his friend's obviously rhetorical query. "I'm sure glad things have changed. I don't want to see Breetai on the other end of an autocannon ever again!"

"Yeah, after serving under Admiral Gloval, it'll be interesting to see what his ex-enemy's like."

"I just wish we knew more about this mission."

"Gloval asked me to bring my whole family along and left it at that."

Rick shook his head in puzzlement. "Why in space would the old man want you to bring Dana along?"

Max shrugged. "I don't know, Rick, but I want you to understand something: I won't put her in jeopardy, mission or no mission."

Rick looked at him squarely and said, "I won't let you."

* * *

"All polarities inside the reflex furnaces have become stabilized, Commander," Claudia told Breetai from her station.

A confusing array of data scrolled across the monitor screens, a mixture of English, Zentraedi glyphs, and the newly devised equivalency-transcription characters—phonetic Zentraedi.

A Zentraedi tech reported to Claudia that fold computations were complete, and she relayed to Breetai that all systems were go. "We can fold any time you like, sir."

He thanked her, then raised his voice to a roar.

"Begin fold operation immediately!"

As the fold generators were engaged, Protoculture commenced its magical workings on the fabric of the real world, calling forth from unknown dimensions a radiant energy that began to form itself around the ship like some shimmering amorphous aura, seemingly holing it through and through. The massive vessel lurched forward into a widening pool of white light; then it simply vanished from its Lagrange point, for one brief instant leaving behind globular eddies and masses of lambent animated light, lost moments in somewhere else's time.

CHAPTER SIX

Up until the end of the Second Robotech War (how Pyrrhic, how bittersweet that victory!), Protoculture was literally in the employ of the Robotech Masters; not only did it in effect keep tabs on itself for their benefit, but alerted them to changes in the fabric of the continuum. Not a single Zentraedi ship could fold without their being made aware of it.

Dr. Emil Lang, as quoted in *History of the Second Robotech War*, Vol. CCCLVII

YES . . . I FEEL IT . . .

The three Masters linked minds and once more laid their bony hands against the Protoculture cap. The mushroom-shaped device reacted to their touch, radiating that same pure light which spilled into the known universe when Breetai's ship had folded. The cap took them through the inverse world, through white holes and rifts in time, allowing them to see with an inner vision.

They were no longer in their space fortress now, but back on their homeworld, back on Tirol.

—Our former charges have allied themselves with Zor's descendants; our former charges would replace us as Masters.

—We must try again to resurrect a simulacrum of Zor.

Twenty clones had been created from Zor's body; they had been grown to maturity in biovats and held weightless in a stasis sphere. All matched his elfin likeness: handsome, dreamers all of them, youthful and graceful. But none of them had the spark of life that would replicate his thoughts and mind, that would allow the Masters to learn the whereabouts of the Protoculture matrix and the secrets of that rare process.

The Masters left the cap and stood gazing up at the stasis sphere that housed the remaining clones.

"I suggest we begin the prion synthesis immediately," said one of the Masters.

Away from the Protoculture cap they were forced to rely on ordinary, primitive speech to convey their thoughts.

"Yes, Master," a synthesized voice responded.

Three Masters positioned themselves around a saucer-like device fitted with numerous color-coded sensor pads grouped circumferentially around a central viewscreen, while a visible antigrav beam conveyed one of the lifeless clones from the stasis hemisphere of a circular biotable. The clone was placed flat on its back on it, as if it were resting on a sheet of pure light.

The three Masters placed their hands on the saucer's control pads. Roller-coaster-like readouts, hypermed schematics and X-ray displays began to flash across the circular viewscreen beneath them. Meanwhile the unmoving clone was bathed in a fountain of high-energy particles that rose from the biotable like an inverted spring rain.

"Altering positronic bombardment," said the gold-cowled Master, frowning as he watched the disappointing displays take shape.

"There's some bilateral cellular inversion," observed a second, the same one who had called for prison synthesis. "Commencing symphysis . . ." he announced, the sensor pads flashing like a light box.

The Masters concentrated, focusing the powers of their telepathic will, then broke off their attempts momentarily.

The clone showed no signs of cerebral activity.

"Cranial synapses are still not responding . . . There is the same disintegration of molecular substructures as in previous attempts."

"Yes, it has happened again . . . This time I think we've

taken the clone from the suspension before complete maturation . . . We must stimulate its life function regardless," the red-cowled Master said, leaving the saucer pod.

"I suggest we alter the prionic bombardment of the upper strata," said the third Master.

Master two nodded his head and moved his left hand to a new location along the control rim. "We'll try . . . Augmenting prionic bombardment in increments of four . . ."

"Positronic emission is at maximum capability!" observed the third, his arms at his sides.

"Good—cellular agitation is critical . . ."

Still the clockwork schematics revealed no activity.

"It is useless . . . We are down to the minimum suspension material—we cannot waste it like this."

"Life is such an elementary process," said the first, standing over the now useless clone, its neural circuits fried. "Where have we gone wrong?"

Miriya relaxed back into the couch and sighed, her fingers playing absently with Dana's curls. Would she keep her dark hair? Miriya wondered; each day it seemed to be growing lighter and lighter . . .

The baby was peacefully asleep on her breast, and just looking at her, it was all Miriya could do to keep from weeping for joy. A miracle, she told herself ten times a day: that she and Max could produce such innocent loveliness; that she, a former warrior, could feel this way about anyone or anything. Such unknown contentment and pure rapture.

"Max." She smiled. "Look at our child. She's so peaceful."

Max glanced out from the kitchenette of their quarters aboard Breetai's ship. He was carrying a trayful of tall cocktail glasses to the sink—the aftermath of an afternoon's partying with Rick, Lisa, and Claudia—and wearing a knee-length apron that read: MAX AND MIRIYA: LIVE!

Peaceful and beautiful, both of them, he said to himself. But while Miriya seemed to be having all the fun, he was the one who was stuck with all the dishes and the cooking and more than half the time the midnight feedings.

So what he said to her in the end, without betraying any of these thoughts and just grateful for a few minutes of blessed peace, was: "Yeah . . . but we'd better keep our voices down or we'll wake her up."

Rick, Lisa, and Claudia were a somewhat unsteady trio returning to their quarters after the afternoon drinks they'd shared with the happy couple. Combined with the thrill of deep space (after so many planetbound months) and the effects of hyperspace travel, the drinks had left them with more than an ordinary buzz.

". . . and I held little Dana the whole afternoon, and she didn't cry a bit the entire time!" Lisa was saying.

"Yes, but I don't think Miriya should have *thrown* Dana to you. She has to learn to be more careful!"

Lisa nodded, biting her lower lip. "Well, it's an adjustment for her. After all, her role model was probably the neighboring test tube."

Claudia cracked a smile in spite of herself and looked over Lisa's head at Rick, but he was too bleary-eyed to catch her gaze. "Sometimes I envy Max and Miriya for just having such a beautiful little girl," she said loudly.

"Mm-hmmm," Lisa agreed.

They had reached Lisa's quarters now, and Rick was standing off to one side vaguely thinking about how he was going to spend the rest of the day, while Lisa and Claudia exchanged good-byes. Suddenly Lisa turned to him and said: "Rick, I'm going to walk Claudia to her quarters, but if you have a minute, I'd like you to wait in my room for me—there's something I want to talk to you about."

Her request somehow managed to cut through all the cotton inside his head, and he found himself stammering, "Uhh . . . but . . ." all the while knowing that there was no way around it. It just didn't seem like she had *official* business on her mind, and he wasn't at all sure he was up to a heart-to-heart.

Claudia cleared her throat. "May I remind you, Mr. Hunter, that Lisa *is* your superior."

"But I'm off duty," Rick protested, definitely not in top form today.

"So is she," Claudia laughed, throwing him an exaggerated wink.

The two of them left Rick standing there with some half-formed reply caught in his throat while they continued on down the corridor sharing a whispered exchange.

"Now then, Lisa, what can I do for you?" Claudia asked when they were some steps away.

"I just wanted to thank you for being understanding these past few weeks. It really helps to have someone to lean on."

"I know what you mean," Claudia said at the door to her quarters. "It can be rough sometimes—when you find you're in love."

Lisa still grew a little wide-eyed at hearing it stated so matter-of-factly. She blinked and swallowed hard, ready to defend herself, but Claudia cut her off.

"Go get him, okay?" A wink for Lisa also, and she was through the door.

Inside, she dropped herself on the bed and kicked off her heels, sighing: *I hope those two get it together soon.* Lisa had a habit of pushing "understanding" to the limit. And Hunter . . . Hunter was starting to remind her of Roy in his early days. And that wasn't necessarily a good sign.

Alone in Lisa's quarters Rick felt nervous and trapped. *His superior, huh?* Just how long was he going to have to put up with that remark? Almost three years ago—*on this very ship!*—Lisa had used that remark, and he had held it against her ever since.

Lisa had unpacked some of her things, and Rick was wandering around inspecting this and that when he saw a framed photograph on the room's desk. He picked it up and regarded it. By the look of it, it had to have been taken ten years ago. But here was Lisa looking cute in short hair and chubby face, standing alongside an older guy, taller than she was by a foot and wearing what looked to be an Afghani woven cap. Nice-looking couple, he decided. But there was something familiar about him . . . something that reminded him of . . . *Kyle*! Then this had to be Riber, Rick realized. Karl Riber, Lisa's onetime true love, who had bought it along with Mars Sara Base years ago.

His attention was so fixed on the photo that he didn't hear Lisa enter the room. She realized this and stood in the doorway a moment, not wanting to startle him or make him uncomfortable. Finally she called his name softly, and he reacted like a sneakthief caught in the act, dropping the photo sideways to the desk and apologizing.

"Oh, I'm sorry, Lisa. I didn't mean to snoop."

This angered her: after all they had been through together, after all the *time* they had spent together, sharing secret thoughts and feelings, after all the time *she* had spent at his place in New Macross familiarizing herself with *his* things . . .

"What do you mean 'snoop'? I have nothing to hide from you, Rick. Be my guest, look around—not that there's much here . . ."

"Uh, sure," he said, at a loss. "So, uh, what did you and Claudia have to say?"

Lisa dismissed her conversation with Claudia as nothing special and asked him if he wanted some tea. "You know, just a little chat," she told him from the kitchenette.

Rick righted the photo when she left the room. He joined Lisa on the couch afterward.

"Didn't sound like just a little chat to me," he braved to say, tea cup in hand.

"Well, as a matter of fact, we were talking about you."

Rick squirmed in his seat. "If it concerns me and Minmei, I don't want to hear about it!"

"It wasn't at all about Minmei," she said cheerfully. "What would I possibly want to talk about her for?"

Lisa was unpracticed at this sort of thing and wished for a second that Claudia could stand over her shoulder during moments like these, feeding her the right lines or something. But oddly enough, Rick was apologizing for his tone.

"Minmei and I haven't seen much of each other in several months, and . . ."

"Oh, Rick," she said, perhaps too tenderly. "I know

how you feel about her, so . . . well, there's nothing more to say about it."

Acceptance was the one tack she hadn't tried yet.

Rick breathed a sigh and was puzzling over how he could just politely excuse himself, when Lisa added:

"I don't know why, but I get the feeling sometimes that you . . . well, that's there's something you *want* . . ."

Who doesn't? Rick asked himself, wondering just what she was getting at now.

"What are you talking about?"

She made an exasperated sound. "Rick, you know what I—"

The PA chose just that moment to intervene: A female voice was calling Lisa to the bridge.

Frustrated, Lisa said, "The usual perfect timing," then laughed. "You've managed to escape unscathed once again." She stood up and bade him a resigned good-bye. "We'll try this again some other time."

Rick reacted as if a dentist had just told him to make another appointment.

Claudia had also been summoned to the bridge. She stood stiffly with Lisa now on the automated walkway that was actually the curved top rail of the observation bubble, her back to the astrogation hold. The ship had unexpectedly defolded from hyperspace, and they were once again feeling a bit shaky.

Exedore was manning one of the human-size duty stations. Breetai was seated in his command chair, a grim look on his face. When Lisa said, "Reporting as ordered," he uttered a throaty growl and inclined his head a fraction to the left, as if to indicate the object of his attention.

Claudia and Lisa about-faced and eyed an image now filling the rectangular field of the projecbeam. It was like nothing either of them had ever seen—a twisted convoluted dark mass of armor, tentacles, reflex thruster ports, and sensor devices, smoothed and eroded-looking along its dorsal side, like a monstrous hunk of extraterrestrial driftwood.

"What in space is *that*?" Claudia asked.

"That, my dear Commander Grant, is a ship from our reconnaissance force—a fairly late model if I'm not mistaken."

"B-but I've never seen anything like it!" Lisa exclaimed.

"That is not unlikely," Breetai told her.

Lisa turned to Exedore and ordered a status report.

"I have made a positive identification, and it is in fact a late-model reconnaissance vessel. It has been somewhat modified for hyperspace travel. Moreover, our scanners indicate no biological activity whatsoever."

Lisa noticed the concerned look on his face as he studied the image and attendant glyphic readouts. Sectional views and close-ups of salient features of the thing flashed across his monitor screen to illustrate his report.

Lisa sucked in her breath and turned to Breetai once more.

"Commander, we have to investigate!"

"That is completely out of the question," he snapped.

"Sir," she tried, "isn't it possible your scanning systems may have missed something? Perhaps there are Zentraedi aboard? Isn't there any margin for error?"

She didn't believe a word of it, and judging from the look on Exedore's face, neither did he. But it was possible there were weapons aboard—pods, tri-thrusters, something the Earth forces could use to beef up their arsenal.

"The information assimilated is in accordance with the galactic code," Exedore told her sternly. "'Errors' are not possible."

"We can't waste an opportunity like this—we must investigate!" she answered him, filing away "galactic code" for some future discussion. "The possibility of Zentraedi—"

"Your *compassion* is commendable," Exedore interrupted, still unconvinced. "However, it looks to me as though the vessel could be a trap."

"A trap?!"

"Yes," he continued. "We Zentraedi are known for such 'Trojan horses,' as you call them. It is not wise to take such a risk."

Claudia decided to step in. "He's right—we can't jeopardize the mission, Lisa."

"I suppose . . ." she said uncertainly.

"It is worse then you realize," Breetai intoned behind her. "This vessel belongs to the Robotech Masters. It is one of many which act as their eyes and ears."

The Robotech Masters, Lisa exclaimed to herself.

"You're saying that they could monitor our presence."

Breetai grunted. "I fear they already have."

CHAPTER SEVEN

Your Earth scientists are a fanciful lot: all this talk about time travel, relativity, looking through a telescope and being able to see the back of your own head... I suppose it all looked good on paper.

Exedore, as quoted in Lapstein's *Interviews*

DEFOLDING FROM HYPERSPACE ONCE AGAIN, Breetai's flagship materialized in real time hundreds of parsecs from Earth.

If the image of the Robotech surveillance vessel had awed Lisa, the form and appearance of the automated factory satellite positively stunned her. It had the same vegetal look as the smaller vessel, the same external convolutions, cellular armor, and incomprehensible aspect, but all similarities ended there. The satellite was enormous, almost organically rose-colored in starlight, shaped in some ways like a primate brain, with at least half a dozen replicas of itself attached to the factory's median section by rigid stalklike transport tubes. In orbit around it were hundreds of Zentraedi craft: dreadnoughts, battle mecha, and Cyclops recons.

"My dear colleagues," Breetai announced as a close-up of the factory appeared in the projecbeam field, "we have arrived."

Lisa, Claudia, and Exedore looked up from their duty stations.

"It's incredible!" Claudia exclaimed breathlessly.

Lisa made a sound of amazement. "Whatever powers created that must be light-years beyond us," she said softly, recalling her first glimpse of Dolza's command center and the surveillance vessel they had left behind only hours ago. "It's still hard to believe that such things exist in our universe."

"Well, all I can say is you *better* believe it, Commander," Max Sterling chimed in from Lisa's monitor, his helmeted image filling the screen. Max and Miriya's Veritechs were in position on the docking bay elevator, preparing for launch.

Lisa went on the com net. "Max, remember: You must convince Reno that we possess the Protoculture."

"Right, Captain." He saluted and signed off.

"Exedore," Breetai said from behind Lisa. "Summon Commander Hunter to the bridge immediately."

Lisa swiveled in her seat to face the commander while Exedore carried out the order.

"What do you have in mind, Commander?" she asked him.

Breetai showed a roguish smile. "I must apologize for not having informed you sooner, but you are of course aware that diversionary tactics will be necessary if our plan is to be successful."

"I support the tactic," she said warily. "But I thought we had agreed to broadcast Minmei's voice."

"Correct," he responded, suddenly turning to Exedore. "However, we have devised a small modification."

Lisa didn't like the sound of it, especially when she saw Exedore return the commander's grin and add, "Your Lordship, that was your plan from the beginning, was it not?"

Breetai issued a short laugh. He was pleased to see that his adviser had not been completely changed by the Micronian ways; Exedore still refused to take credit for a plan, even when his inspirations had guided it.

"Your modesty equals your intelligence," Breetai told him. Then, turning again to Lisa: "Captain, *we* have decided that *the kiss* would be a more effective counterattack. Wouldn't you agree?"

Lisa's eyes went wide and unfocused; she began to slump down in her chair, her stomach in knots. "Umm . . . I suppose . . ." she managed.

"I'm sure you recall the extraordinary effect produced when you and Commander Hunter touched lips," Breetai was saying.

Claudia meanwhile had left her station and was coming Lisa's way, a sly smile already in place. "Liisaaa . . ." she said playfully, putting her hand on her friend's shoulder. "Come on, Captain, can't you see it's a *brilliant* plan! Nothing to get upset about."

Lisa was staring blankly at the monitor. *Plan?* she asked herself. Yeah, but what plan were they all talking about: the one to fool the Zentraedi Reno, or were these galactic events suddenly taking second place to a universal conspiracy meant to bring her and Rick together?

"Lord Breetai," a Zentraedi voice announced. "A transmission from Commander Reno. Shall I put it through, sir?"

Breetai raised himself out of the command chair.

"Yes. And use the translator so that our friends can understand him."

Reno's face and shoulders took shape in the projecbeam field. A swarthy male with large eyes, dark busy brows, and a square jaw, Reno wore a blue uniform with red piping and a green command tunic. He opened with formalities, although wariness was suggested by both his voice and his stance.

"Welcome," he told Breetai, the English translation out of synch with the movements of his full lips. "It has been a long time, Commander."

"Indeed," said Breetai flatly. They hadn't seen each other since that fateful day long ago when Zor had been killed; when Dolza had ordered Reno to return the scientist's body to the Masters; when Zentraedi and Invid had fought to the death . . . Breetai unconsciously stoked the faceplate that concealed scars from those less confused times . . .

"Do you come as friend or foe?"

"We have retrieved the Protoculture matrix from Zor's dimensional fortress, Reno. Our powers are limitless. I have come to demand that you surrender the satellite to me. Join me and my friendship is yours. Oppose me and perish."

Reno snorted. "So you've stolen Zor's science, have you? . . .And of course you and your new Micronian playmates plan to keep it from the Masters . . .Any other amusing anecdotes you wish to relate, Breetai?"

The commander smiled knowingly. "Actually, I do have something else you might enjoy—it should be arriving at any minute."

"I'll attempt to contain my boundless excitement," Reno responded sarcastically.

Rick was at just that moment arriving on the bridge. He saluted Breetai from the curved walkway.

"Right on time," said the pleased commander. He turned to Reno and issued his ultimatum: "This is your last opportunity to comply."

"Ridiculous!" Reno started to say. "The very fact that you have rejected the ways of the Robotech Masters indicates—" But his own projecbeam now closed on Lisa and Rick standing together on the walkway. Reno's bushy brows went up. "What?! A female talking to a male?!"

Breetai's one eye sparkled. "Yes, that's right, Commander. And now . . ."—like a master of ceremonies—"if you watch closely, you will witness the strange and glorious freedom that comes from Protoculture."

Rick meanwhile was baffled, casting confused looks to Breetai and the projecbeam image of Reno. He turned hopelessly to Lisa and whispered, "What the heck is going on?"

"It's all right," Lisa said soothingly.

Rick stiffened. If Lisa was telling him it was all right, he was *really* worried!

"Max," Miriya said over the tac net after hearing him laugh, "is there any chance Rick won't go along with the change in the diversionary tactics?"

Their Veritechs were wing to wing in deep space, closing fast on Reno's command ship, thrusters blue in the eternal night. The drama on the bridge was being carried over the com net.

"I don't think I'm going to like this one little bit," Rick was grumbling.

Max grinned. "Don't worry about him, Miriya. Remember: Rick Hunter is a *professional.*" The humor was of course lost on her.

Miriya recognized Lisa's voice now: "Yes, mister, I'm making it an order!"

"It's his *job* to take orders," she heard Max comment. *He's so serious,* she thought. Perhaps there was another side to kissing that she wasn't aware of—some *strategic* method Max had yet to teach her. As a mother she was somewhat alarmed; but the warrior and fighter ace was downright angered. This was, after all, a dangerous mission they were flying. There might not be another opportunity...

"Do you think we'll ever have a chance to touch lips again, Max?"

Max regarded her red-suited image on his commo screen and smiled. "I *promise* we will," he assured her.

"The Veritechs are within range of the tracking systems now," Claudia reported from her duty station.

"Commence broadcast," Breetai told Exedore, ignoring for a moment the minor battle that was in progress on the walkway below him.

"No, Lisa!" Rick was shouting. "I'm not going to consent to the kiss, orders or no orders! I'm sorry, but my mind is made up!"

Diversionary tactic, Rick said to himself with distaste. Of all the cheap shots Lisa could have taken! Just something to divert him from thinking about—

Minmei?!

Rick blinked: Minmei's "Stagefright" was booming over the bridge PA system, and he seemed to be the only one surprised by it.

Although that wasn't quite true: Reno's crew wasn't prepared for this, either. Nor had they the chance to become gradually accustomed to singing, as Breetai's crew had. Consequently, they reacted as though a combination of nerve gas, high-frequency sound, and unbridled electricity had suddenly been leveled against the ship.

"Aaargh! Blast it!" screamed Reno, throwing his hands up to his ears.

"Can't stand it!" yelled his crew members, who were dropping like flies at their duty stations.

"No more!" Reno pleaded. "Please turn it off!"

It never failed to amaze Rick that Minmei's voice could elicit such contrary responses from beings who supposedly had common ancestors; but he had scarcely a moment to dwell on it. Lisa had grabbed him by the shoulders and was now putting all she had into *offensive osculation.* And *whew!*—this was a different Lisa from the one who'd kissed him closed-mouthed in front of Breetai three years ago!

"Well, Reno," Breetai was saying at the same time, a self-satisfied smile on his face, "perhaps *this* will please you."

Reno, who had averted his gaze from the projecbeam, turned back to it now that Breetai had lowered that "sound weapon." But the image that greeted his eyes was even more debilitating: Here were two Micronians . . .

"*—touching lips??!!*" Reno wailed. He stared at the field, nauseated by confusion and some *feeling* even more alien to his system. From the ship's astrogation hold came shrills of protest, pain, and caterwauling. Reno covered his eyes with his hand: He had barely enough strength to deactivate the projecbeam and felt close to fainting when he managed to do so. Below him, several of his troops had collapsed. But he would never admit to defeat.

"Breetai," he said into the mike, his voice a harsh croak. "That display gained you nothing."

Breetai looked exulted nonetheless, ready to lay down his trump card now.

"Reno has discontinued transmission," a tech informed him.

Then Claudia relayed that the Veritechs were approaching their mission objective.

"Contact in three seconds . . ."

* * *

Reno was just regaining his composure when a fiery explosion breached the starboard hull of the astrogation hold, the force of it throwing several of his goliath crewmen clear across the vast chamber. He cursed and at the same time complimented Breetai for the brilliant execution of his plan; his diversionary tactics—*those Micronian secret weapons*—having completely disarmed his crew. Regardless, he had the presence of mind to bellow:

"Attack alert!"

On Breetai's ship, Claudia updated that the Veritechs had made a successful entry.

"The baby is with Max and Miriya," Lisa said worriedly to a still dazed and confused Rick.

"Huh?!" he stammered in response, promising this was the last time he'd permit himself to be so far removed from mission planning.

When the smoke and fire had been sucked from the hold of Reno's ship, the hull self-repaired, and two Micronian battle mecha, one red, one blue, rested side by side on the deck, fully encircled by Zentraedi troops wielding pulsed-laser rifles.

"All units prepare to destroy Micronian fighters on my command!" Reno growled, his troops snapping to and arming their weapons. He asked himself just what Breetai was hoping to gain by the insertion of such a small strike force, then directed his orders to the pilots of the Veritechs, using what little he knew of their language. "Micronians! You are completely surrounded! Surrender immediately and you will be allowed to live!"

The augmentation packs of the fighters elevated.

"This is it, Max," Miriya said over the net. "Wish me luck."

"You've got it," Max returned. "Everything'll be fine —I'm right here."

From the observation bubble high above the deck, Reno watched as the canopy of the red fighter went up. The Micronian pilot stood up and removed its helmet, shaking its long green mane free. Reno's mouth fell open when the Micronian spoke.

"I am not a Micronian," Miriya announced in Reno's own tongue, "but a micronized Zentraedi warrior."

Reno didn't doubt it for a second; in fact, he recognized her. "You are Miriya Parino!" he said in disbelief. "You were second in command under Azonia!"

Miriya pointed to Max's Veritech. "Allow me to present Lieutenant Maximillian Sterling, an officer with the Earth Forces . . . and my *mate.*"

Max removed his "thinking cap" and stood up in the cockpit.

"What is this thing, 'mate'?" Reno was asking. "He is merely a Micronian."

Max said loud enough for Miriya to hear: "Show him the baby."

And Miriya did just that, lifting Dana from the cockpit and raising her into view. The infant was cradled in her arms, wearing the same helmet and Dr. Dentons EVA suit.

For a moment Reno didn't know what he was looking at, but there was something about the thing that filled him with fear nonetheless. From his vantage it appeared to be some sort of . . . *micronized Micronian*!

"But this is impossible!"

His rough and ready troops were similarly nonplussed.

"What is that thing?" one asked.

"By the twelve moons—it's deformed."

"Look—it moves!"

"A mutant!" someone insisted.

In an effort to rub her eyes, Dana had brought her tiny gloved fists up to the helmet faceshield.

Miriya resumed, "In the Micronian language, this is what's called an 'infant'—actually created inside my own body. By both of us," she hastened to add, indicating Max.

Max nodded, humbly, and smiled.

"It is *love* that is the basis of Protoculture," Miriya continued. She lifted Dana over her head, the baby smiling and cooing in response. "You cannot conquer *love*!"

Reno's face began twitching uncontrollably at Miriya's mention of the shibboleth—*Protoculture!*

Still holding Dana aloft, Miriya pivoted through a 360-

degree turn, preaching to the full circle. "Observe the power of Protoculture—the power of love!"

"It's a mutation," one of the troops shouted, letting his weapon fall and fleeing the hold.

"It's contagious!" said another, also fleeing.

More discarded weapons crashed to the deck.

Dana, innocent, continued to wave her arms and smile.

Overcome, the troops began to desert their posts.

Beads of sweat pouring from his face, Reno was ranting into the mike: "Stay where you are, you cowards! Come back! It must be a trick!" Ultimately he backed away, turned, and ran from the observation bubble.

CHAPTER EIGHT

Love, like size, had lost all meaning—love was a battle maneuver, kissing a diversionary tactic. The only one among us who seemed to know anything about that elusive emotion was Miriya, wedded to the infant she'd given birth to as much as she was Max.

The Collected Journals of Admiral Rick Hunter

REPORTS FROM MAX AND MIRIYA VERIFIED THE success of the third stage of the ruse.

Breetai reasoned (correctly, as it would unfold) that Reno would retreat just far enough from the cruiser's command center to restabalize himself and sound general quarters. It was possible that the three-act tactic had convinced him to surrender—and indeed, Breetai was more than willing to give him the benefit of the doubt before mounting a full-scale assault on the heavily guarded satellite—but unlikely.

At her duty station well below Breetai's thoughtful look, Claudia Grant laughed. "I can't imagine why Reno's crew reacted like that," she was telling Lisa Hayes. "I think Max and Miriya's baby is pretty cute, don't you?"

"Oh, stop it, Claudia," said Lisa.

Breetai noticed that Commander Hunter appeared

somewhat debilitated by the kiss he performed with Lisa before he had rushed from the bridge. It was no wonder that Hunter had expressed such initial reluctance, Breetai thought. *Obviously, kissing is something not to be taken lightly.*

"None of you should underestimate the opposition's capability," Breetai warned the humans now, putting a quick end to the jokes. "Inform your mecha pilots to stand by."

Claudia followed through immediately, ordering Blue, Green, and Brown teams to their launch platforms. And not a minute later Max reported that Reno had called for a counterstrike; he and Miriya were going to make a break for it.

Dana! Claudia recalled, suddenly full of concern.

"Launch all mecha!" Breetai bellowed.

Human and Zentraedi mecha launched themselves from the warship's bays while the vessels of Reno's fleet massed for attack.

Rick led his small squad of seven Veritechs against them, side by side with the Zentraedi's ostrich-like Battlepods, tri-thrusters, and pursuit ships. Two years had passed since he had engaged any enemy in deep space, but it suddenly felt like no time had elapsed. The silence, the zero-g spherical explosions that bloomed in the night like flowers of death, the eerie glow of thruster fire, the disinterested shimmer of starlight, the cacophony that poured into his helmet through the tactical net a hallucinatory symphony of panicked commands, frenzied warnings, and final screams.

He knew that he would need to clear his mind of all thoughts, righteous and otherwise, to come through this unscathed. Out here thoughts were a pilot's number one enemy, because they invariably impeded productive interface with the Veritech. So he let it all go—the questions still there after four years of combat, the faces of those left behind—and the mecha picked up that vibe transmitted through the sensor-studded gloves and "thinking cap" to its Protoculture heart and led him once more through hell's gates.

* * *

"I don't want your excuses!" Reno screamed, slamming his fist down on the substation console—an elaborate control center even by Zentraedi standards, salmon-colored and organic in design with no less than a dozen circular monitor screens. "Now order your troops to battle stations! Do you understand?!"

The face of Reno's red-haired lieutenant seemed to blanch in the projecbeam. He raised his shaking hands into view.

"But sir, our troops are terrified of Micronian contamination!"

"Nonsense!" howled Reno. "You have your orders: Destroy the infected mecha at once! I have spoken!"

"We are within range, m'lord," Exedore reported calmly.

Breetai regarded the projecbeam. Reno's fleet had foolishly formed up on the commander's own cruiser, now itself bracketed in Breetai's deadly sights. *So much the easier, then,* he said to himself.

At one time the strength of Breetai's conditioning would have made such a thing impossible, but the Zentraedi imperative had been altered beyond recognition by the campaign directed against Zor's dimensional fortress. To remain on the side of the Robotech Masters was to be Breetai's enemy.

"On my command, Exedore . . ." said the commander.

Skull One's lateral thrusters edged the Veritech out of the arena—momentarily. There were still half a dozen Battlepods on his tail crosshatching space with angry bolts of cannon fire, *and these guys were on his side*! The nonallied pods were of course a concern, but the crazed random firing of Breetai's troops was life-threatening! From the sound of the shrieks and comments coming through the net, Rick knew that he wasn't alone in his fear.

Now, with no advance warning from the bridge, the warship's main cannon had been armed. Pinpoints of dazzling light had erupted across the blunt nose of the battlewagon; in a moment, Rick knew from previous battles, a lethal slice of orange death would streak from each of these, holing their targets with an immeasurable force.

Breetai's ship was within point-blank range of Reno's, taking aim at the bow of the smaller ship where the bridge and astrogational section were located. Rick went on the tac net, warning his fellow pilots to steer clear, and voiced a prayer that Max and Miriya had escaped safely.

The Robotech factory satellite, its secondary modules like small moons, spun slowly on its axis—a small world unto itself, barely visible now in the blinding light of a thousand small novas.

Miriya held Dana in her lap, her right hand gripping the Veritech's Hotas. Flashes of stroboscopic light threw flaming reds and blazing yellows into the cockpit. In no other battle (and there had been many) had she been possessed by such fury. Even that on-and-off dogfight she had waged against Max couldn't measure up to the intensity and *need* she now felt. It was as though her entire body was rallying to the cause; as though the small life she held in her arms was a treasure more precious than any the universe could offer, a life worth preserving at all costs . . .

She and Max had blasted free of Reno's ship, but they were far from safe.

"Enemy projectiles bearing 977L!" Claudia told her through the com net, the alarm in her voice unmasked. "Two triple-fins attempting interception!"

"Watch it, Max!" said Miriya, as concerned for his safety as she was for Dana's. "I've got them!"

She thumbed the trigger button on the Hotas, releasing four white-tipped heat-seekers, which tore from the Veritech's missile tubes. They found one of the tri-thrusters, blowing it to pieces, while the second craft disappeared beneath Miriya's own. She engaged the underside lasers as the enemy made its pass, the intensified light searing open the cockpit of the triple-fin, decommissioning it.

Miriya heard Max breathe a sigh of relief and thank her.

She returned the sigh and clutched Dana more tightly to herself, the infant waving her arms joyously at the fiery spectacle.

"Fire!" said Breetai.

A rain of supercharged energy ripped from the nose of the warship, converging on Reno's ship, individual bolts tearing through it as if it wasn't there. And in scarcely a second, it wasn't—its superstructure flayed and bow blown open beyond self-repair.

Like a whale swallowing a stick of dynamite, Rick decided. He imagined Reno's swift death: energy brilliant as blizzard snow wiping him from life . . .

"Dead ahead!" one of his wingmen said through the net.

Rick looked forward into a swarm of Officer's Pods, triple-fins, and tactical Battlepods.

"Fire all proton missiles on my command," he told his squad. "Now!"

Hundreds of missiles dropped from their pylons and fuselage tubes, blowtorching into the midst of the enemy cloud, taking out fighter after fighter.

Meanwhile, Breetai's dreadnought had loosed follow-up fusillades against two more warships in what had once been Reno's fleet. Explosions lit local space like a brief birth of suns, Robotech husks drifting derelict in the perpetual darkness. On the observation balcony, Breetai stood rigid with his hands behind his back, impassively watching projecbeam views of the battle. Victory was assured: one more blow struck against the Masters. But he was aware that this was a minor triumph in the war that would someday rage at Earth's gateway; and as bright as this moment might seem, he would be powerless when that day arrived—

"Squadron leader requesting assistance in the Third Quadrant," one of his officers interrupted.

"Is the neutron cannon ready?" Breetai asked.

"Eighty percent," Claudia reported sharply.

"We have positive lock and focus on photon particle tracking beam," Lisa added, her monitor schematic resembling a star map overlaid with doodles. "All Veritechs and pods have cleared the field of fire."

"Neutron exchange complete," Claudia updated.

Breetai's lips became a thin line.

"Sanitize the area," he ordered.

Rick led his squad—Max and Miriya among them now—to the safe coordinates Lisa had supplied him. Hearing the go signal for the neutron cannon given, he glanced back at Breetai's ship, expecting to witness an outpouring of energy to make all previous discharges pale by comparison. But he saw no sign of fire, only the invisible particle beam's awesome and horrific effect: Nearly every mecha in the cannon's line of fire was disintegrated. Some exploded, others came apart, while still others simply vanished without a trace.

The number of dead was beyond his ability to calculate. And he found himself thinking about the Zentraedi on Earth—the micronized ones who were struggling to adapt to a new culture, the malcontents who wandered the wastes in search of new wars. With Reno's defeat (according to Exedore), the race would be close to extinction.

It was as if they knew somehow that their time had come. They had honored their imperative; they had chased Zor's fortress for their Masters and done their best to reclaim it. But in truth, they had traveled clear across the galaxy to fulfill a greater imperative: *They had come to Earth to die.*

"Lord Breetai," said Exedore. "The remaining troops have agreed to surrender." His voice gave no hint of sadness at the nearly total annihilation of Reno's forces; if anything, it carried a suggestion of relief. His commander's reign was now supreme—as it was always meant to be, with or without the Protoculture matrix.

Breetai was seated in the command chair. Regally, he stated, "Let the prisoners know that we will gladly accept all who wish to join us."

Exedore spoke into the mike at his duty station. "Lord Breetai extends his greetings to all Zentraedi prisoners.

Furthermore, it is his pleasure to extend a full pardon to those who wish to join the United Forces under his command."

Standing now, Breetai announced: "Our victory may very well mark the dawn of a new era in galactic relations."

His ship was already closing on the Robotech factory satellite, a biluminescent mollusk in the blackness of space, strings of lights girdling it like some Christmas ornament. The prize had been won. And if those defeated troops on bended knee weren't testament enough to the win, one had simply to look out on that seemingly limitless field of mecha and cruiser debris through which his ship moved, the remnants of the last remaining Zentraedi fleet.

CHAPTER NINE

The transport of the Robotech factory satellite to Earthspace was another one of the malign miracles visited upon us. Certainly Gloval and Breetai had only our best interests in mind, but shouldn't it have occurred to them that if the Robotech Masters had been able to track Zor's dimensional fortress here, they could surely do the same with the satellite? Like Zor before him, Breetai thought he was doing Earth a favor... This renders his comment (upon manifesting in Earthspace with the factory) doubly ironic: "We've made it," he is quoted as saying. "It is good to be back home."

Dr. Lazlo Zand, *On Earth As It Is in Hell: Recollections of the Robotech War*

ARMAGEDDON PLAYED IN FULL COLOR ON AN oval-shaped viewing screen in Tirol's central ministry, an organic room like those in the Masters' space fortresses, cathedraled by columns that might have been living ligaments and sheathed neurons. Representatives from the Council of Elders, the Robotech Masters, the Young Lords, and the Scientists were in attendance—the Elders and the Masters in unvarying groups of three at their Protoculture caps. The Young Lords, a bearded trio, balding in spite of their relative youth, were intermediaries between the Masters themselves and the Empire clones. Three was sacred, three was eternal, the irreligious trinity ruling what remained of Tirol's social structure—what remained of a race long past decadence. Such had been the influence of the tripartite Invid flower, the Flower of Life...

One of the Masters had the floor now: With Reno's

defeat at the hands of the traitor, Breetai, their hopes for reclaiming Zor's fortress had been dashed.

—I think that the best plan is to completely educate another deprivation tank tissue, so that by the time we get to Earth, it will appear human.

One of the Scientists risked a question, approaching the Masters' station arrogantly, leaving his partners in the Triumvirate to labor at the spacetime calculations.

—What makes you think this clone will be different from the others that have been generated and failed?

—Mmmm?!

A second Master took up the challenge, regarding the Scientist with distaste. An exotic-looking, blue-lipped, and scarlet-haired androgynous clone. What had they accomplished, the Master asked himself before replying, in creating this young generation of long-haired, toga-clad beings who walked a thin line between life and death?

—Such insolence! Have you forgotten that these previous efforts have been undertaken without proper attention to the basic matrix generation process? This clone will have ample time to mature, but we must begin programming the tissue immediately. Of the fourteen remaining in the tank, one will surely take on the full psychic likeness of Zor.

—One more thing, Master: Why don't we check the matrix figures on the remaining Protoculture? Perhaps such a journey is unnecessary.

—The figures have been checked and rechecked. We don't even have enough to make the hyperspace-fold to the Earth system.

The female member of the Triumvirate turned from her calculations.

—I understand, Master.

—*So!* We will begin the trip under reflex power and rely on the remaining clone matrix cell tissue to complete our mission.

—Twenty long years by their reckoning. . . . And how many of us will survive such a journey?

—If only three of us survive, it will be enough. This is our only chance to regain control of the Protoculture.

One of the Masters gestured to the oval screen—a

view of deep space captured by their surveillance vessel: the mecha debris and litter that was once Reno's fleet.

—After all, look what is left of *their* culture; observe and survey the remnants of their once-great armada. We must have that Protoculture matrix! Even if it takes twenty years and the last developing clone from our tank! We have no choice but to proceed. I can see no other solution. *So!* If there is nothing further...

A member of the Elder Triumvirate spoke through lips as cracked as baked clay, a face as wrinkled as history itself.

"Elder Council is with you."

The central speaker of the Masters inclined his head in a bow.

"We acknowledge your wisdom and appreciate the generosity of your support, Elder. It is out of loyalty to you and our forefathers that we have decided thus."

"We understand the importance of this mission, not only for our race but for all intelligent life in the quadrant."

A second Elder bestowed his blessings on the voyage.

"Proceed with your plan, then; but know that there can be no margin for error without grave consequences."

"The future of all cultures is in your hands."

A twenty-year journey through the universe, the Masters thought in unison. Twenty years to regain a prize stolen from them by a renegade scientist. Would they prevail? Was there not one loyal Zentraedi left?...Yes, there was. But could even he succeed where so many had failed?

Khyron!

Khyron was their last hope!

Human and Zentraedi teams labored long and hard to ready the factory for a hyperspace jump. In less than a week's time it defolded in lunar orbit, winking into real time without incident, Breetai's dreadnought, his Human and Zentraedi crew, and thousands of converted warriors inside the satellite's womb. The commander's prime concern had been the removal of the factory from the Robotech Masters' realm; their reach, however, was to prove greater than even he had anticipated.

The Veritech Team, as well as Lisa and Claudia, returned to New Macross, and in their place arrived scores of Lang's Robotechnicians, who dispersed themselves through the factory like kids on a scavenger hunt. Finally, Admiral Gloval himself was shuttled up to Earth's new satellite; well aware that the factory was now Earth's only hope against a potential follow-up attack by the Robotech Masters, he traveled with his fingers crossed. Claudia Grant was his escort.

Dr. Lang and several of his techs were on hand to greet them. Pleasantries were dispensed with, and Gloval was led immediately to one of the factory's automated assembly lines, where alien devices, still only half-understood by Lang, turned out Battlepod carapaces and ordnance muzzles.

Gloval marveled at the sight of these machines at work: Pods were being fabricated as though they were chocolate candy shells. From a basic sludge vat of raw metals to finished product in minutes; servos, arc welders, presses, and shapers doing the work of thousands of men. Unpiloted pods, controlled by computers even Lang refused to tamper with, marched in rows, one above the other, along powered transport belts, pausing at each work station for yet another automated miracle. All the while a synthesized Zentraedi voice actually *spoke* to the devices, directing them in their tasks. Exedore had substituted a translation, which was playing as Gloval stood transfixed.

"Make ready units one fifty-two to one fifty-eight for protobolt adjustments and laser-bond processes. Units one fifty-nine to one sixty-five are on-line for radio-krypto equipment encoding . . ."

"But what does it mean?" Gloval asked Lang.

The scientist shook his head, marblelike eyes penetrating Gloval's own. "We don't know, Admiral. But do not be deceived by what you see. This entire complex is but a ghost of its former self—nothing is running to completion." Lang made a sweeping gesture. "Whatever fuels this place—and I see no reason to suppose that it is any different than that which runs the SDF-1—has lost its original potency."

"Protoculture," Gloval said flatly.

Lang gave a tight-lipped nod and pointed to the line of half-finished pods along the conveyor belt. "Observe . . ."

Gloval narrowed his eyes, not sure what he was supposed to be looking at. But shortly the Doctor's meaning became obvious.

"Warning! Shut down! Warning! Damage! . . ." the synthesized voice began to repeat. Suddenly one of the pods on the belt was encased in a spider web of angry electrical energy. Servowelders and grappling arms flailed about in the fire, falling limp as the pod split apart and the great machines ground to a halt.

"Status report on the way," one of Lang's techs said to Gloval.

The admiral rubbed his chin and hid a look of disappointment.

No one spoke for a moment, save for a human voice from the PA calling maintenance personnel to the process center. Then Exedore arrived on the scene. Gloval had not seen him since the evening the satellite mission was first discussed.

"How are you, sir?" Exedore asked, concerned but having already guessed Gloval's response.

"Not as well as I was hoping," Gloval confessed. "When can you start operating again?"

"I'm afraid the situation is worse than first thought." Never one to mince words, Exedore added: "We may be down permanently."

"Are you certain?"

The Zentraedi adviser nodded, grimly.

Claudia gasped. "But our defense depends on continued operation!"

Gloval clasped his hands behind his back, refusing to accept the prognosis. "Carry on," he told Exedore. "Do what you can to get things running again. Do something —*anything*!"

* * *

"Veritech team leader," said the female voice over Rick's com net. "We have a disturbance in New Detroit City. Can you respond?"

Rick accessed the relevant chart as he went on the net. "Roger, control." He glanced at the monitor: His team was over the southern tip of Lake Michigan, close to what was once the city of Chicago. "We are approximately three minutes ETA of New Detroit City. What's up?"

"Zentraedi workers have broken into Fort Breetai. They've taken over the sizing chamber and are attempting to transport it from the city."

Rick gritted his teeth and exhaled sharply. "Listen up," he told his wingmen. "We're on alert. Hit your afterburners and follow my lead."

New Detroit had risen up around a Zentraedi warship that had crashed there during Dolza's apocalyptic attack; its mile-high hulk still dominated the city and the surrounding cratered wastes like some leaning tower of malice. The population of the city was predominantly Zentraedi, many micronized by order of the New Council and hundreds more who were full-size workers in the nearby steel factories. In addition, though, there was a sizable contingent of civil defense forces stationed there to guard a sizing chamber that had been removed from the derelict ship but had yet to be transported to New Macross, where similar ones were being stored.

Rick caught sight of the chamber on his first pass over the high-tech fort. A convoy of vehicles was tearing along the rampart that led to the underground storage facilities. Updated reports from control indicated that at least twelve Humans and three Zentraedi giants lay dead inside.

The clear-blue nose-cone-like device had been placed on an enormous flatbed, hauled by a powerful tug with tires like massive rollers; two micronized aliens were in the drivers' seats, three more up top, along with three blue-uniformed giants, two of whom were attempting to stabilize the hastily guy-wired and turnbuckled chamber. Behind the flatbed were two more enormous eight-wheeled transports, each bearing malcontents armed with autocannons. Rick saw them open fire on the laser-sentry posts. At street level, they turned their cannons on everything that moved, scattering workers and pedestrians alike.

"We're over the disturbance now," Rick reported in. "Left wing, wait until they've reached the outskirts, then go in low and give them a warning."

The renegade Zentraedis spotted the Veritechs and opened up with indiscriminate volleys as the fighters fell from the sky. Rick and his team rolled out, dodging autocannon slugs and gatling spray as they broke formation.

So much for scare tactics, Rick said to himself, Skull One flying inverted and low over the tortuous landscape outside the city limits.

"Left wing, knock one of the giants off the lead unit immediately!"

Rick completed his roll as his wingman went out, reconfiguring the Veritech to Guardian mode and swooping down on the convoy. The Zentraedis were loosing continuous fire, but Rick could discern the early stages of panic in their flight. The highway was full of twists and turns here, and the converter had made the flatbed dangerously top-heavy.

The armed alien on the flatbed got off one last shot before Rick's wingman, now in Battloid mode, blasted him from the vehicle. The road was also proving too much for the drivers to handle; Rick watched the vehicle screech through a tight S-turn, leave the road, clinging to a raised course of shoulder, then bounce back to the tarmac, where the giant's micronized accomplices decided to call it quits.

Meanwhile, the rest of the Veritech group had reconfigured to Battloid mode and put down ahead of the halted convoy.

Rick completed his descent and advanced his mecha in a run, chain-gun gripped in the metalshod right hand and leveled against the giants on the flatbed. One Zentraedi was dead on the road. The others began to throw down their weapons as Rick spoke.

"Don't move or you'll be destroyed!" he called out over the external speakers. The Battloids came to a stop and spread out. "It's useless to resist," Rick continued. "You are completely surrounded. You must understand that what you have done is unacceptable behavior by Human standards and that you will be punished." Rick stepped his mecha forward. "Now, the Protoculture chamber will be returned to the fort."

Three hundred miles to the northeast of New Detroit a thick blanket of newly fallen snow covered the war-ravaged terrain. Khyron's ship had landed here, having used up almost all of the Protoculture reserves that drove its reflex engines to free itself from Alaska's glacial hold.

Zentraedi Battlepods sat in the snowfields like unhatched eggs abandoned by an uncaring mother. Deserters from the Micronian population centers and factories continued to arrive in stolen transports and tugs. The hulk of a Zentraedi warship overlooked the scene, its pointed bow thrust deep into the frigid earth like a spear, alien tripetaled flowers surrounding it, hearty enough to pierce the permafrost.

Khyron had followed a trail of such ships clear across the northern wastes, salvaging what he could in the way of weapons and foodstuffs, marveling at the resilience of the Invid Flower of Life, gone to seed and flower as the Protoculture in the ship's drives had disintegrated.

Now in the command center of his ship, he received word that his plan to steal the sizing converter had failed.

"Idiot!" Khyron said to his second, Grel, standing in stiff posture before the Backstabber. Azonia was seated in the command chair, her legs crossed, a mischievous look on her face. "Your feeble plan has failed us again!"

Grel frowned. "I'm sorry, sir, but our agents failed to eliminate the communications center and the Veritechs—"

"Enough!" Khyron interrupted him, raising his fist. "Our soldiers couldn't even defend themselves!"

"But sir, if you had only listened to . . ." Grel started to say, and regretted it at once. The plan had been Azonia's, not his; but there was little chance that Khyron would blame her—not now that a *special* relationship had been forged . . .And especially since his commander had begun to use the dried Invid leaves once again. As if that wasn't enough, the troops had all seen the Robotech satellite appear in Earth's skies, and that meant only one thing: The Micronians had somehow defeated Reno!

"Shut up, Grel!" Azonia barked at him. "Under your leadership they couldn't possibly have succeeded!"

"Well, I wouldn't exactly say—"

"Do not interrupt," she continued, folding her arms and turning her back to him.

Khyron too mocked him with a short laugh, and Grel felt the anger rising within him despite his best efforts to keep his emotions in check. It was bad enough that he and the troops had been forced to live these past two years with a female in their midst, but now to be humiliated like this . . .

"You should have had no trouble capturing the sizing chamber," Azonia was saying when he at last exploded, murder in his eyes as he leaned toward her.

"It might appear that all of this is my fault, but the truth is that you—"

"Enough!" Azonia screamed, standing, nearly hysterical. "I don't want to hear any excuses from you!"

Khyron stepped between them, angrier and louder than the two of them combined. "Stop arguing, Azonia! And Grel, I want you to listen, understand me?! I don't have to tell you what the appearance of that satellite signals—the last hope for the Masters lies with *us*!"

"Sir, I'm listening," Grel said, spent and surrendering.

Khyron, spittle forming at the edges of his maniacal snarl, waved a fist in Grel's face. "Excellent . . . because my reputation is on the line, and I need that sizing chamber to save *face*, and if I don't get it. . . . *I shan't spare yours!* Now, get out of here!"

Grel stiffened, then began to slink away like a beaten dog.

When he had left the room, Azonia moved to Khyron's side, pressing herself against him suggestively, her voice coy and teasing.

"Tell me confidentially, Khyron, do you really think he can handle it?"

"For his sake, I hope so," Khyron said through gritted

teeth, seemingly unaware of Azonia's closeness until she risked putting a hand on his shoulder.

"You know how to handle your troops, Khyron," she purred in his ear.

He pushed her away with just enough force to convey his seriousness, not wanting to confront the hurt look he was sure to find on her face. There was no use denying the bewildering attraction he had come to feel for her in their joint exile—these novel pleasures of the flesh they had discovered; but she had to be made to understand that there was a time and place for such things and that war and victory still came first—*would always come first*! No other Zentraedi had more right to these sensual gifts than he, but his troops deserved more than a commander who was less committed to them than they were to him. He had promised to return the deserters to full size, and he meant to do it—with or without Grel. And, should it come down to it, with or without Azonia.

"Now, listen," he confided. "There is something I couldn't tell Grel but I'm going to tell you . . .I'm going after than sizing chamber myself—I can't count on him to do it. I want you to stay here and take command while I'm gone."

He turned and walked away from her without another word, unaware of the smile that had appeared on her face.

Azonia savored the thought of commanding Khyron's troops in his absence. "This is starting to get good," she said aloud after a moment.

CHAPTER TEN

If we accept for a moment the view expressed by some of our twentieth-century colleagues—that children live out the unconscious lives of their parents—*and apply that to the Robotech Masters and their "children," the Zentraedi, we will arrive at a most revealing scenario. It is clear at this point that the Masters were the ones devoid of emotions. War though the Zentraedi did, their true imperative was centered on individuation and the search for self. . . . One has to wonder about Zor, however: He served the Masters yet did not count himself among them. Who can say to what extent he himself was affected by Protoculture?*

Zeitgeist, *Alien Psychology*

RETURNED TO NEW DETROIT, THE SIZING chamber was being hoisted back into its cradle, a four-poled hangar similar to those used to support freestanding tents. A large crowd had gathered, Humans and coveralled Zentraedi giants as well as their micronized brethren. Rick was supervising the crane operation, while the rest of his team, still in their Battloids, patrolled a cordoned-off area in front of Fort Breetai. There was palpable tension in the air.

"That's it . . . just a little more and we're there," Rick instructed the operating engineer. "Fine, fine . . . just keep it coming . . ."

As the chamber's round base was sliding down into the cradle's cup, a black sports car screeched to a halt nearby. Rick glanced over his shoulder and spied Minmei in the passenger seat.

New Detroit's Mayor, Owen Harding, a well-built man

with a full head of thick white hair and a walrus mustache, was in the back seat. He recognized Rick from the days he himself had served with the RDF aboard the SDF-1. Harding stepped out and asked if everything was well in hand, whether there was anything he could do. Minmei had been recognized by the crowd, and two policemen moved in to keep them from gathering around the car.

Rick saluted and gestured to the sizing chamber. "I need your people to provide security for this device."

"I can't do that, Commander," the mayor said firmly. "Most of the population here is Zentraedi—as you can see. Securing this 'device,' as you call it, is a military matter. We've already had enough trouble, and I'm not about to add to it by throwing my police force into the middle of it. Let's not beat around the bush, Commander, we all know what this machine is for."

Rick shook his long hair back from his face and squared his shoulders, trying not to think about the fact that Minmei was only fifteen feet away. "That's exactly why I need your support, sir—just until my superiors dispatch a proper unit to guard it. We can't afford to allow this chamber to fall into the wrong hands."

The crowd didn't like what they heard. Even before Rick finished, they were letting the mayor know where they stood.

"What're you saying, *Commander*—that we're all thieves?!" someone shouted.

"Just who is the 'wrong hands,' flyboy?!" from another.

The mayor made a hopeless gesture. "You see what I'm up against."

"Look," Rick emphasized, "I know you don't want any more trouble here, but I'm only asking for your cooperation for a matter of days—"

"I can't become involved in this."

"It's for *their* protection, too," Rick said, pointing to the crowd. "We all agreed to honor the Council's—"

"Then tell all the facts," a familiar voice interrupted.

Rick turned and saw Kyle walking toward him from the car.

"Military business, Kyle—stay out of it!" Rick warned

him sternly. Kyle was the last thing this situation needed: Mr. Agitation.

"This isn't just military business," Kyle started in, addressing Rick and the crowd. "It's everyone's, *Commander,* because you're talking about the Zentraedi's right to return to their normal size whenever they want."

Rick was incredulous. *Sure, why not let them all change back—especially now that they are hungry for warfare again and the closest targets are one-tenth their size.*

"You're nuts, Kyle."

"If you think I'm kidding, you're even a bigger fool than I thought. And I'm sure that most of the people in this city would agree with me. . . . isn't that right?"

Rick didn't bother to look around. Shouts of agreement rang out; micronized Zentraedi raised their fists, and the giants growled. Kyle's violent scene with Minmei in Granite City replayed itself in Rick's mind, along with Max's remarks about Kyle's false pacifism. *Minmei,* he said to himself, giving her a sidelong glance and reading some sort of warning in those blue eyes. *How could you be blood with this—*

"Well, do you . . ." Kyle was demanding. Picking up on Rick's inattention, he followed his gaze, reading his thoughts now. . . . *So he's still in love with her.*

Rick heard Kyle snort, then say to the crowd:

"When they take away your right to use the Protoculture chamber, it's the first step toward martial law! You lived under that for long enough before you came to Earth! This chamber should be controlled by the people of *this* city!"

One of the giants stomped his feet, rocking the area.

"You better listen to us right now!" he bellowed.

"This is our city," said a human female, much to Rick's amazement, "not the military's!"

Was there some sort of reverse *contagion at work here?*

"Why don't you just climb into your little plane and get out of here while you still can!" yelled a second giant.

"Listen to me!" Rick pleaded, actually managing to quiet them for a moment. "Isn't it better to have this machine secure from people who would use it against you than to endanger the whole city with it!"

"I'm getting sick of your lies, Hunter!" Kyle ranted at him, furious.

"Beat it!" the crowd shouted.

"We're not going to take this anymore!"

The mayor edged over to Rick, eyes on the alert for airborne bottles or rocks. "They mean business," he said warily.

"I've heard enough!" Rick began to shout back at them. "This is military property! I've been ordered to secure it, and I intend to carry out those orders!"

"We'll see about that!" one of the giants threatened.

Rick signaled his squad lieutenant. Two of the Battloids raised their gatlings and stepped forward.

The crowd took a collective intake of breath, but the comments persisted, helped along by Kyle, who was now attempting to lead them in a chant: "Leave here now! Leave here now!" punctuating his call with raised arm gestures.

The crowd joined him, holding their ground.

"Please, *Commander,*" said the mayor. "You have to go."

Rick narrowed his eyes and shot Kyle a deadly look. He scanned the crowd—angry faces and towering Zentraedi. If the Battloids opened fire, there would be all hell to pay; and if they didn't . . . if they just let the chamber sit . . .

No win! Rick screamed at himself, sending a tormented look Minmei's way before he turned his back on all of them and walked off.

In the snowfields at civilization's edge, Khyron received word of the turnabout in New Detroit. He couldn't have been more pleased.

He stood now at the head of a double-rowed column made up of twelve of his finest troops, each, like himself, suited up in Zentraedi power armor.

"Listen to me," he instructed them. "We are the *last true Zentraedi!* We must take that sizing chamber! *No* sacrifice is too great!"

With that, he fired the body suit's self-contained thrusters and lifted off, his elite squad following him into the skies.

Having left two of his Veritech corporals to stand guard over the chamber, Rick and his remaining team were on their way back to New Macross. Bill "Willy" Mammoth, one of Skull One's wingmen, had raised Rick on the tac net.

"Go ahead, Willy, I'm reading you," Rick told him.

"It's just that it's bothering, sir. All that power. Leaving it there'n . . . well, forget it . . ."

"Say it, Willy. I told you, I'm reading you."

"Well . . . I just hate to see a bunch of innocent people get hurt because of some hare-brained troublemaker."

An image of Kyle's angry eyes flashed in Rick's memory. That fight long ago in the *White Dragon,* Kyle's *pacifist* speeches, his violent temper . . .

"Yeah, so do I," Rick said grimly.

Mayor Harding was having misgivings. Two of Hunter's Battloids along with one of New Detroit's own civil defense Gladiators were supervising the transfer of the sizing chamber from Fort Breetai to its new resting place inside the city's exposition center, a sprawling complex of pavilions and theaters constructed in the "Hollywood" style—a pagodalike multistoried building here, a Mesoamerican temple there.

"But will it be safe?" the mayor wondered aloud.

Lynn-Kyle and Minmei were with him in the center's vast rotunda, observing the transfer procedure.

"Something's bothering you, Mr. Mayor?" Minmei asked leadingly, hoping Harding had had a change of mind and would recall Rick and his squad.

The mayor bit at the ends of his mustache. "To be honest, I was just thinking about the consequences of having the sizing chamber here should we be attacked. . . . I only hope I made the right decision."

"Attacked by whom?" Kyle said harshly. "The war's *over.*"

"Not to hear Commander Hunter tell it." Harding

shrugged. "All these disaffected Zentraedi who have been leaving the cities and setting up camps *out there* . . ."

Kyle made a dismissive gesture. "Forget about it—all that's just disinformation. They'll say anything to convince us that we still need their protection. Besides, there are a lot of peaceful Zentraedi citizens here. They'd help us if things got bad."

"I hope you're right."

"Don't worry. We did the right thing, and the people appreciate it. This chamber rightfully belongs to the Zentraedi people, and that's all that really matters."

The mayor cleared his throat.

Kyle said, "Trust me."

Harding, however, remained unconvinced. Kyle noticed that Minmei seemed preoccupied and uneasy, her face inordinately pale. The mayor had insisted on taking them on a tour of the center's new theater, and it was here that Kyle decided to change strategies.

"I've got an idea," Kyle told both of them, a lighter tone in his voice now. "How about a goodwill concert to promote brotherhood between the Human and Zentraedi citizens of New Detroit?"

All at once Harding grew excited. "Why, that would be great! I mean, if Minmei would consent . . . on such short notice and all . . ."

"Of course she'll do it," Kyle continued, although Minmei hadn't so much as acknowledged the idea by word or movement.

"The whole city'll turn out," said Harding, the wheels turning. He began to lead them down one of the theater aisles toward the large stage. "We can seat almost three thousand in here, and wait till you see our lighting system." Cupping his hands to his mouth, he called to the balcony: "Pops! Open up the main curtain and hit the spots!"

An unseen old-timer answered, "Sure thing, Mr. Mayor," and the curtain began to rise. Kyle took advantage of the moment to turn to Minmei and whisper, "What's you problem today, Minmei? You're going to upset the mayor."

"I just don't feel like singing," she said firmly.

Kyle raised his voice. "And just why not?"

"Because I don't think this place is safe with that Protoculture chamber here and because of what you did to Commander Hunter," she answered, not looking at him. "He *is* my close friend, you know. *He saved my life.*"

Kyle smirked. "You make it sound like it's a lot more than friendship, Minmei."

"You asked me, so I told you."

"Take it easy," he said. "First of all, we're not in any danger. And second, it didn't hurt your flyboy any to have his feathers ruffled. It keeps him sharp."

Minmei gritted her teeth.

"Here they come, Mr. Mayor!" the veteran stagehand yelled.

Two intense spots converged center stage, and Mayor Harding turned to Minmei proudly.

"How 'bout that?"

Kyle put on his best smile and stepped forward. "I think the whole *place* looks great, sir."

The mayor beamed and started to say, "Thank you—" when a loud concussion rocked the theater. A second and third explosion followed in quick succession, violent enough to send them all reeling in the aisle.

"What the—"

"Quick! Outside!" Kyle ordered.

No doubt a Minmei concert would have worked wonders in New Detroit, but how could Kyle have known that Khyron had made a previous booking?

Immediately upon his return to New Macross, Rick was ordered to report to Admiral Gloval in the briefing room of the SDF-1. There he found the admiral, Exedore, Lisa, Claudia, Max, Miriya, and the infamous Terrible Trio—Sammie, Vanessa, and Kim—seated at the room's circular table. Rick made his report directly to Gloval, summarizing the events that had transpired in New Detroit.

Gloval wore a look of despair. "I want to commend you for exercising good judgment, Captain," he told Rick after a moment. Then he gestured to the table. "I wanted you to be included in this. Exedore . . ." he said, sitting back to listen.

The engimatic Zentraedi inclined his head. "I have finished my research on the relationship between Protoculture and the Zentraedi," he began rather soberly. "My race . . ." Exedore's face appeared to blanch. "My race was bio-genetically engineered by the Robotech Masters for the sole purpose of fighting. Protoculture, the discovery of the Tirolian scientist Zor was utilized in both the initial cloning process and the enlargement of our physical being."

Miriya gasped. "You're saying that the Masters *created* us? It can't be true, Exedore. I have memories of my youth, my upbringing, my training . . ."

Exedore shut his eyes and shook his head sadly. "Implants, engrams . . . The Masters were clever to equip us with both racial and individual memories. But they neglected what is more important . . ."

Gloval cleared his throat. "Exedore, if I may? . . ."

Exedore gestured his assent, and Gloval addressed the table.

"These people you call the Robotech Masters were extremely proud of their advanced and powerful civilization. Hyperspace drives and advanced weaponry were already a part of their culture. But soon after the discovery of Protoculture and the science of Robotechnology, they dreamed of ruling a galactic empire. And they decided to develop a police force to protect their acquisitions—the Zentraedi."

The table went silent.

"For hundreds of years," the admiral continued, his eyes finding Miriya and Exedore, "you secured worlds for them—these *Masters* you were programmed to obey. But this scientist, Zor, the very genius who designed and built this ship, was silently working at tearing down what his co-opted discoveries had unleashed. It was believed that he hid his secrets somewhere in this ship and tried to send it from the Masters' grasp.

"And you, Exedore, and Miriya, Breetai, the old one you called Dolza, even Khyron, you were ordered to reclaim this ship at all costs—because without Zor's secrets the Robotech Masters won't be able to fulfill their dreams of empire. Without *Protoculture*, they will fall, as surely as their race of giant warriors fell. Confronted with emotions and feelings for the first time, the Zentraedi were powerless. For surely that race of perverted genuises had no love left in their hearts. And they will be defeated for the very same reasons."

Exedore looked up now. "Do not underestimate them, Admiral," he cautioned. He was impressed by Gloval's summary and evaluation, but the admiral spoke as if all of this was behind them, when in fact *it was just beginning*. "We Zentraedi no longer pose a threat to you, it is true. But believe me when I say this: The Masters are out there waiting, and they will not rest until that Protoculture matrix is theirs. Earth has been brought once to the brink of extinction by their power. Do not mislead yourselves by thinking that it can never happen again."

Gloval absorbed this silently. "Are there any questions?"

"Are the people of Earth . . . are they Protoculture?" Miriya asked, full of concern as she looked at Max. There was Dana—how could they explain *Dana*!

Gloval said, "I know what you're thinking, Miriya. But no. You see, we go back millions of years. And the Zentraedi . . ."

"But how can you explain that our genetic structures are nearly identical?" Max wanted to know.

Exedore spoke to that. "Nearly identical. *Nearly* identical. What is most plausible is that our genetic . . . stuff was cloned from the Masters themselves. They are, after all, er . . . Micronians like yourselves. Look for a similarity there, Lieutenant Sterling, not among the Zentraedi."

Max shook his head in a confused manner. "But I don't see that it matters any!"

"It doesn't," Miriya said, putting her hand over his.

"Then it must figure," Lisa pointed out, "that the people of Earth and the people of Tirol *did* have a common ancestry."

"I no longer believe that to be so," said Exedore. "A coincidence, I'm afraid."

Rick's eyebrows went up. "A *coincidence*!? But Exedore, the odds on that have to be nothing less than... ah—"

"Astronomical," Lisa finished.

Gloval snorted. "And the odds against our coexisting together?...They might be even greater."

"So the truth is," Exedore concluded, "that although our races are similar, they are not identical. My race, the Zentraedi, were Protoculturally devoid of everything save for the bio-genetically engineered desire to fight. We were nothing but *toys* to our creators—*toys of destruction.*"

CHAPTER ELEVEN

I had wandered into an inviting, friendly-looking house that sat flush with the street, thinking it would be a shortcut to Rick (who was speeding away in his Veritech). The house was filled with antiques from the last century, and I was running around touching everything. But then when I remembered Rick and began to search for an exit, I couldn't find a way out! I started opening doors only to find more doors behind them, and more doors behind those, and more doors!... I woke up more frightened than I've ever been in a long time. It was more frightening than real life.

From the diary of Lynn-Minmei

KYLE, MINMEI, AND MAYOR HARDING REACHED the theater's main entrance in time to see the descent of Khyron's airborne assault team.

They fell upon the city like a storm loosed from hell itself, resembling deep-sea divers and Roman gladiators in their powered armor. Civil defense Destroids were already in the streets, pouring missiles and transuranic slugs into the skies. An Excalibur MK VI, its slung cannons blazing, caught two enemy projectiles, which blew it off its feet, continuous fire from one of the cannons holing storefronts all along the avenue. Nearby, a Spartan was faring better, having taken out two of the enemy raiders with Stilettos launched from the mecha's drumlike missile tubes. But it too fell when one of the Zentraedi, easily as tall as the Spartan and better equipped to maneuver, barreled into it, sending the thing reeling back against the facade of the exposition theater, sparking out as it collapsed to the street, missiles dropping from one of its shattered drums.

Kyle and the others pressed themselves deeper into the theater's doorway, shivering with fear, as cries for help rang out from the demolished Spartan.

"Our worst fears are realized!" yelled Harding.

Minmei clutched Kyle's arm, eyes shut tight, mouth wide in a silent scream.

Khyron's troops were bent on nothing less than extermination; they had had two years to work up to this, two unrelieved years, just waiting for an opportunity to make the Micronians pay for all the hardships they had been forced to endure. Now all the tension and hatred left them in a frenzied rush, with New Detroit left to reap that violent harvest.

Everything was a target, and no one was spared—Human or citified Zentraedi.

"Fight to the end!" the Backstabber yelled into his comlink. "Find that chamber! No sacrifice is too great for a cause dearer than life itself!"

Still, the Earth forces would not surrender; courage and valor were the words of the day, although few remained by battle's end to sing the praises of those who died.

A Gladiator went hand to hand with one of the alien berserkers, dropping the Zentraedi with a left uppercut when its own cannons were depleted of charge, only to have the downed enemy blow it to smithereens with a blast from its top-mounted gun.

Another of Khyron's elite paused before a parking lot simply to incinerate the vehicles and huddled groups of Humans inside.

"I'm getting high reflex-activity readings," Khyron announced, his suit displays flashing. Locaters were helping him zero-in on the exposition hall. "All troops converge on my signal immediately!"

Minmei and Kyle, wrapped around each other in the theater's entrance alcove, watched as enemy troops made for the hall, the streets vibrating to the crash of their metalshod boots.

What have I done?! Kyle asked himself, close to panic.

Inside the hall, the RDF sentries received word that the first defenses had been overrun; the enemy was headed their way. A battloid raised its chain gun at the sound of pounding on the hall's foot-thick steel door. The three-member crews of the Gladiators readied themselves.

Mayor Harding had left Kyle and Minmei and rushed to the basement of the building. He and an unfortunate office worker were looking in on the hall and sizing chamber now, a Permaglass shield the only thing separating them from fire, as the door was suddenly blown open and Khyron's troops poured in.

One of the Gladiators stepped forward to engage a Zentraedi, spitting harmless machine gun fire into the face of its enemy as the two of them grappled. Khyron's soldier got hold of the mecha's face plates, swung it clean off its feet, and sent the hapless thing crashing through the buildings reinforced concrete wall.

The second Gladiator was similarly engaged, one-on-one and winning his close-in fight . . . until a Zentraedi appeared without warning overhead, blasting his way through the ceiling and descending on the mecha forcefully enough to split it wide-open, crown to crotch.

All this time, the Battloid was emptying its gatling against a Zentraedi wall of armor. When the pilot saw the Gladiator take that terrible overhead blow, he ran his mecha forward, autocannon raised high like a sledgehammer, only to receive a paralyzing spin kick to the abdomen by an enemy with eyes behind its head.

"That finishes it!" exclaimed the mayor, turning away from the carnage. "We've lost the sizing chamber!"

"Chances are, no matter how much they are exposed to Humans, the Zentraedi are still a war-loving race," Exedore told the admiral after the session. He, Gloval, and Claudia had walked together from the briefing room to one of the fortress's enormous supply holds.

"But many of your people have discovered an entirely different kind of life here on Earth, Exedore," Gloval argued. "You shouldn't be so . . . *hard* on yourself."

"Admiral Gloval's right," Claudia added. "Many of your people supported peace as soon as they were exposed to the possibility, and most still do."

"I agree that many want it," Exedore countered, unmoved by their obvious attempts to put him at ease. After all, it wasn't a question of *feeling* this way or that way about it; it was simply a fact: The Zentraedi were warriors. Exedore wondered sometimes if Humans didn't carry the emotional mode too far. "It's just that I now worry about those who still want to fight. Surely you understand that, Admiral."

"Yes," Gloval admitted, lifting his pipe to his lips, uncertain where this discussion was headed.

"Doesn't it seem strange, then, that no matter how far even *superior* civilizations have progressed, there never seems to be a solution to the problem of aggression and warfare?"

"How true, my friend."

"That applies to Humans, too," Exedore continued. "In fact, there is no known species in the whole of the Fourth Quadrant that has ever turned its back on war."

"Regrettably so," Gloval said.

A comtone sounded, and the admiral reached for a handset, grunting yeses and nos into it, his nostrils flaring. He recradled it with a slam and barked at Claudia:

"Find Hunter immediately!"

Claudia stepped back somewhat. "Sir?"

"Zentraedi have attacked New Detroit!"

"A toy of destruction," Rick was repeating to Lisa. "That's what he called himself, right?"

The two of them were standing in one of the SDF-1's open bays, twenty feet above the shimmering lake, staring into orange and pink sunset clouds.

"Genetically programmed for fighting . . . it's pretty sad."

"If you ask me, it sounds a lot like us," said Lisa.

Rick frowned at her.

"Aren't *we* always fighting?" she asked him.

"That's not fair, Lisa."

"I wasn't trying to be . . . Just making a point."

"Oh, yeah?"

"Rick! Lisa!"

They turned together to find Claudia striding toward them.

"I'm glad I found you two," she said, out of breath. "Zentraedi forces have attacked New Detroit!"

Rick's eyes went wide. "Forces?! What d' ya mean? Who—malcontents?"

Claudia shook her head. "Not from the sound of it. Their communication signal was lost about ten minutes ago, but one of our recon ships spotted the fighting. It looks a coordinated attack. At least a dozen Zentraedi in power armor."

Lisa watched Rick go livid. He clenched his fists and cursed.

"Rick, it's not your fault!" she said quickly, reaching for him. But he was already through the doorway in a run.

"Who?!" Lisa demanded of Claudia. "Who?!"

The reinforcements from New Macross arrived on the scene too late. Rick, in Skull One, had a bird's-eye view of the battle's aftermath: fire, smoke, and several square blocks of total devastation. New Detroit's central avenues were torn up and cratered; civil defense mecha lay smoldering in the streets, while rescue crews worked frantically to free trapped crew members. The area around the exposition hall was unrecognizable. The main buildings had been reduced to rubble.

Rick blamed himself.

It had been his assignment to secure the Protoculture chamber, he told himself, but he had let Kyle and those easily influenced Zentraedi take charge.

Below him now, cranes and bulldozers worked to haul a damaged Excalibur MK VI to its feet; the mecha's twin cannons had been blown from the body. Elsewhere, the hulk of a Gladiator was being towed from an intersection; it looked as though it had been split down the middle by an ax.

Though Rick was shouldering the blame, he couldn't very well charge himself with the attack, and this was what began to concern him. The only incident that approached the level of destruction here was the raid on New Portland some weeks ago. There, renegade Zentraedi had broken into one of the armories, commandeered three Battlepods, and indulged themselves in a brief orgy of terror. But that was the isolated case; most often, the trouble was confined to fighting—the recent fistfight in the streets of Macross was a perfect example. But now, within twenty-four hours, there had been two major raids.

The recon pilots who had witnessed the attack saw no battlepods; Zentraedi power armor, they said. Rick thought about it: Many of the warships that had crashed on Earth had been stripped of weapons during Reconstruction two years ago. But of course it was possible that a band of outlaw giants had chanced upon a ship and found the power suits . . . but what would they want with the sizing chamber? A blow for independence? Furthermore, the attack on New Detroit had been too well coordinated: It was purposeful, nothing like the sprees of random violence Exedore was worried about—the resurgence of the Zentraedi programming.

Rick found himself thinking about the Zentraedi's raid on Macross City, when it was still located in the belly of the SDF-1. As he looked over New Detroit, he began to feel that there was something familiar about this patterned ruination, almost as if it bore the earmarks of someone thought to be dead—someone whom the Zentraedi themselves had feared . . .

While Rick was dropping the Veritech in for a closer look, searching for an uncluttered stretch of street to put down on, Kyle and Minmei were preparing to flee the city. The black sports car, which had been parked near the theater entrance, had miraculously survived the destruction, and Kyle was behind the wheel now, twisting the ignition key and cursing the thing for not turning over. Above the sleek vehicle towered the lifeless body of an Excalibur, spread-eagle in a death pose against the theater facade.

"You crummy no-good pile of junk!" Kyle shouted at the car, pumping the accelerator pedal for all it was worth.

"Hurry, Kyle!" Minmei yelled from the street. "They might be coming back!"

"I'm doing the best I can!" he told her angrily.

Minmei was wringing her hands and pacing, a victim of fear and self-torment. Like Rick, she was blaming herself for the tragedy.

I could have stopped Kyle, and none of this would have happened! How could I let him do that to Rick?! If I had just stepped in when Rick looked at me like that...

The sports car's engine fired, and Kyle hurrahed.

"Minmei, get in! Let's go!" She was either in shock or lost in thought, he decided, because he wasn't getting through to her. *"Minmei!"* he tried again.

She turned to him as if they had all the time in the world, pure loathing in her eyes. She reached for the handle of the back door and threw it open.

Rick spotted her.

He had the Veritech reconfigured to Guardian mode and was setting down on the theater street several blocks behind Kyle's sports car. Kyle was revving the engine, too preoccupied to take notice of the mecha's descent, but Minmei caught sight of it in the rearview mirror and spun around in her seat.

She sucked in her breath. "Kyle, please don't leave yet—it's Rick!"

Skull One had landed. The radome of the Veritech was on the ground, tail up in the air like some mechanical bird searching the earth for worms. Rick had sprung the canopy and was climbing out of the cockpit.

Kyle said, "We're late already!" and gunned it, patching out on the pavement.

Rick was chasing them on foot, and Minmei could read his lips: He was calling her name, asking them to stop.

"Turn around, Minmei!" Kyle yelled at her from the front seat. "It's too late!"

Her eyes filled with tears.

"Good-bye," she said softly to the small figure in the distance. *It's too late!*

CHAPTER TWELVE

The Zentraedi are not inferior beings, nor should they be treated like second-class citizens. They should enjoy the same freedoms the rest of us do—life, liberty, and the pursuit of happiness! No one can say for sure that some of them won't turn to crime or evil purpose, but at least we won't have repressed their right to express themselves—we won't have acted like fascists!

From Lynn-Kyle's *Pamphlets on Pacificism*

"THE LINE FORMS TO THE RIGHT!" ONE OF Khyron's shock troopers bellowed, gesturing with his massive hand.

Forty feet below the giant's angry face, a micronized Zentraedi, recently returned to the fold, wondered whether he had made the right decision in joining the Backstabber's battalion. It had been an arduous journey from New Detroit to reach these snowbound wastes. And now there was a certain *hostility* in the cold air...

But all at once the shock trooper was grinning, then laughing and slapping his knee. Other soldiers were, too, and all along the line of micronized Zentraedi the laughter was spreading.

"Well, that's what the *Micronians* are always saying, isn't it?" the shock trooper asked his diminutive counterpart. " 'Line forms on the right,' 'no parking,' 'no smoking'... I mean, we Zentraedi warriors have *learned* something from the Micronians, haven't we? We want to do things orderly from now on—*peacefully*!"

"Yeah, we're *all* for *peace*!" said a second trooper, brandishing his laser rifle.

A third added: "We love their homeworld *so much* that we're just gonna *take* it from them!"

And everyone laughed and threw in comments of their own, giants and micronized Zentraedi alike.

The line led to the sizing chamber, back where it belonged in Khyron's command ship now, where one by one, Zentraedi were doffing their Micronian outfits and being returned to full size in the conversion tank. It was a slow and tedious process, but no one seemed to mind the wait.

Khyron least of all.

He and Azonia were sitting some distance from the tank, sipping at tall glasses of an intoxicating drink one of the former micronized Zentraedi had introduced to the growing outlaw battalion. Khyron had taken a fancy to sipping straws, and his consort humored him by having one in her glass also. Close by, Grel watched them nervously.

Word had spread quickly through the wastelands that Khyron had captured the sizing chamber and was ready to make good his promise to return to full size any who would join his army. Each day the lines of micronized Zentraedi males and females grew longer, and Khyron was reveling in his victory. He had instructed his spies in the population centers to make it known just who had taken the chamber.

Let them know that Khyron *had returned!*

Laughing hysterically, the warlord lifted the glass in a toast to a soldier who stepped from the chamber, naked and powerful once again.

"Now that Khyron is in possession of the chamber, he will rebuild his army and crush the Micronians! This wretched world will have known better days!"

With that, he heaved his glass at the line, shattering it against the interior hull of the ship and showering those waiting with glass and liquid.

Azonia looked at her lord and grinned proudly. She

was half in love with his insanity, though "love" was hardly the word she would have used.

But suddenly Khyron wasn't smiling.

He made a guttural sound, stood up, and began to pace back and forth in front of her, his clenched fists at his hips holding the campaign cloak away from his scarlet uniform.

"Not enough," he said at last. "Not enough!" He whirled on her without warning, devilish fire in his eyes. "We must have the Protoculture matrix itself—Zor's factory. It's somewhere still in that rotting fortress, and we will have it!"

"But m'lord, surely the Micronians—" Azonia started to say.

"Bah!" he interrupted her. "Do you think they would even bother to guard this chamber if they had the factory in their possession?! No, I don't think they've found it yet."

"Yes, but—"

Khyron smashed a fist into his open palm. "We will do what we should have done all along. We will *take* something from them—something they deem *precious*. And we will hold it in exchange for the dimensional fortress. There is a Micronian word for it . . ." He turned to Grel and said, "The *word*, Grel— what is it?"

" 'Ransom,' m'lord," came the speedy reply.

"Ransom, yes . . ." Khyron repeated softly. He gestured to the sizing chamber and instructed Grel to speed things along. "We're going to be leaving here shortly," he told him. "But we must not forget to leave a little surprise for our Micronian friends . . ."

New Detroit had been placed under martial law. There was little reason to expect a follow-up attack, but the theft of the chamber had the resident Zentraedi up in arms. Some of them believed that the Earth Forces had *staged* a Zentraedi raid in order to gain possession of the chamber. Reconstruction crews and civil defense reinforcements had been flown in from New Macross, and a field headquarters (with Lisa Hayes in command) had been set up outside the city limits.

Whether a band of malcontents from the wastes were responsible for the assault had yet to be confirmed, but reconnaissance flights north of the city had revealed the existence of a base of some sort, hastily constructed around the remains of a crashed warship whose towering presence dominated that snowy region. A squadron of Veritechs under Rick Hunter's command was on its way to the site now, Lisa Hayes monitoring their progress from field HQ.

Her screen had indicated no activity at the base, but when the Cat's-Eye recon dropped in for a closer pass, the displays had lit up: Enemy missiles had been launched at the approaching fighter group. Lisa went on the com net to warn them.

"Uh, we roger that, control," said one of Rick's wingmen. "Enemy projectiles maintaining tracking status. Onboard computers calculate impact in twenty-three seconds."

"Evasive!" Lisa heard Rick say over the net.

Lisa watched her screen: The missiles were altering course along with the fighters.

"They're still on your tail, Captain Hunter."

An elisted rating at the adjacent duty station turned to her suddenly. "Picking up a sudden heat emission."

Lisa was already back on the net. "The projectiles have activated protoboosters."

"All units," said Rick. "Send out ghosts."

Lisa studied the screen once more. The missiles had gained on the group, but the false radar images had confused them. Only momentarily, however. "They've swung around, Commander."

"Roger, control," Rick answered her. "We've got them in our tracking monitors. We're planning a surprise of our own."

Skull One led the group in a formation climb and rollout that brought them nose to nose with the incoming projectiles. Though eyes saw nothing but blue skies ahead, the Veritech screens read death.

"Impact in seven seconds," said Rick's wingman.

"Hammerheads on my mark—*now*!"

Missiles tore from launch tubes as the group loosed a

bit of their own death; projectiles met their match head-on, annihilating one another in a series of explosions that fused into an expanding sphere of fire. The Veritechs boostered through this, scorching themselves but holding their own, the route to the enemy base clear as day.

They came in hugging the barren terrain, the tail section of the leaning hulk looming into view over the horizon. Rick ordered reconfiguration to Guardian mode when they hit the edge of the target zone and released a score of heat-seekers to announce his arrival.

The ground at the base of the Zentraedi warship was instantly torn up. Snow and dirt were blown from the area, and when the smoke cleared, there was a newly formed crater fully encircling the ruined warship. But no return fire or signs of activity. Rick guessed what the Cat's-Eye indicators would reveal.

"Scanners indicate no sign of life," the recon plane's pilot said after a moment.

Rick ordered half the team to put down and reconfigure to Battloid mode for entry into the warship itself.

The fact that the hulk might contain unknown traps was on everyone's mind, so they were to proceed slowly and methodically, compartment by compartment, checking for timing devices or infrared trips.

Three hours in, they reached a central cargo hold filled with Zentraedi ordnance and supplies. Still there was no sign of occupation.

"Looks like the place was deserted when we hit it," Rick proposed. "The missiles must've been controlled from a remote outpost."

Rick's wingman gestured the arm of his Battloid to the weapons cache.

"Take a look at all this stuff."

Rick did just that: If whoever had been here could afford to leave all this behind, he didn't want to think about what they were packing when they left.

He moved his mecha toward one of the supply crates, absently brushing dirt from the lid. As he did so, the insignia of the Botoru Battalion began to take shape.

Khyron's battalion!

* * *

One thousand miles west of New Detroit, through land that had once been home to dinosaurs and buffalo, ran the strangest group of creatures to appear in many a day: a small band of giant humanoids and ostrichlike machines—in some cases a commingling of the two, with giants riding piggyback on the pods, hands clamped tightly on plastron guns, legs wrapped around the pods' spherical bodies. Inside an Officer's Pod at the head of the pack sat the Backstabber, a crazed smile on his face while he addressed the images of Azonia and Grel on the mecha's circular screens.

"Everything is going just as I planned," he congratulated himself. "These Micronians are so easily fooled."

"Battlepods are now approaching objective," his consort reported.

"No sign of any resistance," said Grel.

"They fell for it!" Khyron cackled.

As a cowboy would the rump of a horse, he slapped the console of the pod to hurry it along. He could hear the mechaless giants give out a war cry as they crowned a small rise in the terrain and moved on the city.

Denver, Colorado, as it was once known, had been rebuilt so often since the Global Civil War and had undergone so many name changes that people now referred to it simply as "the City." An enormous hangar used decades before by America's NORAD had been converted to a concert hall large enough to accommodate several thousand Humans and close to a hundred giants. There was a small crowd tonight, but Minmei was singing her heart out nonetheless, memories of the raid on New Detroit fresh in her mind and the *need* to cement relations between Human and Zentraedi foremost in her thoughts.

She had the crowd, small as it was; the band was tight, and there were moments of perfection in her performance. For a while she could put Kyle from her list of concerns; he hadn't said ten words to her on their cross-country trip from New Detroit, and even now she was certain that he was glaring at her from the stage wings.

Minmei, in that same ruffled dress she had sported in

New Macross, was two verses into "Touch and Go" when the real trouble began. The giant Zentraedi seated in the upper tiers were the first to notice it: a rhythmical undercurrent of mechanical articulation, the beat of metalshod hooves in the streets, a sound like distant thunder.

The singer herself became aware of the noise a moment later and stopped midsong. Most of the audience was on its feet, staring up at the curved roof of the hangar: Something was *moving* up there . . .

When the building began to quake, everyone made a run for the exits, but they were a bit late: The roof seemed to tear open, and all at once it was raining Battlepods. Several more broke through the hangar walls, followed by Zentraedi shock troopers armed with laser rifles and autocannons. The hall was pandemonium, even though not a single shot had been fired.

Minmei stood paralyzed center stage, Battlepods close enough to be reflected in her azure eyes. She was aware of Kyle's presence at her side but incapable of moving of her own free will.

"Minmei," he was screaming, "they're heading right for us! You've got to snap out of it!"

An unusual-looking pod had positioned itself in front of the stage; it had a red snout, a top-mounted cannon, and two derringer-like hand-guns—one of which it slammed against the stage as Kyle was leading her away.

She felt herself thrown off her feet by the violence of the force, but even that wasn't enough to restore her will.

So she surrendered herself to Kyle, allowing him to pull her up and lead her to the stage steps, down into the orchestra pit, down into that grouping of pods closing in on them . . .

"Well, look what we have here . . ." an affected voice boomed out far above her.

Minmei looked up into a handsome, clean-shaven face framed by attractive blue hair. The giant Zentraedi who had climbed from the unusual-looking pod was wearing a scarlet-colored uniform trimmed in yellow and an olive-drab campaign cloak that fastened on itself over one shoulder. He reached his hand out and grabbed hold of her and Kyle, crushing them together in his grip as he lifted them high above the stage.

"Let us go!" Kyle managed to yell. "You're going to kill us!"

The warrior titan held them up in front of his face; Minmei saw the devil in his steel-gray eyes.

"I wouldn't dream of it," he said, some unspoken purpose in mind.

"No harm must come to Minmei, Commander!" she heard one of the other giants insist. She craned her neck to see past the warrior's thumb, fighting for breath to get a look at the one who had spoken in her defense.

Khyron gestured to one of his Battlepods, and without warning the mecha kicked the friendly Zentraedi, catching him in the groin and sending him sprawling back against the wall of the hangar, where he rolled over in agony.

"I will not tolerate disobedience!" Khyron bellowed, raising his other fist.

He shot Minmei a look that chilled her heart; then he threw his head back and roared with laughter.

Khyron's name was being shouted in the streets of New Portland, New Detroit, and several other cities that had seen incidents of Zentraedi uprising. Lisa Hayes had heard as much at field headquarters, and she was the one who first reported the rumors to Admiral Gloval. But Gloval remained skeptical: If history had taught him anything, it was that heroes, regardless of their orientation toward good or evil, were often resurrected in times of cultural stress. The Zentraedi were no exception, so it was natural for them to suddenly *believe* that Khyron, their evil lord, had not perished along with Dolza and the commanders of the armada but had somehow escaped and had merely been lying in wait these two years, ready to strike back at the Earth with an equally ghostlike battalion of warriors when the time was right.

Of course, there was no actual *proof* that Khyron had met his end in battle, and the most recent attack on New Detroit and the theft of the sizing chamber were suggestive of his style. There was also Commander Hunter's discovery of an arms cache bearing the Botoru Battalion insignia . . .

The admiral ran through all of it once more as he paced in front of the large wall screen in the SDF-2 situation room. He was about to put a match to his favorite briar when Claudia called to him from her duty station.

"We're receiving a transmission from someone claiming to be *Khyron*," she told him. "Shall I put it on the screen?"

"Yes, by all means," he replied, stoking the pipe. "And be sure to get a fix on the source of the transmission."

Gloval fully expected to encounter the likeness of an imposter. After all, no one in the Earth Forces had met the so-called Backstabber face to face (although God knew how many had met him mecha to mecha and regretted it). The admiral had, however, seen trans-vids of Khyron supplied by Breetai and Exedore during the long debriefing sessions following the defeat of the Zentraedi armada.

. . . Which explains Gloval's sudden start when Khyron's devilishly handsome face appeared on the wall screen. A collective gasp went up from the command center personnel; even those who hadn't been privy to the trans-vids recognized the real item when they saw it.

Khyron sneered: "What a pleasure it is to interrupt you, Admiral Gloval."

"He sounds like that sixties actor," someone in the control room commented. "James Mason."

Gloval made up his mind that he was not going to allow himself to be rattled. He cleared his throat and chomped down on the mouthpiece of the pipe. "On the contrary," he said with appropriate sarcasm, "the disgust is all mine, I assure you."

Khyron seemed to like that and said as much. He made a gesture with his hand to indicate something off to his left, and the camera swung slightly to find a second Zentraedi officer—a female, at that. She was not unattractive, with close-cropped blue-gray hair, fine features, and a pointed chin, but she wore the same malicious look on her pale face as that worn by her commander. Gloval didn't have to guess: This had to be Azonia, also believed to have been killed, the dreaded Quadrono leader who was Miriya Parino's superior.

"I have some friends of yours here," Khyron was saying quite matter-of-factly.

Gloval didn't have time to wonder to whom or to what Khyron was referring. Azonia had raised Lynn-Kyle into view, pinched by the scruff of the neck between her thumb and first finger. Khyron, too, raised his fist, shoving Minmei toward the remote camera. The singer looked pale and frightened.

"Minmei!" Claudia said in surprise.

"This can't be happening!" seethed one of the techs.

Dropping his act of feigned indifference, Gloval pulled the pipe from his mouth. "You filthy swine!" he said to the screen image.

"You're mad!" someone added.

Khyron reacted by tightening his fist around his helpless captive, his face suddenly contorted in anger. "Don't try my patience, Micronian—I am known to have a violent temper!"

The implication was obvious, and Gloval signaled everyone to remain calm. "We're sorry," he told Khyron.

The Zentraedi laughed shortly. "Well, then, your apologies are *humbly* accepted. But listen to me carefully: I want you to know I mean business, Admiral."

"We understand. What do you want?"

"Don't hurt her—I beg you!" a tech shouted.

Khyron smirked. "Then deliver the dimensional fortress to me tomorrow by twelve hundred hours."

No one had expected this, least of all the admiral.

"That's impossible! The fortress is no longer spaceworthy."

"Don't lie to me, Admiral. I'm warning you . . ."

"I'm not lying," Gloval told him firmly. "Listen to me for a moment . . . The war is *over*, Khyron. Dolza and his armada—"

"The war is not over, Admiral!" Khyron threw at the screen. "Not until I have that fortress in my possession!"

Gloval knew what was on his opponent's mind. "The

Protoculture matrix doesn't exist," he tried calmly. "Ask Exedore and Breetai if—"

Khyron was livid. "Those traitors are alive?!" Suddenly he laughed maniacally. "Just deliver the fortress to me, Admiral—if you value your little . . . songbird."

"You *are* mad!" said Gloval.

"Ah, but there's method to my madness," Khyron returned with a grin. "First, the fortress for Minmei. Then, the Robotech factory satellite for this second hostage." He gestured to Kyle, who was dangling by his coattails from Azonia's pinch.

"Don't do it!" Kyle exploded. "Don't listen to them, Admiral!"

"You mind your manners," Azonia said playfully, wiggling him about roughly.

"It's too dangerous," Kyle managed, in obvious pain. "You can't . . . you can't just give in to this guy. . ."

"You're hurting him!" Minmei screamed.

Khyron gestured to his consort to take it easy. "I'd of course prefer to avoid *violence*, Admiral. But believe me, I'm more than willing to carry out my threats."

"I'm sure we can arrange something," Gloval answered him. In fact, he wasn't at all sure *what* could be arranged, but it was essential to start by buying time.

"That's better." Khyron sneered.

Just then a third officer entered the screen's field of view, a large, square-jawed man who deferentially tapped his commander on the shoulder.

"Uh . . . excuse me . . ." said Grel.

Khyron turned to him briefly, then back to Gloval. "I must take my leave now, Admiral. But remember: tomorrow by twelve hundred hours."

He flashed a smile, V-ed his fingers, and cut off transmission.

Gloval bowed his head and chided himself silently for believing that evil could so easily be laid to rest.

CHAPTER THIRTEEN

When I first heard Khyron announce his demands for the SDF-1 in exchange for the hostages he'd taken, my fear was that his agents had actually penetrated our most top-secret operations. Then, when I realized that his request was more in the nature of a formality, I began to relax some. But the knowledge that he did in fact present a continued threat to our security made me reevaluate the plans I had so carefully formulated for the coming months.

From the log of Admiral Henry Gloval

SOMEONE HAD THOUGHT TO CALL THE DENVER hangar/theater "Zarkopolis"—as close a translation from the Zentraedi as the Micronian language allowed. The structure bore no resemblance to the original Zarkopolis—the Zentraedi mining base on Fantoma—but it was in keeping with the rekindled spirit of conquest to rename it thus.

Cross-legged on a raised portion of the stage that had become their command post sat Khyron, Azonia, Grel, and Gerao. In attendance were several aides and shock troopers in full battle armor. Stationed in the vast hall below were troops of Khyron's elite strike force and half a dozen battlepods. Minmei stood bravely in the Backstabber's open palm; Khyron regarded her as though she were some zoological specimen.

"It's hard to believe that this helpless little creature in my hand is the key to our freedom," he mused aloud. "To think they'd give up the fortress for you..." His closed his hand on Minmei. "This Micronian sentimentality—it makes me quite ill just to think about it!"

Khyron got to his feet, striking an orator's pose.

"Oh, to be free of this miserable planet! . . . I can hardly wait, I assure you . . ." He had turned his back on his audience and was once again eyeing Minmei, now on her knees in his open hand. "Well . . . why doesn't Minmei perform for us, eh?"

He swung around again and extended his hand, a small stage for her act, almost forty feet off the ground.

Minmei was quick to comply; in fact, she'd been waiting for just such an opportunity. Hers was the voice that had toppled a mighty empire, so surely a handful of disaffected warriors would present little problem. She feared and hated Khyron, but somewhere in the back of her mind endured the idea that she possessed the power to open his heart to love and peace.

"To be in love . . ." she began, standing up and looking him in the eye. ". . . must be the sweetest feeling that a *man* can feel . . . To be in love, to live a dream . . ."

Khyron's expression was softening. The giant hand that was sweeping her in front of a shocked and dumbfounded audience of hardened soldiers was shaking and sweating.

". . . with somebody you care about like no one else."

Minmei was practically shouting out the lyrics now as choruses of groans and words of disbelief rose from Azonia and the others.

Khyron's body was trembling; his eyes were rolled back in his head.

"A special woman, a dearest woman . . ."

And suddenly, his knees were buckling and he was down on the floor, seemingly ready to release her from his hold. Minmei started to step from his palm, singing: ". . . Who needs to share her life with you alone . . ." Without warning, he grabbed her again, a sly grin splitting his face as he squeezed the song and breath from her.

"Well, it was a brave attempt, Minmei. But unfortunately for you, as you can see, I am immune to your witchcraft."

"You had me fooled!" Azonia laughed, her hand to her mouth.

But Khyron silenced her. "I am speaking to my little songbird." He looked hard at Minmei. "And she's going to help us get what we want, isn't that so, my little pet?"

Minmei flailed about in his hand, struggling to free herself. "I won't help you—you big overgrown... *clown*!"

Khyron faked a look of hurt. "That was not very nice, Minmei... In fact, I'm rather surprised at you—losing your temper like that. Very unladylike."

Minmei folded her arms in defiance, fighting back tears.

"I may have to teach you some manners," her captor was threatening, his anger building, his grip on her tightening. "You think that just because you're the *magnificent* Minmei, you're better than we are... Well, I despise your *music*! Despise it! Do you hear me?!"

She could no longer breathe. Khyron was ranting and raving, and she was rapidly losing touch with the world. Blackness circled in on her from the edges of her vision, silencing thoughts and fears alike.

Khyron felt her go limp in his hand and realized he had gone too far. Azonia was shouting at him to be careful, but he was certain he'd already overstepped himself.

"Cosmos! What have I done?!"

Minmei was unmoving in his hand, deathly still. "She enraged me so, I forgot how important she was to our plan..." Gently, he poked at her with his finger, hoping she'd revive; and in a moment she did, dazed and possibly hurt but certainly nowhere near dead. Khyron acknowledged his relief with a smile.

"She's all right," he told Azonia. "They're well-built little things."

Azonia had picked up Kyle and was now holding him by one foot and one arm, twisting him about as though he were made of pipe cleaners. Kyle was far less important to the plan, so she wasn't concerned about breaking him up a bit.

Kyle, on the other hand, felt differently about it, and it was only his many years of martial-arts training that kept him from suffering major dislocations. The blue-haired Amazon seemed hell-bent on *reconfiguring* him like some sort of mannikin mecha.

She joked: "Surely this is as much fun for you as it is for me!"

And Kyle could only hope he would see the day when she micronized herself; because if he lived through this, there was going to be a score to settle.

Admiral Gloval called an emergency session with his chiefs of staff following Khyron's transmission, which had been traced to New Denver. They had less than twelve hours to decide on a course of action. Claudia Grant, General Motokoff from G3, and several officers from various departments of the RDF were gathered around a long table in the SDF-2 briefing room. Exedore, still aboard the factory satellite, was in communication with them via comlink; his image appeared on one of the monitors.

"The situation is without precedent," Motokoff was saying. He was a young man in spite of his rank, former head of the CD forces aboard the SDF-1 during its two-year ordeal in space. "Since the Zentraedi have never taken hostages before, we have no way of knowing if they'll make good their promises."

Gloval drew at his pipe, nodding. "Or their threats," he told the table.

"May I respond to that, Admiral?" Exedore said from the screen.

"Go ahead, Exedore," said Gloval.

The Zentraedi looked squarely into the remote camera. "Khyron will make good his threats, of this I can assure you. Lord Breetai concurs with me that this hostage taking suggests he has gone beyond the bounds of his Zentraedi conditioning, which would have rendered such an act unthinkable. There is no telling how far he is willing to go now. But I must caution you *not* to accede to his demands under any circumstances. Lord Breetai wishes me to inform you that he is at your service should you require him in settling this most unfortunate matter."

Gloval took the pipe from his mouth and inclined his

head. "That will not be necessary, Exedore, although you may convey my appreciation to the commander. Your people have already spent far too many years acting as a police force. We won't ask you to fight our battles for us."

"I understand, Admiral," Exedore said evenly.

One of the officers stood up to address Gloval. "I agree with Breetai, Admiral. Putting the SDF-1 into Khyron's hands would be an act of suicide!" The officer had gotten himself so worked up that the pencil he was holding snapped in his hands.

"Calm down," Gloval told him gruffly. "I have no intention of giving in to his demands."

"I hope you're not suggesting that we ignore Khyron's threats to Kyle and Minmei," said Claudia.

"No," everyone was quick to say.

"We're all in agreement on that, sir," said another officer. "But this is a blatant act of terrorism, and we must refuse to bargain with him."

Claudia nodded in agreement.

Gloval cleared his throat. "For two years now the Zentraedi have lived with us as equals. And in that time we have all come to know many of them as friends and allies. Khyron took advantage of this by infiltrating his spies into our cities. We have no way of knowing who they are or where they might be."

"I don't see what bearing this has on the problem, Admiral," Motokoff interjected.

Gloval made a dismissive gesture. "I'm coming to that. We don't know who our enemies are, but we *do* know our friends..." The chiefs of staff waited for him to finish. "So, I suggest we use the Zentraedis to trick him, as he used them to trick us."

"Commander Hunter, engage your scrambler," Lisa said over the net from field headquarters.

The Skull had been ordered out of the deserted Zentraedi base where the arms cache had been discovered. In minutes the place was going to be a memory, thanks to the explosive charges they had set to self-destruct.

"Engaging voice scrambler for encoded transmission,

control," Rick radioed back after tapping in a series of commands on the Veritech's console.

He had been expecting new orders since word had been received that Khyron was responsible for the attack on New Detroit. Unlike Gloval, Rick saw no reason to doubt that Khyron had survived the Zentraedi holocaust. Khyron had always been the most self-serving of the lot; he was a born survivor, and it was not unlike him to go in hiding for two years—to *stage* his own resurrection. Rick recalled the many times he had faced Khyron in battle; without adequate proof, he blamed Khyron for Roy Fokker's death. And as anxious as he felt about a renewed contest, one part of him was actually looking forward to it.

Lisa wasn't sure she wanted to break the news to him about Minmei, but orders were orders. "Operation Star-Saver," the High Command was calling it.

"It looks like it's going to be a tough one, this time," Claudia had told her. *"But you, you lucky devil, you'll be coordinating for Commander Hunter once again."*

Somehow Claudia had missed the point: *Rick was being ordered to save Minmei—again!* How much longer was fate going to build these rescues into their relationship? Lisa wondered. Just when the singer was no longer a threat to what little happiness Lisa and Rick shared, another crisis would present itself.

"And why was it that Rick is called to respond to every crisis?" she had asked Claudia, not really expecting a response and certainly not having to be reminded that *Rick was the best there was.*

That was why she wanted him.

"Good to hear your voice again, Lisa," Rick was saying.

Lisa sucked in her breath and decided to take the plunge.

"Rick," she began. "Your team is to report back to New Macross for special orders. Khyron has kidnapped, ah, two . . . people. He's holding them hostage in New Denver for the return of the SDF-1."

"That's insane! The fortress isn't even airworthy, is it?"

"Of course not. But—"

"Man, somebody really must have slipped some elephant juice into the punch bowl when that guy was cloned... And since when do the Zentraedi take hostages?"

"Since Khyron got back to town."

"So who'd he grab? Lynn-Kyle, if it's my lucky day."

Lisa raised her eyes to the domed ceiling. "It's your lucky day," she told him.

She heard his gasp, then: "Who's the second person, Lisa? Give it to me straight."

Make it short and sweet, she told herself, and said: "Minmei. Khyron attacked a club in—"

"Where are they?!"

Lisa stiffened at her station. *He'd fly to the sun and back,* she said to herself. But to Rick, she cautioned: "There is no place for amateur heroics on this mission, Commander."

Rick went silent, and it was too late for her to take it back.

"Uhh, really?" he said after a moment, cold as ice. "I wasn't aware that amateur heroics were my stock in trade."

Lisa fumed, her face coloring. The woman tech at the adjacent station was staring at her as if assessing her professionalism. "That is all! Out!" she hollered, and slammed her palm down on the comlink button.

Four hours later, Skull Team was assembled on the flight deck of the *Prometheus*; they had been briefed and were ready for action.

Lisa, also recalled to New Macross, was braving the cold evening winds to wish Rick well. She couldn't bear the thought of his going off into combat while that foolish argument remained unresolved. But he wasn't helping her out at all, clinging to his anger.

"Please be careful, Rick," she called up to Skull One's cockpit. "Khyron will stop at nothing, you know that."

Rick stopped on the top step of the Veritech's ladder and turned to her, "thinking cap" in place. "Look, I appreciate your concern, but we've been over the operation, and I know what I have to do."

"That's not what I'm talking about," she said as he climbed in. "I'm just afraid you'll lose your objectivity and do something rash . . ."

Again her words brought him to a halt, but this time he leaped from the Veritech and strode toward her.

"Rick—"

"Yes. I love her very much—I won't lie to you, Lisa. I've never tried to conceal that from you. But I settled my feelings about her a long time ago. Minmei and I can *never* be together . . . I'm flying this mission as a pilot."

"And you're a fine pilot, Rick. Just don't lose your perspective, that's all. If anything happened—"

"I'm commanding an entire squadron, Lisa! Do you think I'd jeopardize their safety just because of my feelings for Minmei?!"

"Emotions are so compelling . . ." she said, averting her eyes. "I just can't be sure . . ."

Rick struck a challenge pose, gloved fists on his hips. "What? You can't be sure of *what*?!"

She lowered her head. "It's nothing . . . Forget I said anything."

Rick put his hands on her shoulders. "Look, I'll be back," he said, hoping to put her at ease. He didn't even know why they were going at each other like this. Two hostages: It didn't matter who they were . . .

"Good luck," Lisa said as he walked away.

In celebration of his imminent victory, Khyron had emptied the coffers of the last remaining Zentraedi foodstuffs and provisions—bottles of Garudan ale and sides of yptrax from Haydon VI, too long in the freeze-dry bins. Most of the Zentraedi subsisted on chemical nutrients, but Khyron had always strived to individualize himself. *To be unique in all things*. He respected the Micronians' taste for organic food; it was only fitting that life feed on death, as death fed on life . . .

Khyron toasted their success, took a long pull from the bottle of ale, and refilled Azonia's glass. She was on the floor to the left of Khyron's improvised throne—an enormous storage crate turned on its side—Grel, a drumstick of meat in hand, to the right.

"There you are, my dear."

Khyron and Grel watched her empty the glass and laughed drunkenly.

"She's amazing, my lord," Grel commented. His feelings toward Azonia had changed somewhat, especially now that there were other Zentraedi females in camp. And of course the ale helped considerably.

"I believe I'll have another," said Azonia. "Fill it up."

Khyron smiled and poured. "My dear Azonia, I believe you could outdrink all of us."

"And I'm just starting." She beamed.

Khyron leered at her. "Excellent, Commander... excellent."

Minmei and Kyle were imprisoned in an ingeniously designed cage fashioned from a circular arrangement of giant-size forks—the downward-pointing tines anchored by the inner lip of a shallow bowl—and a similarly sized pan lid that enclosed and held fast the backward-bending upper ends of the fork stems. To offset the fear, and really for lack of anything better to do, the two captives pulled at their makeshift bars to no avail.

Exhausted, Minmei fell to the bowl floor, Kyle beside her, breathless, his body racked with pain from Azonia's manhandling.

"We'll have to try another way," she managed, gasping for air.

"There *is* no other way—we'll never get out of here!"

"No, Kyle, don't say that..."

"Whatever happens to us—no matter what he does to us—Gloval must never give in to that barbarian's demands." Kyle wiped sweat from his brow. "Imagine the SDF-1 in Khyron's hands!"

"Won't they try to rescue us?" she asked, suddenly even more frightened.

"I wouldn't hold my breath, Minmei."

It was difficult to know just what Kyle wanted. He didn't want the admiral to give in to Khyron's demands, but at the same time he was already condemning him for not mounting a rescue. This was all too typical of his recent behavior, and Minmei was further saddened.

"Then there isn't much to hope for," she sobbed. It

didn't seem possible: Hopes and dreams were so very *real*...

Kyle was getting to his feet. "There's *nothing* to hope for."

"But we *can't* lose hope—that's all we've got," she told him, unsure whom she was trying to convince.

But Kyle came back at her with his usual: "All the hope in the world is useless in a situation like this."

Minmei felt sad for him. She didn't want to hurt him but nevertheless found herself saying, "If only Rick was here—*he'd* save us."

Kyle didn't hear it or perhaps didn't want to hear it; in either case, he had turned his attention to their captors and was now leaning between the forks and shouting at them.

"Hey, you Zentraedi! Hey, you overgrown gorillas! What a bunch of brainless baboons! All you can think about is your own bellies, huh?!"

Khyron and the others fell silent, listening to him.

"What about your own comrades? What do you think about that? Does it make you happy knowing that you've slaughtered your own people?!"

Minmei noticed Khyron's eyes narrowing. She wanted to tell Kyle to stop. What was he trying to gain by this, anyway? but he went right on provoking them.

"Why can't you goons learn to live in peace for a change? I'll tell you why—because that would take courage, and you're all a bunch of cowards, that's why!"

Khyron had been getting a kick out of it—the spunk displayed by this tiny creature—but accusations about *cowardice* were never amusing, especially since the defeat of the armada and Khyron's decision then to absent himself from the battle...

The Backstabber got to his feet in a rush, smashing a bottle of ale down on the table that held the cage.

"Careful, Khyron," Azonia said as her commander stomped toward Kyle and Minmei. "Remember the fortress..."

"You puny little things," Khyron sneered, towering over them. "If it weren't for the fact that I need you, I'd...I'd *crush* you—just for pleasure!"

Minmei was shaking uncontrollably, ready to feel that hand come down on their cage. She stammered, "Be careful, Kyle, he's been drinking!"

The female, Azonia, was by his side now, and Khyron suddenly reached out for her and pulled her to him, passionately.

"You see," he whispered to his captives, "I've learned something about *pleasure* . . ."

And with that he embraced Azonia and kissed her full on the mouth, savagely; she responded, groaning and holding him fast. Kyle and Minmei were aghast—every bit as shocked as Dolza had been by Rick and Lisa's kiss years before, the one that had started it all.

Kyle dropped to his knees as though defeated while the two Zentraedi drank in each other's lust. And there was no telling just how far Khyron and Azonia might have been prepared to go. But fate, as is its wont, chose that particular moment to intervene: Grel, nervous at the prospect of disturbing his lord, stepped forward with news to drain the life from the best of parties.

"I'm, er, sorry to have to interrupt your . . . *demonstration*, Lord Khyron," Grel faltered, "but I, uh, thought you might want to know that we seem to be, uh, under attack."

CHAPTER FOURTEEN

Hierarchy, hegemony . . . these words have no meaning to a Zentraedi. They were a . . . compartmentalized *military body. Dolza was created to oversee them, Exedore to advise them; Breetai, Reno, Khyron, and innumerable others to command; and the rest, to serve. But there was never any male/female fraternization. And that very* repression *of natural drives and instincts was in part responsible for the tremendous energy they consequently gave over to warfare—*displacement drive *as it was once called . . . How like the matrixed seeds of the Invid Flower itself, the basis of Protoculture.*

Dr. Emil Lang, *Ghost Machines: An Overview of Protoculture*

PART OF AZONIA'S INITIATION INTO SENSUAL PLEAsure was to be pushed aside and told that the time wasn't right.

Khyron had rushed to the nearest viewscreen, leaving Azonia where he had pushed her to the floor, hungry for more of his attention. A red-haired Zentraedi soldier stationed at a forward outpost saluted the Backstabber from the screen.

"Greetings and salutations, Lord Khyron, master of the peoples of—"

Reflexively, Khyron leaned back from the monitor as a fiery blast erased the soldier's words and carried him clear out of the remote camera's field of view.

"What's happening there?!" Khyron shouted into the comlink, fooling with the console control knobs. In a minute, the soldier rose into view once again, hand to his head where he'd been wounded.

"Fighters are everywhere, sir! They've taken us completely by surprise! We'll try to hold them off for as long as we can!" Earth mecha streaked across the screen's starry background, leaving contrails in the night sky. "Please, sir, you must send reinforcements—" And the monitor blanked out.

Khyron frowned. Behind him, one of his shock troopers suggested that the Micronians might be mounting a diversionary raid, but Khyron didn't think them foolish enough to risk such a thing.

"So this is how they answer my demands!" he said, suddenly getting to his feet. "Well, it seems as though our little songbird has outlived her usefulness—to them *and* to us!"

Khyron ordered his troops to their pods and began to suit himself up in Zentraedi armor, bandoliers, and hip belt. Azonia approached him cautiously.

"Khyron, may we please continue the . . . demonstration?"

"Just as soon as I return," he told her firmly. "But why don't you come with us? The Micronians won't stand a chance with you by my side! We'll enjoy a moment's pleasure with them."

Azonia hesitated; it was certainly an inviting notion, but she had been trained to lead, not to follow. Besides, it would mean that one of the troops would have to give up his mecha, and they were looking forward to battle to the last man.

"And what about Minmei?"

Khyron glanced over at the cage he had fashioned and spat.

"We'll deal with her later." He put his arm around Azonia and offered to find her a Battlepod, as if offering to take her on a vacation.

"That would be wonderful!" Azonia gushed.

"We'll share the experience our people love most!"

"Yes, we'll go into battle together!"

"Good." Khyron smiled. "I sense a great victory!"

Outside the hangar theater, the Zentraedi commander lowered himself into a harness seat astride an Officer's Pod, which had been modified to support four top-mounted cannons. The mecha was piloted by a three-man crew of micronized warriors. Somewhat below him, Azonia clambered into one of the standard versions. "Show no mercy!" she shouted to the troops lined up behind them.

Khyron kicked the side of Officer's Pod to signal the pilots to move out. Inside, one of the crewmen asked whether one kick meant "forward" or "reverse."

"Neither, you fool!" said a second. "It means advance to the left."

"What does it matter?" asked the third. "We better do *something* or he'll start screaming at us again."

Sure enough, Khyron opened the hatch to the control room and snarled: "Get moving, you idiots!"

Zentraedi war cries filled the air as Khyron's alliance of troops and mecha charged into the night.

Undiscovered by Khyron's sentries, two members of an RDF long-range reconnaissance team witnessed the charge from their position atop a granite outcropping not far from the hangar theater. They were outfitted in sensor-reflective antirad suits, complete with jetpacks, full helmets, and survival gear. The radio man had raised SDF-2 control.

"Pelican Mother," he whispered. "This is Eyes-Front. The Dark Star has fallen; repeat: The Dark Star has fallen . . ."

"Roger, Eyes-Front, we copy you loud and clear," returned Lisa Hayes. She then switched over to the com net.

"Skull Team, you now have green light, over."

Winging his way toward New Denver in Skull One, Rick copied the message.

"Roger," he told Lisa flatly. "We're going in."

There was so much more she wanted to say, so much more.

Khyron's forces crested a small rise and dropped into a barren hollow in time to see three of their comrades locked in hand-to-hand combat with three RDF Battloids.

"Micronians!" Khyron snarled from his seat. "Prepare to meet your doom!"

Vastly outnumbered, the Battloids turned and fled as expected, but the sight of the three Zentraedi giants fleeing along with them came as a complete surprise. Khyron began to shout: "Where are you going?! We have come to save you!" He didn't bother to repeat himself, though. His warrior sense told him that he'd been led into a trap. Ordering his team to a halt, Khyron spent a moment puzzling out Gloval's move.

Of course! he said to himself. *Gloval had managed to infiltrate his unit with Zentraedi traitors!* Khyron turned in his seat and regarded his forces warily. But there was no time to pick out the good from the bad: On the high ground all around them, Micronian mecha were popping into view.

"Fire!" ordered Khyron, barely getting the command out before the enemy guns opened up. Six of his Battlepods were taken out in an instant, and an explosive close call almost toppled him from his seat.

"*Fire!*" he yelled again, hearing the immediate report of friendly cannons. "*Charge!*"

"Skull Team, this is Pelican Mother: The trap is sprung! Over!"

"Roger, Pelican Mother," Rick's wingman radioed Lisa. "Approaching assault objective."

"Commander Hunter," said Lisa. "That's your signal to begin."

"Roger."

The heck with rules, she told herself. "Be careful, Rick. Khyron left several Battlepods behind to guard the hostages."

"Going in low," he replied, Lisa's last words to him echoing in his mind. *Don't lose your perspective.* But Minmei's voice was running at the same time in wishful daydream thoughts.

It can't end this way, Rick, she was telling him lovingly. *Soon we'll be together.*

Rick's face had a determined look as he nosed the Veritech still lower, the target looming into sight.

Inside the hangar, three Zentraedi giants were playing cards, trying to shake off the buzz from that premature celebration bash. The fork cage was beside them on the table. Before they had time to know what hit them, a Veritech had blown its way into the building, swept-back wings bringing down two soldiers in its flight path.

Three Battlepods guarding the entrance had already been blown to smithereens.

The hangar was pure chaos; every soldier with an autocannon or assault rifle was loosing fire and bolts of deadly energy against the fighter, a bird of prey streaking overhead.

Rick circled the stage, looking for Minmei and Kyle while he dodged steady bursts of ground fire, blinding searchlights in the dark building. In Guardian mode now, he nosedived his mecha to within twenty feet of the floor and made a pass between two Zentraedi, bowling them over with the Veritech's wings. When he put down, a third giant wielding a depleted autocannon rushed at him, connecting once with a blow that narrowly missed the cockpit canopy before Rick dispatched him with a savage thrust of the mecha's metalshod left fist. The warrior was propelled a good three hundred feet to his final resting place.

Rick walked the mecha forward to the cage, pulling off the lid as he dropped the Veritech's radome to the tabletop.

"Minmei, are you all right?!" he called anxiously through the external speakers.

She was standing inside the fork enclosure, somehow tidy-looking and effervescent despite the ordeal she'd suffered through.

"Yes, Rick! I knew you'd come for me!"

"Of course I would."

Looking up at him in the cockpit, she felt her heart suddenly swell with love and longing. Rick was like some guardian angel in her life, always there when she needed him—for support, protection, *affection.* And in that moment, she vowed to act on the strength of these renewed feelings, to demonstrate to him how much he meant to her.

"It's been a . . . long time," she said softly.

But it was doubtful that Rick heard her over Kyle's shouts.

"Will you get us outta here!" he was demanding.

Rick thought the mecha through a series of motions that allowed him to rip open the remainder of the cage, flattening the forks like a hurricane wind. As Minmei and Kyle clambered up the mecha's left hand and arm, Rick raised the base:

"This is Skull Leader, Operation Star-Saver . . . Mission accomplished!"

Lisa Hayes was already on her way to New Denver's theater when word arrived that the two hostages were safe and sound. But no sooner had her plane put down than she began to get an earful of complaints from an infuriated Lynn-Kyle.

"I'm telling you," he was hollering in her ear, "he came blasting in without any regard for our safety!"

Lisa could never figure Kyle out, but she had no patience with anyone who criticized a successful mission—especially when that mission had saved two lives.

Kyle thrust his forefinger at her like a weapon. "That maniac almost got us killed!"

"We executed the mission to the best of our abilities," she countered, angered beyond control. "If Commander Hunter's conduct was unacceptable, then file a report."

"A report?!" Kyle screamed, flexing his hands. "Just lemme get my hands on him!"

Suddenly Minmei was between them, holding her arms out like a crossing guard—a living cross to Kyle's vampire. "Stop it!" she shrieked. "Can't you see that all these people risked their lives for us, you ungrateful oaf!"

Lisa waited for Kyle to deck his cousin, but Rick's equally sudden appearance caught Kyle off guard. The Skull Leader came walking out of the night shadows cast by his crouched Veritech, helmet cradled in his right arm.

"I did it for *you*, Minmei," he said, approaching the three of them. "I sure didn't do it for *Kyle*."

Kyle took a step forward, threateningly. "I'd expect that from you, Hunter." *Now,* Lisa said to herself. *Now all hell is going to break loose.* Things had been building to this showdown for three years . . .

But thankfully, the argument didn't escalate to violence. Quite the opposite: Minmei stepped out from between Kyle and Lisa with a warm "Thank you" for Rick, and he smiled. "I was happy to do it."

She seemed to stand there staring at him for a moment, then broke out into a run that led her straight into his arms.

Lisa heard Rick tell her: "You must know that I'd be willing to risk my life for you again and again." And as Lisa's mouth dropped open, the two of them began twirling around together, sobbing with joy like long-lost lovers.

Just that, in fact.

Elsewhere, Khyron's troops and the Earth Forces were annihilating each other. The last thing the RDF commander had expected was a charge; but then, he had never faced the Backstabber in battle.

Battlepods and Gladiators met head-on, going at it with a ferocity neither side had experienced before. Here, a pod rammed itself into a MAC II cannon, self-destructing on impact, while close by two pods down on their backs and cracked open like eggs fought their assailants with blasts of heat and fire sent blowtorching from their foot thrusters. Azonia, the Protoculture charges of the Officer's Pod weapons system depleted, windmilled the mecha's hand-guns against its Battloid opponent. Zentraedi infantry troops armed with control rods torn from ruined Battlepods dueled Excaliburs, swinging autocannons like baseball bats.

Khyron was still astride his undamaged cannon pod, directing rotating fusillades of fire against ridge guns and attacking mecha. Battloids challenged his position, charging in from all sides and scaling the four-cannon machine to engage him one on one.

He wrestled a gatling away from one of these would-be heros and turned the gun on it, blowing off the top of the pod. As the Battloid hit the ground and exploded, Khyron emptied the gun on a new wave of Micronian mecha, laughing maniacally, as was the Zentraedi way to welcome death.

Khyron was cursing the depleted gatling when one of his micronized crewmen appeared briefly in the cockpit hatchway to inform him that the cannon's Protoculture charge was likewise used up. Distracted, the commander didn't see a second Battloid that had reached the top of the cannon until it was almost too late. He sidestepped the mecha's lunge and knocked it off balance with a gatling blow to the abdomen. But now a third had suddenly appeared behind him, and again he twisted and swung the gun, nailing the mecha with a shot to its chest.

Grel had also survived the initial surprise attack and was contributing his blood lust to the kill zone. Out of weapons charge, he ran his Battlepod at full throttle into the swarm of Battloids attacking his commander's position. But a miscalculation inadvertently brought him crashing against one of the mecha's hand-guns, setting loose the cannon's final charge. The force of the blast threw Grel's Battlepod into a back flip, while the slug itself ripped from the muzzle and blew away the arm of Azonia's Officer's Pod.

Khyron saw her go down in a fiery fall and leaped from the cannon seat to run to her aid. Bolts of energy crisscrossed overhead and explosions erupted around him as he ran, a broken-field runner in hell. A Battloid thought to stop him, but he felled it with a gatling blow to the thing's head.

He lifted the plastron hatch of Azonia's smoldering pod and called out to her, the first time he had ever demonstrated such feeling for one of his own kind. She was lying injured inside, on the brink of unconsciousness, until she saw him and felt the light return to her.

Was she all right? he wanted to know.

She smiled slightly, even though there was nothing good to report; oh, she was unhurt, but the pod's weapons were empty. And it didn't matter, she wanted to tell him, because she had at least lived to experience the joy of battle and the knowledge that he had cared enough to come to her side.

But Khyron surprised her by ordering a retreat.

She got the pod to its feet and scooped Khyron up in its one good arm, running away with him into the dawn light, a badly beaten band of Battlepods trailing behind.

Lisa and Kyle stood silently side by side, identical scowls on their faces, while the happy reunion continued. Lisa was thinking: *We must look like twins.*

She wasn't aware of the female flight officer who approached her from the shuttle plane until she felt the light tap on her shoulder.

"Khyron is in full retreat," the woman reported.

Lisa glanced back at the lovers. The sun was up, and it would have made a pretty picture—the two of them embracing, the Guardian behind them against a powder-blue sky—if only Rick hadn't been a featured subject. But this sudden news had presented her with a way to break it up. After all, it was Rick's *duty* to go after Khyron, wasn't it. *He was the best there was . . .*

If Lisa wrestled with the idea of using her rank to come between them, she didn't show it. She turned to the woman officer and told her to notify Admiral Gloval that she was sending Commander Hunter in to mop up.

With that, she walked over to them, tapping Rick roughly on the shoulder to put a swift end to their lingering kiss. She demonstrated none of the nervous reserve Grel had shown earlier with Khyron and Azonia.

"I hope I'm not interrupting anything *important*, Commander, but Khyron is on the run, and Skull has been ordered to give pursuit."

"Huh?" Minmei said, as if waking from a dream.

Rick shot Lisa an angry look. "I almost didn't make it back the *first* time—isn't that enough for you?!"

"Are you refusing orders, mister?!" she said, raising her voice.

Rick threw his helmet to the ground. "You're darn right I'm refusing! You want Khyron so bad, you go out and get him!"

"Fine!" Lisa shot back, squatting down to retrieve the helmet. "I'll go bring him in, and you can just go put yourself on report!"

Minmei made a startled sound, looking back and forth

between them. Rick snatched the helmet away from Lisa's grasp.

"Forget it! I've come this far—I might as well finish the job, Captain!"

Lisa berated herself silently. *How could I allow myself to do this to him?* She started to apologize, but he cut her off.

"It's my *duty*, right?!" He turned affectionately to Minmei and told her that he'd be back soon.

"I know you will," she sighed.

Lisa stood with her arms folded, her foot tapping the tarmac fitfully. She wanted to throw up, apologize again, scream, do *something*!

Rick donned the "thinking cap" and made an athletic jump to the lowered nose of the Veritech. As he was snuggling down inside the cockpit, Minmei saluted and said, "I'll be waiting for you."

He returned both her smile and her salute before bringing the canopy down.

The Guardian righted itself as Rick fired up the rear thrusters, and some sort of silent communication passed between Minmei and himself: words and thoughts from the past, suddenly intertwined and confused with these renewed trusts.

Minmei stood unmoving while the Veritech initiated its launch, riding over the barren land on its own blasting carpet. But when it had reached the end of the field, she began to chase after it, shouting out Rick's name, afraid all at once that she would lose him forever.

Lisa took off after her, concerned for her safety. She saw Minmei collapse a short distance off, burying her face in her hands.

CHAPTER FIFTEEN

I don't know who I want to strangle more—Lisa or her idiot flyboy. I only know that if something doesn't put a quick end to this little duet they're dancing, I'm going to get myself transferred to the factory satellite, and I'm going to see to it that Lisa Hayes comes with me.

The Collected Letters of Claudia Grant

THE ISSUE, LISA DECIDED AFTERWARD, WAS CONTROL. It had nothing to do with Minmei, Kyle, or even Rick. She couldn't bring herself to blame him no matter how much effort she put into it; she couldn't accuse him of deceit—he had been honest about his feelings for Minmei all along—lack of consideration, or outright selfishness. Nor was his behavior manipulative or *controlling* in any way. Damn him. That left only herself to blame, unless she could somehow pin the whole thing on *Khyron*!

This made her laugh: Here she was, sitting in the officer's mess feeling like the world was about to end because she and Rick had had another tiff, when *Khyron* was on the loose, kidnapping people, demanding the return of the SDF-1, and threatening to wipe out what little remained of the human race. But her preoccupation with the *little* things didn't surprise her. For what could one person do up against the *big* ones? She played her part, Rick played his; all of them, Minmei included, had roles to enact. Sometimes, though, it felt as if someone else had written the lines they all delivered with such force and passion. But in the end it all came back to control: how she was going to regain control of herself.

Lisa sat there sipping at lukewarm coffee, so wrapped up in replaying dawn's events that she took no notice of Claudia's arrival.

"I thought I might find you in here," her friend said, slipping into the seat opposite her. "Why so glum, chum?"

Lisa looked up, startled and in no mood for good cheer.

"Come on," Claudia pressed. "Tell me what Rick has done now, Lisa."

"Please, Claudia . . ."

"Not in the mood for talk, huh? Well, honey, sometimes it clears the air . . . just helps to get it in the open."

Lisa loved Claudia dearly, but ever since Roy's death she seemed to have become the absolute font of optimism. Whether this was simply *her* way of running from reality—her path of control—Lisa had no idea. Just now she didn't feel like "clearing the air"; instead, she tossed her head back as if to shrug off her dark mood and asked Claudia what made her think she was upset.

Claudia almost smiled. "Uh, woman's intuition. And even if I'm wrong, I want you to try my prescription for pain." She produced a box of blended teas from her jacket pocket and slid it across the table. "Hot tea can do wonders for open wounds."

Indefatigable optimism and a reliance on health potions and panaceas, thought Lisa. But after a moment she surrendered.

"Is it really all that noticeable?"

"Only if someone happens to be glancing in your general direction," Claudia told her. "Or maybe to someone who's been there . . ."

Lisa could only shake her head.

Claudia reached out for Lisa's hand. "I know how it is . . . but you've got to loosen up. Stop trying to control how you feel—just *tell* him."

Claudia stood up.

"What am I supposed to tell him?"

Now Claudia shook her head. "How you *feel* about him, silly."

Lisa thought about it as Claudia walked off. She picked up the package of tea and began to fool with it absently. *Rick Hunter,* she said to herself. *This is the way I feel about you: I-I love you.* Suddenly she gave the box a sort of hopeless toss. Even her inner voice was stammering! This was not going to be easy.

Mirroring the emotional state of its pilot, Skull One came in fast and furious, rocking side to side as it screeched along the *Prometheus*'s flight deck.

Rick was like a raw nerve just waiting to be touched. Effectively he'd been in high gear since leaving the abandoned Zentraedi base over forty-eight hours ago. For the past eight, the squadron had been scouring the countryside for signs of Khyron's forces. Beginning with the site of the surprise attack (now a place of unspeakable carnage, littered with the remains of scores of Battlepods and RDF mecha), Skull Team had traced Khyron's retreat north to yet another hastily abandoned base. Sensor readings indicated that a Zentraedi warship had been launched from the base shortly before Skull's arrival, but there was no trace of its heading or any way to determine the strength of Khyron's remaining army. Given the number of Zentraedi who had deserted the cities, the size of the ship (Zentraedi cruiser class), and the fact that Khyron was in possession of a workable sizing chamber, troop estimates ranged anywhere from one to three thousand.

Then there was Lisa to think about—the other front in this war without end. Bad enough that most of his walking life was spent following orders, but to have to take them from someone who expected to regiment his personal life as well was more than he could stand. Even the memory of Minmei's sweet embrace wasn't enough to wash away dawn's sour start.

"We'll put her away for you, Commander!" one of the ground crew said as Rick was raising the canopy.

It took Rick a second to realize that the man was talking about Skull One. He took a deep breath of fresh air and climbed from the cockpit, dead on his feet.

The ground crew chief called out to him as he was leaving. "Excuse me, sir, but Captain Hayes wants you to report to her as soon as possible."

"Did she say why?" Rick asked him.

"No, sir."

Rick turned and stormed off. It was time to have a showdown with *Captain* Hayes.

Lisa, meanwhile, was at her station in the SDF-2 control room. She had made up her mind to apologize to Rick, perhaps go a step further if her courage held up. Humming to herself now while she toyed with the tea package, she didn't notice Rick's vexed entry. Vanessa, at the adjacent duty station, tried to whisper a warning, but Lisa had turned and caught sight of him, somehow misreading his mood.

"Oh, hello, Rick," she said cheerfully.

He answered her by practically throwing his written report at her. "With my compliments, *Captain.*"

Lisa's eyes went wide; she hadn't anticipated this.

"Will that be all?" he continued in the same sarcastic tone. "I don't want to take up too much of your time."

"Rick, I—"

"I said, will that be all, Captain?"

"What's the matter with you?" She raised her voice, but it came out confused-sounding.

"What's the matter with me?! I come in after chasing Khyron halfway across the continent and the first thing I hear is that I'm supposed to report to you—you think I don't understand military procedure by now, or what?!"

He was standing over her, red-faced and shaking.

"If you'll just give me a chance to explain . . ."

"And another thing." He made a fist. "My personal life is just that—*personal*! D' ya understand, Captain?! I'll speak to whoever I want, whenever and wherever I want!"

So that was it, Lisa thought. He believed that she had manipulated this morning's situation for her own purposes. In other words, her motives had been transparent.

"I understand," she told him meekly.

"Like Vanessa here, for example," Rick added suddenly, walking over to her station. "Am I right or not?"

Vanessa adjusted her glasses, glanced briefly at Lisa,

and slid down in her seat, wanting no part of this. "Uh, I don't really think I'm . . ."

But Rick was bending over her, his hand on the back of her chair, full of false charm. "Hey, why don't we grab a bite to eat?"

Vanessa blanched. "Please," she told him, not wanting to have to state the obvious. "As you can see, I'm still on duty. . ."

"So what? You can still play hooky, can't you?" Rick stole a look at Lisa; she was getting to her feet, her back to both of them.

"If you'll excuse me," Lisa said, "I think I've had enough of this." She was hurt, but at the same time she felt sorry for Rick. That he would stoop to such transparent gestures to get even with her; that he would drag her friend into it; that he was a *man* . . .

When Lisa was out of earshot, Vanessa turned sharply to Rick and told him off. "That was the worst, Hunter. I mean it."

He had an arrogant look on his face. "Oh yeah, why's that?"

Vanessa shook her head in disbelief. "You've been relying on instruments too long, flyboy. Open your eyes: Did you stop to think about how Lisa feels about you?" This was none of her business, and she knew she had no right to be speaking for Lisa, but *somebody* had to get this guy to wise up.

"Feels about me?" Rick was saying as if he couldn't believe what he was hearing. "You gotta be kidding—the only thing Lisa cares about is her job."

Vanessa frowned, and Rick walked off. She gave herself a moment to calm down, then went over to Kim's station to fill her in on this latest chapter in the Hayes-Hunter miniseries.

"What's Lisa's problem?" said Kim after she'd been briefed.

"She doesn't have any problem," Sammie defended her commander. "It was just a lovers' quarrel. It's none of our business."

Vanessa disagreed. "You weren't there. She loves him, but she doesn't have the courage to tell him."

"That's absolutely ridiculous!" said Kim, suddenly angry. "Why doesn't he just be a man about it and tell her how he feels?"

Vanessa gave her a quizzical look. "Has it ever occurred to you that he doesn't share the same feelings? He asked me out, you know."

"Oh, come on," Kim said, dismissing it. "He knows how she feels about him, and he *does* feel the same. He's just being a stubborn idiot."

Vanessa restated her doubt. Sammie, though, had a dreamy look on her face. "Well, if I felt that way about a man, I'd come right out and tell him."

Kim turned to her and laughed. "Yeah, but you do that with almost every man you meet!" This cracked Vanessa up as well. But it didn't last long.

Kim sighed. "The only reason we're laughing is because it isn't happening to us."

Vanessa nodded. "The only other man Lisa ever loved was killed in action."

"This makes me so sad . . ." Sammie said tearfully.

Yeah, Vanessa thought, putting her hand on Sammie's shoulder. *But what would we do for entertainment around here without Lisa and Rick?* What was there in her own life—or in Kim's or Sammie's—that even approximated passion and the dream of a new start? Rico, Konda, and Bron? That was a dead end on several counts. She grew tearful herself, for all of them. For the emptiness at the center of this brave new world they had all been thrown into.

In spite of the threatening skies, Lisa had decided to walk home from the base. The clouds opened up before she had made it halfway to the New Macross burbs, drenching her instantly and chilling her to the bone. A long winter was on its way.

When the world is out of synch with your inner life, you come to think of it as a heartless, godless realm; and yet when it mirrors those thoughts and feelings, you dismiss it as pathetic fallacy.

She stood thinking this to herself in front of Rick's quarters. There were lights on inside, and once she saw his silhouette pass briefly behind the picture window permaglass. It wasn't aimless wandering that had brought her here, but she couldn't summon up the nerve to go up to the door. Rather, she had a peace offering in mind: She'd leave Claudia's tea in Rick's mailbox, go home and phone him, and—

"Planning to drink that tea in the rain?"

All at once there was an umbrella overhead and Claudia was beside her, smiling. "Why don't you go up and knock?"

"He doesn't want to see me," Lisa told her, raising her voice above the sound of the rain.

"You've made up his mind for him, huh? Well, listen, if you're not ready to talk to him right now, why don't you come on over to my place? We'll dry off and talk some—what do you say?"

Lisa hesitated, and Claudia put the umbrella in her hand.

"Well, while you're thinking about it . . ."

"Claudia, I . . ." Lisa began, but her friend was already trotting off. Lisa gave another hopeless glance toward Rick's window and followed after her.

"I've made some nice hot tea," Claudia called out from the kitchen.

Lisa was on the living room sofa towel-drying her hair. Tea sounded all right, but the chill she was feeling ran clear through to her heart. "At the risk of sounding like a pushy guest," she said when Claudia entered with the tea serving, "you wouldn't happen to have anything stronger lying around, would you?"

Claudia's eyebrows went up. "Like what?"

"You hiding any wine around the house?"

A big grin appeared on her friend's handsome face.

"You got it."

"Well, go get it!" Lisa said playfully. She had a low tolerance for alcohol and drugs of any sort, which was both a good and a bad thing: On the one hand, her body simply rebelled at overindulgence, a fact that kept her from turning to drugs for escape in times of stress; while on the other hand, she could count on a little going a long way—one or two drinks and inhibition was a thing of the past. A classic "cheap date," she reminded herself.

"Burgundy all right?"

"Right now I'd settle for Zentraedi zinfandel."

Claudia returned with two wine goblets and sat down facing Lisa on the matching recliner. A framed photo of Roy held center stage on the low table between them. She pulled the cork from the bottle and poured two full glasses. Lisa offered a silent toast and drained the entire glass, sensing an almost instantaneous warmth suffuse her body. She settled back against the couch and smiled at Claudia.

"So how long does it take for the hurting to stop?" she asked her.

"You sound like you're giving up."

"When he came in with his report this morning, I really wanted to apologize, but then, before I could, he started chewing me out."

Claudia refilled Lisa's glass. "What did he say?"

"Only that his personal life was his own business and that I should stay out of it." Again Lisa drained the glass.

"What did you expect?" Claudia was saying. "He doesn't know how you feel about him. You've both shared some ordeals and some close conversation, but as far as he knows, you're just his fellow officer and sometime friend."

"I know . . . I've *tried* to be honest about it . . . but I don't think it would matter anyway."

Claudia had never seen her friend quite so loosened up. Lisa was holding her glass out for yet another refill, but she already looked pretty low-lidded. Claudia didn't want her to get sick or pass out, but she poured a little more burgundy, anyway.

"You don't *know* that it wouldn't matter to him. Stop trying to outguess him all the time. Just do it, Lisa."

Lisa blinked and shook her head. "Okay, toss it up to the wine."

"Fine. But you weren't drinking out there in the rain twenty minutes ago when you decided he wouldn't want to see you . . . The situation's *not* as hopeless as you think—at least the man you love is still alive . . . Of course, I know that you've had that experience also," Claudia was quick to add.

Both women turned to the photo of Roy.

Claudia continued. "When Roy passed away, *this*," she said, holding up her wine, "became a very necessary crutch for me . . . Now, nothing seems to be important anymore."

Lisa was stunned, almost brought back to the edge of sobriety. *But what about all that optimism?* she wanted to ask—all those *teas*? Instead, she said: "There's a difference, anyway . . . You and Roy hit it off from the very start . . . Rick and I were . . . emenies, I mean, enemies." Lisa stopped and took a breath: *"Enemies."*

Claudia chuckled, then grew somber. "It wasn't like that at all—Roy and I were at each other's throats all the time. It nearly drove me crazy."

A second revelation! thought Lisa.

Claudia reached for Roy's photo. "Do you want to laugh? I'll tell ya 'bout him!"

Lisa laughed up front. "Lemme tell ya something—right now I'll take all the laughs I can get!"

Rick was too exhausted to sleep; it was as if he had somehow passed beyond the need for rest. And that cold prewinter rain beating down on the flat roof of his small modular barracks home seemed to be keeping time with his racing heart.

He had tried to focus his thoughts on Khyron's whereabouts; the latest intel reports pointed to a southern route of retreat. But where, Rick had asked himself while pouring over the reports and reworked maps—somewhere in what used to be Mexico, or the decimated Panamanian land bridge, the Amazon jungles, such as they were? Where was he hiding, and what was his next move likely to be? Even Breetai hadn't a clue.

He gave up on this after a while and collapsed on his back to the bed, still in his uniform, hands locked underneath his head.

Why did I have to go and shoot off my big mouth like that? he asked himself, getting at last to the center of his confusion. *The least I could have done was to listen to what she had to say!*

* * *

That tall, blond, smooth-talking, and guitar-strumming Roy Fokker had been a ladies' man came as no surprise to Lisa; but to hear Claudia tell it, he had also been something of a scoundrel and *womanizer.* Lisa had always known Claudia and Roy as the happy couple—this went back to the early days on Macross Island when the SDF-1 was first being rebuilt. But the stories Claudia had regaled her with for the past two hours painted a much different portrait than the one Lisa had imagined.

Claudia met Roy in 1996, during the initial stage of what would come to be called the Global Civil War, when the two of them were stationed together at a top-secret base in Wyoming; Roy the eager young fighter jock, half in love with death and destruction, and Claudia the naive recruit, easily impressed and often taken advantage of. Claudia described an arrogant Roy to Lisa: a whacko flyboy who would be plying her with gifts one week, then showing up for a date with three adoring women in tow the next. A Roy who would down enemy fighters in her honor but who would rarely call in advance to cancel an appointment.

"Talk about a complex personality," Claudia said. "At first I didn't want anything to do with him, and I avoided him as much as possible. I even told him so, point-blank. But . . . it didn't work—Roy Fokker was nothing if not persistent.

"But what I'm trying to tell you is that our first impressions can be all wrong. Roy and I never really *talked* to each other, or said how we actually felt, until it was too late . . . And then he was gone."

Lisa was momentarily confused; then she realized that Claudia was referring not to Roy's death but to his overseas transfer during the Global Civil War.

For over a year Claudia didn't hear from Roy; but ultimately they both wound up on Macross Island soon after the "Visitor" crash landed. Still, it was rough going. Roy now had a new love: Robotechnology—specifically, the Veritech fighters that Dr. Lang's teams of scientists were developing.

"He used to look at those experimental aircraft the way I wished he would look at me," Claudia explained.

She had actually left unopened all the gifts Roy had given her in the old days and returned them to him years later, hoping he would come clean with her about how he felt. But Roy had simply chalked it up to fate, telling her with a shrug, that you couldn't win them all! And it was Claudia who had ended up hurt. On another occasion she saw him dancing and carrying on with three women in a way that suggested that they knew him much more intimately than she did.

But finally—on a rainy night much like tonight, Claudia went on—Roy confessed his love for her. As obsessed as he was with flying and combat, he was equally obsessed with death; he was certain that he would die in a fighter, and it was only Claudia he could talk to about his hidden fears.

"It was quite a revelation for me to realize that underneath all that mechamorph bravado, there was a sensitive human being, full of real dreams and real fears," said Claudia. "Deep down I knew it all along. But look at all the happiness I lost with him just because I wasn't able to say what was in my heart. I just hope that you won't let the same thing happen to you, Lisa."

Lisa polished off the last sip of wine and set her glass on the table, staring at it absently. Rick had never pulled half the stunts Roy had; she at least had that to be thankful for. But in some ways her problems with Rick ran even deeper than Claudia and Roy's: Their arguments centered on issues like . . . competition and control . . . and *Minmei*! Roy had stepped out from behind his mask, but Rick Hunter didn't wear a mask.

The ball remained in Lisa's court, and even now, after all these hours of wine and honest conversation, she still didn't know how to play it.

While Lisa was visiting Claudia's past, Rick was running through his own. He recalled his first exchange with Lisa, when he had called her "an old sourpuss," and their first meeting after he had embarrassed himself in a lingerie shop. Then there were the countless arguments, most of them over the com net, related to procedure and such. Their capture and interrogation on Breetai's flagship. *That first kiss* . . . The decoration that followed their escape, the complex crosscurrents that developed after Lynn-Kyle entered the scene. The time Lisa had visited him in the hospital—after inadvertently shooting him down. Roy's death, and how she had tried to comfort him . . . Ben's death on that horrible afternoon over Ontario . . . The final battle that brought them all together, the way they ran into each other's arms after he had touched down near Alaska Base, thinking themselves the last survivors of their race. And the two long years of Reconstruction following that fateful day. He and Lisa as a team: planning, supervising, rebuilding. She would come over to his quarters for a late-night snack or just hang out and read while he was off somewhere on patrol—often clean up the mess he invariably left behind. And that day not long ago when she had presented him with a picture of her to add to his album . . .

For the first time he felt as though he were seeing the whole progression of their friendship clearly. And isolated from its various backdrops—Minmei, Kyle, the war without end, Reconstruction blues—their relationship suddenly leapt out as the most significant one in his life. What leapt out with equal clarity was that he had been an absolute *fool*!

How, he asked himself now, could he have run that lame number on Vanessa—just to hurt Lisa?! He realized that his stubborn refusal to believe that Lisa was in love with him was all wrapped up in the Minmei dreams he himself perpetuated. Lisa represented a *threat* to those dreams, much as Minmei was a threat to Lisa's dreams. Dawn's harsh words were crystal clear, and so were Rick's thoughts: He jumped out of bed feeling as though he had slept for a month, refreshed and revitalized, with one purpose in mind—to find Lisa.

He grabbed an umbrella and ran through the rain to her place, but she wasn't there. He tried a spot in town she frequented; no one had seen her. He phoned headquarters, and the SDF-2 duty chief told him that Lisa had signed out hours ago . . . That left only one more possibility.

He deposited another token in the pay phone and tapped in the numbers as rapidly as he could.

"You're kidding," Lisa slurred when Claudia informed her that Rick was on the phone.

"He called from across the street." Claudia smiled, recradling the handset.

"You're serious."

"You bet I am." Claudia picked up Fokker's picture and regarded it. "Now I wanna have a drink with this fella," she said. "So don't plan on hanging around here with your friend."

Lisa was suddenly flustered. "What'll I say?"

"What'll you say? If you don't know by now, then we've wasted the whole evening."

In a moment Rick was pounding on the door, and Claudia was handing Lisa yet another box of tea. "Your Prince Charming is here. Now, go on, and take this with you—it's a great little icebreaker."

They walked silently, shoulder to shoulder beneath Rick's umbrella. Lisa was carrying on a running dialogue with herself, and by the looks of it, Rick was too. After all they had been through together, tonight had all the uneasiness of a first date. Something as yet unspoken had altered the way they reacted to each other.

"Uh, you aren't going to be too cold, are you?" Rick asked her.

"Oh, no . . . Are you?"

Rick suggested they call a cab, even though it was only a few blocks to either of their quarters—and that was the general idea, *wasn't it*? She smiled and said that she enjoyed walking.

Rick agreed: *Yeah, it felt good to walk.*

"I walk a lot at night," said Lisa.

"That's great—it's terrific exercise."

Finally, when she couldn't stand the small talk anymore, she said: "Rick. We've got to talk."

They were at the corner nearest his place. Rick gestured. "We could go to my quarters, but I don't have anything to offer you—er, wine or . . ."

She produced the package of tea. "I've got just the thing."

Rick smiled. "You're a lifesaver," he told her.

CHAPTER SIXTEEN

First and foremost we must accept who we are; only then can we gain a clear view of our motives. How well I recall being one of the important *people, and how well I recall the effect that illusory self-image had on my decisions and motivations. Fallen from grace, I was rescued from what might otherwise have been a transparent existence.* Unimportant, *I learned to know myself. This forms the basis for the following lesson.*

Jan Morris, *Solar Seeds, Galactic Guardians*

NOVEMBER 2014 CAME AND WENT, THANKSGIVING for those who remembered it—not in remembrance of the pilgrims, though, but in memory of the feast held two years before, when the SDF-1 returned to its devastated homeworld and founded New Macross. Wild flowers covered the western slopes of the Rockies, and blue skies had become an everyday event. The cities had been peaceful, and there was no further sign of Khyron. Minmei was back on tour.

Rick and Lisa had been seeing a lot of each other. This morning she was in the small kitchen of her quarters, humming to herself while preparing sandwiches and snacks for the picnic she and Rick had planned. On routine patrol only days ago, he had discovered an ideal spot in the nearby forest. Lisa was in high spirits. She had a map of the area spread out on the table. It seemed like months since she had taken personal leave and years since she had done anything like this. And she owed at least some of her happiness to Claudia for getting her to be more honest with Rick; she had told him how special he was, and surprise of surprises, he had said he felt the same way toward her.

In his own quarters a few blocks away, Rick was getting himself ready. Lisa had said she wanted to take care of the food; all he had to do was show up on time. He was certain he could handle that much. It was strange to be out of uniform, almost frightening to contemplate a return to normalcy, days and days of uninterrupted peace. And that very sense of discomfort made him ask himself how similar the Human and Zentraedi races had become: in their own way grown dependent on war.

The phone rang while he was shaving. He turned off the razor and went to answer it, figuring it was Lisa trying to hurry him along.

"I'm almost ready," he said into the handset, not bothering to ask who was on the line. "I'll be there—"

"Hi there, it's me!"

Suddenly uncertain, Rick looked at the phone.

"It's Minmei!"

"Oh, Minmei!" he answered, perking up. "Where've you been?"

"All *over* the place," she said dismissively. "Where are you now?"

Rick looked at the phone again. *"Home."*

Minmei laughed. "Oops, I completely forgot! I called to thank you . . . for saving me and . . . Kyle. I mean it."

"You don't have to thank me, Minmei," Rick said plainly.

After a moment she asked him if he was free for the day. Rick hemmed and hawed but didn't mention the picnic. She was hoping that he could make it over to Monument City—she had a few hours free before tonight's concert.

"I kinda made plans already."

"Oh, please, Rick," she purred. "I'm only here for today, and I'm sure whoever you're going to meet won't mind."

Rick thought back to his conversation with Lisa, how he'd asked her to cancel whatever plans she had made so they could get together for the picnic. He looked at his watch and wondered what sort of last-minute excuse he could come up with. Sickness? A new war?

"Pleease . . ." she repeated.

"Uh, I guess it's okay," he said, relenting. "It's not every day that I get to spend time with you."

"It'll be fun," Minmei said excitedly. "You can see your friend any time, right?"

"Yeah . . ."

"Great! I'll be waiting for you at the airport. And dress up," she told him.

An old school chum showed up, Rick thought, replacing the handset. *Somebody who just wandered in from the wastelands.* Quickly he punched up Lisa's number, but of course she had already left; more than likely she was already at the Secielc coffcc shop waiting foı him. Better to say nothing, he decided at last. Just not show up at all.

There are a hundred reasons why this is a good idea, Rick said to himself as he dropped his fanjet in for a landing on Monument's new strip, not the least of which was the chance to put his little craft through some paces—it had been months since he'd taken it out. And of course it was good for his relationship with Lisa: putting his feelings for Minmei to rest and such. But "sudden business in Monument City" was what he planned to tell Lisa; he promised himself that he would take her on *two* picnics to make up for this.

He cut quite the dashing figure in his new gray jump suit as he jumped from the cockpit. He had changed from denim and flannel to his one and only suit and was wearing it underneath, a black scarf tied around his neck.

"I'm over here, Rick!" Minmei waved from behind the chain-link fence. "How've you been, flyboy?"

He approached her, smiling. She was wearing a tight-fitting sweater and skirt, heels, a large red hat that matched her belt, and big round tinted glasses.

"I don't think I would have recognized you," he confessed.

She laughed. "That's the point, silly."

Rick got out of the jump suit and stowed it in his carry

case, while she ran to the gate, coming around to his side of the fence.

In a moment they were walking arm in arm, not saying much to each other. Rick felt uncomfortable in his button-down shirt and tie but tried not to convey it.

"Listen, Rick," Minmei said at last, biting her lower lip. "I'm sorry to drag you away from your appointment. I hope he wasn't mad at you, whoever he was."

Rick cleared his throat. "Uh, no, *he* wasn't mad . . . I rescheduled my appointment with him . . ." Minmei pressed herself against him, her hand caressing his arm. People were checking them out as they strolled by. "Aren't you worried that someone might recognize you . . . and me, and, er . . ."

"I'm never worried with you," Minmei sighed. She turned him around and reached for the knot in his tie, adjusting it. "I've never seen you in a suit before. You're very handsome—you look important."

Important? he asked himself. He remembered how good it felt to be in denim and flannel—strange but good. And here he was in a suit, wandering around Monument City with a *star* on his arm, looking *important*, and receiving compliments left and right. What did Minmei have in mind? he wondered. Lisa had wanted to picnic and hike.

Minmei had rented a vehicle for them to use. Rick climbed behind the wheel and followed her directions into the city. Monument was about the closest thing Macross had to a sister city. It had been founded by Zentraedi once under Breetai's command, who had rallied around the crashed warship towering out of its lake the way Humans had around Lake Gloval's similarly situated SDF-l. Monument had spearheaded the separatist movement and had recently been the first to be granted autonomy from the Macross Council.

She sensed that she might have done something wrong, but she had only been trying to show him how she felt about him. If flattery wasn't going to work, she had hopes that the restaurant she was leading them to would do it: beautiful view, great food, soft music . . . It was probably more suited to quiet dinners than early lunches, but it had been difficult enough to block out even a few midmorning hours from her busy schedule. And there were only so many excuses she could come up with to convince Kyle that she needed private time.

Chez Mann was an anachronism, a sumptuously decorated theater restaurant with window walls, crystal chandeliers, and tuxedoed waiters, which, for all its pretensions, ended up looking like an airport cafeteria. An arrogant maître d' showed them not to the secluded table Minmei requested but to a deserted-looking one along the window wall, while a lifeless pianist noodled his way soullessly through an old standard.

"Do you like it?" Minmei said when they were seated. "My producer has a friend who's part owner. Movie stars come in here all the time," she continued, pressing her point.

Rick regarded her quizzically. Minmei seemed incapable of accepting the present state of the world. *Movie stars*: There weren't more than a handful of entertainers left on the entire planet, let alone in Monument City! In fact, if anything, the notion of entertainment was reverting back to much earlier forms of story telling and what amounted to religious drama and reenactments.

"Who cares about movie stars?" Rick said harshly.

Minmei smiled at him. "Well, *I'm* a movie star, and you like *me*."

"I liked you *before* you were a star, Minmei."

Her first reaction was to tell him: *I've always been a star*. Miffed, she said: "You mean you don't like me just because I happen to be famous?"

"I like you," he reassured her, but she had already turned her attention to something else. Rick glanced down at his watch and thought again about Lisa. When he looked up, Minmei was sliding a present toward him.

"Just my way of saying thank you, Rick."

He didn't want to accept it. It wasn't, after all, like he'd done her some sort of *favor*. But she insisted, claiming that she had looked all over for something special. Finally, he shrugged and opened the wrapping; inside was a winter scarf of hand-woven alpaca wool, as rare as hen's teeth these days.

He put it around his neck and thanked her. "I'll think of you whenever I wear it."

"It looks good with that suit," she commented, hoping the nervousness she felt wasn't visible. It was so important to her that he understand how she felt.

"Makes me feel like Errol Flynn," Rick joked, striking a pose.

She laughed. "All you need is a sword."

Minmei wanted to reach out and take his hand, but just then the waiter appeared with cocktails and set them on the table. The moment spoiled, she looked across to Rick and said: "Why do waiters always seem to serve people at precisely the wrong time?"

The waiter, a long-haired would-be actor with a pencil-thin mustache who had had a bad morning, returned: "And why is it that movie stars always seem to find something to complain about?"

Rick stifled a laugh, happy to see Minmei taken to task. But it hardly fazed her. He joined her in a toast to "better times" and began to feel suddenly at ease. They began to talk about the old times—for the two of them, a period of scarcely four years. To Rick it felt like yesterday, but Minmei seemed to think those times a million years ago.

"Some things time can't change," Rick said cryptically.

She nodded. "I know. Sometimes I think my feelings haven't changed at all."

It was an equally vague sort of response, and Rick, recalling Minmei's feelings, wasn't sure he wanted things to return to yesteryear. He decided to be straightforward—the way Lisa had been with him recently—just to see where it would lead.

"I still think about you, Minmei," he began. "Sometimes at night, I—"

There was some sort of commotion at the door; the maître d' was shouting, insisting that the man who had shoved his way past him was required to wear a tie before entering. The long-haired man turned out to be Lynn-Kyle.

Both Rick and Minmei had turned their attention to

the scene; now they were staring at each other blankly. Minmei took Rick's hand, squeezing it, her eyes brimming with tears.

"*Please* Rick, you've got to promise me: Whatever he does, whatever he says, you won't interfere."

"But—" he started to protest.

"Promise me!"

Rick's lips became a thin line, and he nodded silently.

In a moment Kyle was standing over Minmei.

"I've been looking all over for you," he said, controlled but obviously angered. "You knew I scheduled a press conference. Come on, we're leaving."

He made a move toward her, but she refused to budge.

"Don't be obstinate, Minmei! Do you realize the strings I had to pull to get those reporters out here today?!"

Rick held himself in check, the scarf still around his neck; Kyle hadn't bothered to acknowledge him. Rick guessed he was still sore about having had to be rescued. *The dirt bag*. Still, this was business, and maybe Kyle had a right to be angry. He decided to help Minmei out by offering to leave. But instead, she put him right in the middle of things.

"We don't have to leave—I'm not going!"

Now Kyle grabbed her by the wrist. "Oh yes you are!"

"Get your hands off!" she retaliated. "You're hurting me, you bully! Who do you think you are, anyway?!"

Surprisingly enough, Kyle backed off, and Rick offered silent thanks to the heavens, because if it had gone on another second, he would have been all over Kyle, promise or no promise, martial arts or no. The piano player had stopped his noodling, the restaurant patrons having found more accessible entertainment.

Kyle grinned knowingly and turned to Rick. "This is how a professional acts . . . Attractive, isn't it?" He swung back to Minmei, raising his voice parentally. "That's enough of your whining! Why don't you try acting your age for once? People are waiting for you!"

Minmei was standing at her place, her fists clenched. She grabbed her cocktail and downed the thing defiantly, shivering and trying to brave it out. Rick looked out the window.

"I'm tipsy..." he heard her say. "I couldn't *possibly* talk to any reporters now."

Kyle issued a low guttural growl, a dangerous signal that Minmei might have overplayed her part. With lightning speed he scooped up the water glass and threw it in her face.

"That oughta sober you up."

Rick was halfway out of his chair, his teeth bared, waiting for the next move. Minmei had begun to sob, and once again Kyle had her by the wrist.

"Now, stop acting foolish and let's go."

Kyle tugged, she followed; then she suddenly turned and shouted for Rick.

"Kyle!" he screamed, expecting him to let go of her and come after him. Kyle, however, chose a subtler way to disarm him.

"Don't you understand, Hunter?" he said, reasonably and in full possession of himself. "She's got too many things that have to be taken care of. It comes with the territory." When he saw Rick relax, he added: "Oh, and don't worry about lunch: We'll cover it—that's what expense accounts are for. Maybe you should just report back to your base, huh? Get back into your uniform or something."

Rick saw Minmei nod to him, sobbing but gesturing that he should do as Kyle said. Kyle tugged at her again, lecturing her about how he had given up everything, how she didn't care about her career anymore. Most of the patrons were bored by now; many had simply gotten up and left the restaurant.

Rick avoided their stares and reached for his drink, fingering the new scarf. *Some swashbuckler,* he said to himself.

It was almost noon, and the Seciele coffee shop was beginning to gear up for lunch, although the majority of its outdoor tables remained empty. The weather had taken a sudden turn, and most people were electing to take indoor seats. Lisa, however, was still at the table she had occupied since nine o'clock. She had already downed four cups of coffee and was sweating despite the sudden chill in the air. There had been no word from Rick, but she had decided to remain in case he tried to get a message through. Obviously he had been called in, but no one at the base knew anything about it or knew where he might be. If there had been an alert, she would also have been notified, but no such orders had been given. Still, Rick's being called in was the only possible explanation.

The good mood she had enjoyed only hours before had long since abandoned her along with the morning's unnatural warmth. Were these quick turnabouts a sign of the times? she questioned—the mood swings, the reversals, the confusion? Only moments ago she had witnessed a small misunderstanding between a pedestrian and a motorist escalate into a violent argument. It made her wonder if Rick had been involved in an accident, perhaps run over!

Anxiously, she checked the time and hurried to the vid-phone. There was no answer at Rick's quarters, so she toned in the base again, contemplating a fall leaf that had blown her way—the closest she might come to nature all day.

"Communications. This is Lieutenant Mitchell."

Lisa identified herself, but before she had an opportunity to inquire about a possible alert, Nikki Mitchell said: "Captain Hayes, I thought you were with Commander Hunter."

Lisa instantly regretted phoning them. Her life had practically become an open book to the SDF-2 control room crew, Vanessa, Sammie, and the rest. It was one of those damned-if-you-do, damned-if-you-don't situations: When she was cool, calm, and collected, Lisa Hayes "the old sourpuss," no one bothered to interfere with her private life; but now that she had taken some of Claudia's advice and was speaking her mind, everyone was tracking her moves as if she was a regular entry in some sort of gossip column contest.

"Aren't you supposed to be on a picnic?" Mitchell asked.

In the background, Lisa could hear Kim say: "I bet

that creep stood her up." Vanessa reinforced it: "See, I told you he wasn't interested in her."

"Shut up!" Nikki yelled, and Lisa held the phone away from her ear. "You two sound like a couple of old hens!"

"And what does that make you—the rooster?" Sammie countered.

Lisa was furious. Not only was her private life being discussed behind her back, but it was being wagered upon and argued about!

"Oh, never mind!" Lisa yelled, and hung up. "Busybodies," she muttered under her breath.

Cut off by the Chez Mann bartender after countless drinks, Rick had drifted back to the right-hand-drive rented vehicle and started out for the airport. The scene that had taken place between Minmei and Kyle now seemed just that: an orchestrated act put on for the public, with a cameo by Rick Hunter, occasional hero. In the end Minmei had chosen to run along with Kyle, and that was all that really mattered: She hadn't changed, and Rick had been a fool to think she could. Presents, wistful walks down memory lane, postrescue embraces: it was all part of her repertoire. And now he had lost her for the umpteenth time and stood up Lisa to boot.

Up ahead of him on the two-lane airport highway was a roadblock manned by a CD corporal wearing a white beret. The road was closed, Rick was informed.

"Is there an alternate route to the airport?" he asked, leaning out the driver's window.

"Airport's closed," said the corporal. "We've got Zentraedi trouble."

"My plane's out there!" Rick shouted, not clear-headed enough to show his ID.

The corporal's hand edged toward his sidearm. "I told you, buddy, the road's closed."

Rick cursed him and stomped on the accelerator. The minivan shot forward, swerving around the barricade, while the sentry drew his weapon. In thinking about it later, Rick would ask himself why he had done this, wondering whether to blame Minmei or the alcohol. In the final analysis, however, he realized that he had done it for Lisa: He was going to have to tell her *something*!

"Damn fool!" the sentry yelled, thinking twice about firing a warning shot and hurrying to his radio phone.

A Battlepod ambled along the runway, destroying grounded Veritechs with blasts from its plastron cannon, while nearby a giant Zentraedi armed with an autocannon picked off fire and rescue vehicles that were tearing across the tarmac en route to crisis points.

"These Micronians are no challenge at all!" he yelled in his own tongue, the lust for battle erasing all memories of his two peaceful years on Earth.

A second giant in Botoru powered armor lifted a fighter from the field, pressed it over his head, and heaved it at a speeding transport truck several hundred feet away. The Veritech fell squarely on the vehicle and exploded, obliterating both.

Veritechs appeared in the skies now, just as Rick was arriving in the minivan. Dodging gatling slugs, he made his way to the CD hangar, showed his ID, suited up, and commandeered an Excalibur. He had counted five giants—all armed with autocannons—a sixth in powered armor, and at least two Battlepods. Whether these were malcontents or members of Khyron's beaten band was immaterial: The CD unit was outpowered. And yet the base commander was giving him a lot of flack about clearance and warning him *not to damage the mecha*! Rick realized that Monument's recently gained autonomy accounted for this, but without a little help, there wasn't going to be much of a Monument left; so he humored the commander, shaking off the last of his alcoholic stupor.

Meanwhile, a Battlepod was holing the passenger terminal with volleys of fire. His ally with the cannon had tired of firing on the private craft and now turned his attention to the terminal. Peering through a horizonal row of permaglass windows, he spied several Micronians huddled together behind the desks of a spacious office—the most laughable sight he had seen all day. It was too easy to blow them away as a group, so he first drove the muzzle of the autocannon through the plate glass to scatter everyone. Only then did he train the weapon on them, bolts of white energy flinging bodies to gruesome deaths.

One of his less exacting comrades emptied his cannon against the building in an effort to collapse the entire wall.

Rick stepped his mecha from the hangar in time to see a pod with its left foot posed above his small fanjet, preparing to stomp it out of existence. He got off a shot without thinking and managed to take the pod's leg off at the knee, sending the mecha backward and down on its back to the field. This captured the attention of the remaining Zentraedis, who swung around to find themselves face to face with two Excaliburs and a Battloid.

"Zentraedi rebels!" Rick yelled through the external net. "Throw down your weapons at once or we will be forced to take immediate action!" He repeated it even as the soldiers and mecha were leveling their weapons against him.

"Prove it!" said one of the giants, a purple faced, blue-haired clone with gorilla features. He gestured to his fellow warrior and opened fire, autocannon slugs raining ineffectively against the armored legs of Rick's Excalibur.

"They're bluffing!" he shouted when his weapon had expended its charge.

Rick smiled madly inside the cockpit. "Give them a demonstration," he ordered.

Suddenly a drum-armed Spartan was looming into view on the other side of the airport terminal. Rick gave the word, and scores of missiles streaked heavenward from the mecha's launch tubes. The three Zentraedi giants tracked their course with frightened eyes and screamed as the missiles plunged homeward, exploding like strings of fireworks at the giants' feet. The three were blown from the strike zone, one flung to his death against a massive conduit, the others gasping for air as paralyzing nerve gas released from the missiles began to sweep over them.

"Move in!" Rick said over the tac net.

Reconfiguring to Guardian mode, the Battleloid went after the remaining Battlepod; but the Zentraedi mecha juked and sidestepped, facing off with Rick's Excalibur instead. Rick dropped his mecha to a crouch and tackled the pod, shearing off one of its legs as it passed overhead. Out of commission, the mecha hit the field with a ground-shaking crash, its severed leg bouncing along with it.

The one giant who had survived the gas was easily dispatched by the second Excalibur, while the Veritech just as easily dropped the alien in powered armor.

Rick ordered the civil defense units to collect the bodies, separate the living from the dead, and lock the former away for interrogation.

"And radio the SDF-2 for me," Rick added as an afterthought. "Make sure you mention that I was here."

With a little luck, Lisa would receive word of the uprising even before he made it back to New Macross.

Lisa had switched over to cocktails, and by the time the robo-waiter cruised over to inform her that outdoor service was being discontinued, she had had so many Bloody Marys that she was seeing red. The waiting game had become some sort of crazed exercise in self-control. She had visions of Rick finding her skeletal remains here, her withered hand permanently affixed to the thermos or the picnic basket. The temperature had fallen a further fifteen degrees since noon, and the wind had picked up, gusting in autumn leaves that swirled around her feet. Once, a puppy had wandered by and she had fed him snacks from the wicker basket. She had been eyed by more than one Veritech jock and coffee shop poet. But now she was ready to throw in the towel. That Rick Hunter had *died* was the only excuse she was ready to accept.

But no sooner did she hear Rick's voice than she went back on her word. He was running up the street toward her, dressed, oddly enough, in his one and only suit and wearing a long scarf around his neck. Hardly the picnic and hiking outfit she had expected, but she decided to at least give him a chance to explain.

"Let's hear it, Rick," she said coolly from her chair.

Rick was panting. "I didn't think you'd still be here

...I checked your quarters first... You see, there was a Zentraedi uprising in Monument and—"

"An uprising?!" Lisa said, surprised. "Is everything all right?"

"Yeah, now it is. But there were a number of deaths and—"

"Wait a minute," she interrupted him. "We have no jurisdiction in Monument. What were you doing there?"

"Well, I... had some official business—"

"Which is why you're wearing your suit, of course."

Rick looked himself over as if noticing the suit for the first time.

"This was for our date."

Lisa laughed. "It was supposed to be a picnic, remember—not a cocktail party."

"Look..."

She made a dismissive gesture and stood up, taking hold of the basket and thermos. "It's too late for a picnic now. And it's a shame, really, because I spent all morning cooking. It's the first time I've had a chance to do that in years."

Rick stammered an apology.

"You should have called me," she told him. "I've been waiting here all day, worried that something had happened to you and figuring you would try to get a message to me somehow. Now you give me this story about an uprising and some mysterious business—"

"There *was* an uprising! Check with the base if you don't believe me. Besides, I did try to call you..."

She threw him a suspicious look. "You're here now. We can at least take a walk."

Lisa didn't hear Rick's sigh of relief. She was too busy concentrating on the fact that he was cozying up to her, draping one end of that scarf around her shoulders. The temperature was continuing to plunge, and there was a winter dampness in the air. She reached up to feel the weave; it was so soft, she touched the cloth to her cheek. And suddenly stopped dead in her tracks.

She might have had a poor memory for faces and two left feet when it came to dancing and a habit of picking derelicts for boyfriends, but one thing she prided herself on was her talent for remembering aromas and tastes. And she sure as heck recognized the perfume on that scarf: *Innocent*—Lynn-Minmei's favorite!

"Take that thing off me, Hunter!" she exclaimed. "You seem to have wrapped it around the wrong person!"

"Lisa, I can explain everything! It's not what you think!" Rick said, as she threw one end of the scarf over his shoulder.

"I recognize the scent, you idiot! So *that* was your official business, huh?" she began to walk away. "And don't bother calling me!"

She shouted it without turning around because she didn't want him to see the tears in her eyes.

Snowflakes had begun to fall.

"Good evening, ladies and gentlemen of Monument City," Lynn-Kyle announced from that city's bandshell by the lake. "Congratulations on your autonomy from the central government. Tonight, in celebration of that event, we have a special treat in store. Minmei has graciously agreed to come and sing for you. Let's all hang *our* hopes for a bright future on her songs . . . And so, let's have a warm welcome . . . for a great talent—*Lynn-Minmei*!"

The audience of mostly Zentraedi giants applauded and cheered as the orchestra commenced the opening bars of "Stagefright." The bandshell blacked out, and Kyle moved off to the wings. On the stage's upper tier, a wide spot found Minmei; she stood unmoving, arms at her sides, the mike dangling from one hand.

Even *after* the song's intro.

Kyle looked up, full of concern. The band had broken into a low-volume vamp, awaiting her entrance. "Minmei, that was your cue!" Kyle whispered. When she didn't respond, he tried another tack. "Quit fooling around! Are you all right?!"

"Yes," she said with a sad smile. The band had broken off altogether now, and murmurs were running through the audience. Some thought it part of the act—a new form of dramatic effect or something—and a rhythmical clapping began, punctuated with shouts of "Minmei! Minmei! Minmei!"

"What's the problem?!" hissed Kyle. "Sing!"

She had one arm across her chest self-protectively and her eyes averted from the audience. Kyle heard her sigh; then she suddenly turned to them. "I'm sorry—I can't perform!"

The clapping died down.

"I won't sing," she continued, on the verge of tears. "I can't perform when my heart is breaking!"

And with that she dropped the mike, turned, and fled. The audience surged forward, refusing to believe this, and Kyle was all at once stunned and worried about a riot. Quickly, he signaled the stage manager to lower the bandshell's eyelidlike curtain.

The audience fell back to watch its descent. And the moment carried with it a discomforting note of finality; the Zentraedi ship in the lake loomed behind the closed bandshell like a spike driven into the all-seeing eye.

Kyle found her on the littered beach behind the bandshell. She was alone, hugging her knees, staring at the ruined Zentraedi ship. He wasn't sure that anything he said would turn the trick. And for the first time he didn't care. She had moved away from him, withdrawn from the high goals they had both set themselves. Unreachable, she had ceased to interest him any longer; she was beyond his control.

"This is all your fault," Minmei said, sensing somehow that he was standing over her. "Since I've been with you, I've lost touch with the things that are really important to me."

Kyle laughed shortly. "You haven't changed a bit, have you? Still the selfish brat! You know, you only think about what *you* want, just like you've done since you were a kid. Well, it's about time you grew up. Don't you have any idea how those people felt when you refused to sing for them tonight? You should've seen their faces . . . They're your fans, and they love you. And what do you do? You go and let them down. That's just like you!"

Minmei struggled with his words, determined not to let Kyle get to her. She knew what he was up to: pulling out all the stops now to convince her to come around. And she knew it would get worse—*uglier.*

"I just can't do it anymore," she said firmly.

Kyle reconfigured his tone. "If you just opened your heart and let the love flow through you, you could be the greatest talent ever. Through your music, we could transcend all the evil in the universe and bring people together... That's a precious gift, Minmei, but it has to be properly presented. That's why I've worked so hard for three years... But now, this is the end. I'm going to take a long trip, and I probably won't see you again—at least not for some time..."

A ferry was crossing the lake, its mournful horn sounding. Minmei clenched her teeth, hating Kyle for his hypocrisy, his years of abuse. He had almost succeeded in dragging her down to that plane of misery and cynicism he lived on—despite the *noble* sound of his words, the *peaceful* thrust of his speeches. And now he was simply going to walk out on her—his standard approach to interpersonal challenge when martial arts wouldn't do it. So of course it was important for him to make her realize that she'd been rotten all along, that he could do nothing with such flimsy stuff, that she was no longer worth the effort. He had done the same thing to his parents.

He had draped his jacket over her shoulders in preparation for a theatrical exit.

"I hope that someday," he was saying, "you can find happiness for yourself. I'll always love you..."

Creep! she was shouting to herself. *Rat! Fool!* But at the same time she seemed to have a vision of him, off somewhere in the wastelands, probably living among the Zentraedi renegades organizing a new movement... perhaps seeing if he could get himself enlarged to their size—a dream at last fulfilled.

A sudden breeze came up, sending watery crests of moonlit brilliance across the waves. She felt a chill run through her, and when she turned, he had disappeared into the night.

CHAPTER SEVENTEEN

The symbolism of the SDF-1 as New Age Ark wasn't lost on the residents and crew of that fortress—Macross, thrice-born city of the stars. *But unlike the Old Testament Ark, which was really Noah's Ark, the dimensional fortress was thought of by some as the savior itself: the reappearance of the culture hero, the second coming, clothed in the guise of technology—Robotechnology—befitting the times, much as the Nazarene was his own world. This, however, remained the stuff of esoteric cults; underneath it all, the old religions continued to thrive. A return to the basics was universally stressed: the original untampered-with versions of creation and regeneration. And even the Zentraedi found their way over to these.*

History of the First Robotech War, Vol. CCXIII

ALTHOUGH DOLZA HAD RAINED DEATH ON THE east and west coasts of the South American continent, the Amazon basin, with its complex river systems and millions upon millions of acres of virgin forest, was left relatively untouched by his deadly storm. Ironically, many of the indigenous people who had once abandoned their dwellings on the jungled shores of those many slow-moving tributaries for the coastal cities had found their way back into that verdant wilderness after the devastating Zentraedi attack. Green hell or green mansion, its untamed prehistoric disorder was currently home to more survivors than ever before.

And among the most recent arrivals was Khyron.

So different from those bleak icebound reaches he had come to hate, this landscape of perpetual murder—where one waged a daily battle for survival, and where pain, misery, and death ruled supreme—it was hardly his world, but it was most certainly his element.

Chased by unrelenting squadrons of Earth Forces mecha, Khyron had been forced to put down here, his own troops reduced to a mere handful, and his cruiser all but depleted of its Protoculture fuel supplies. The small amounts of precious fuel that had spilled from ruptured Protoculture lines had found sympathetic roots in the forest, working vegetal miracles in the thin surface soil—Khyron's ship, wrapped in creepers, tendrils, orchids, and vines, looked as if it had landed there eons ago. But there were things to be thankful for: Some of his troops had served for many months in the Micronian population center factories, learning about that strange custom called "work" and that more important process known as "repair"; moreover, his agents were still at work in the so-called cities of the north, reporting to him on matters of mecha deployment, Protoculture storage, and the growing separatist movement in the Zentraedi cities such as New Detroit and Monument. Soon the time for his reappearance would be at hand . . .

In addition, Khyron learned that scores of Zentraedi ships had crashed in the jungle, and already the survivors of those wrecked ships were finding their way to his new stronghold.

For several weeks the tech crews had worked feverishly to effect repairs on the cruiser's weapons and navigational systems, while squads of giants had scoured the thick forests for food and supplies, often raiding the simple Micronian settlements they stumbled upon. The hot, steamy jungle succeeded in dragging them down to its own primitive levels, *humanizing* them in ways even Khyron didn't notice. Discipline had loosened somewhat, especially with regard to fraternization between males and females and the wearing of uniforms. The men, sometimes stripped to the waist or in tank-top undershirts, grew accustomed to sweating—something new to their bodies, despite their having labored on infernal worlds like Fantoma. And Khyron got used to his troops calling him by name.

"Commander," called one of the techs now. "I can give you auxiliary power."

"Then do it," Khyron told him.

There were four of them in the control center of the cruiser, all in sleeveless T's, enervated by the afternoon heat. The man who had addressed Khyron was seated at one of the many duty station consoles; he engaged a series of switches, and illumination was returned to the bridge.

"Good," Khyron complimented him. He reached for his communicator and inquired after the reflex furnaces.

A tech wearing an earphone, a flex-mike communicator, and a monocular enhancer responded from elsewhere in the ship. He was one of those who had spent more than a year in the New Detroit mecha factories.

"Not yet, Khyron. And probably not at all unless we acquire some Protoculture soon."

"What is the status of the main reactors?" Khyron asked.

"Barely functional. Takeoff is still impossible."

"Not good enough! Is there some way to shunt primary power to one of the smaller ships?"

"Yes . . ." the engine room tech said hesitantly. "But its range would be very limited."

"Enough to get us to New Macross and back?"

"Yes, but—"

"That's all," Khyron said, breaking transmission. He adopted a thoughtful pose for a moment; then, wiping sweat from his brow, he turned to Grel, who was tinkering with a monitor at the opposite end of the control room.

"Grel, are your spies in the Micronian cities to be trusted?"

"I believe so, m'lord," Grel said over his shoulder.

Khyron walked over to him, bending down to repeat his question. Again Grel stated that the agents could be trusted.

"I have a plan . . ." Khyron began. "This 'hollow day' that approaches—"

"'Holiday,' m'lord. A feast day of sorts."

"Holiday," Khyron repeated, trying the word out. "Yes . . . 'Christmas,' you called it. The Micronians will have their minds on celebration."

Grel smiled. "I understand, Commander. It would be an ideal occasion to strike."

"And you're certain about the whereabouts of the

Protoculture matrix, Grel? Because I warn you—if you're not . . ."

Grel swallowed hard. "Certain, m'lord."

Khyron ordered him to open all communications channels within the cruiser. When Grel nodded, Khyron picked up the comlink mike.

"Now hear this," he anounced. "We are mounting a raid on a Micronian population center. Our objective: the Protoculture-matrix drive housed in the storage facility at New Macross. I want all of you to go on standby alert."

Khyron signed off.

"What is this 'Christmas,' Grel?"

Grel raised his eyebrows. "A feast celebrating the creation of one of the Micronian culture heroes, I believe."

"Culture hero?!" Khyron spat. "It is the name 'Khyron' they will speak of after our raid! Khyron the destroyer of worlds!" He threw his head back, laughing maniacally and crushing the communicator in his hand. "Khyron, the *Protoculture* hero!"

"Sometimes I think life was easier when we were Zentraedi," Konda said sadly.

Bron and Rico responded at the same time:

"You don't meant it!"

"We're still Zentraedi, Konda!"

Konda pushed his long lavender hair out of his face and looked at his comrades. "I know that. But I mean when we were soldiers." He turned and motioned to the shelves of Christmas toys that lined the back of their small Park Street stall. "We wouldn't have to worry about selling all this stuff!"

Snow had begun falling on New Macross two hours ago, lending further enchantment to an already cheery and magical Christmas Eve. It was the first snowfall in several weeks, the first Christmas snow many of Macross City's residents had seen in a decade. Shoppers and pedestrians moved along the sidewalks in a kind of wonder, as if questioning their surroundings: Was it possible after four long years of war and suffering that joy was finally returning to their hearts? One could almost feel the radiant warmth of their collective glow.

All except Rico, Konda, and Bron, that is.

Their jobs at the laundry had come to a sudden end months ago, when they had returned from a routine-pickup with a stack of expensive linen sheets, each bearing Lynn-Minmei's indelible ink autograph. There had followed a succession of menial jobs since, culminating with this Park Street stallful of toys—transformable robots, lifelike dolls, and huggable stuffed puppies, all of which had peaked three seasons before and were little more than memorabilia now. They had managed to sell two items during the past week—and that was only by reducing the prices to less than they had paid.

"We just have to learn to be more *aggressive*," Rico said knowingly.

"What d' ya mean?" said Konda.

Rico thought for a moment. "Uh, you know: *forceful*."

Bron looked confused. "Are you *allowed* to do that?"

"That's what someone told me." Rico shrugged.

"Well, okay," Bron echoed, beginning to roll up his sleeves to expose his brawny arms. "But I don't see how we can do that from inside this stall."

"He's right," Konda suddenly agreed. "We should put all these toys in sacks—"

"Like Santa Claus," Bron interjected proudly.

"Right. And take them over to the mall. We'll have more knee room there."

Rico stared at the two of them. "Elbow room, you idiot."

Konda grinned sheepishly. "Whatever."

"I say we do it!" Bron said decisively, slapping his friends on the back. "We'll be the most *aggressive* salesmen in town!"

In the deserted children's playground across from the mall where Park Street emptied into Macross Boulevard, Minmei rocked herself side to side on one of the swings. The newspaper gossip columns were filled with rumors linked to her sudden disappearance from Monument City almost three weeks ago, and this was the first time she had ventured out of the White Dragon since returning to Macross. Even so, she wasn't disguised, dressed in a plain burgundy-colored dress and black sweater barely heavy enough to keep her warm. She reasoned—rightly so—that people wouldn't recognize this *new* Lynn-Minmei, who was as far removed from that eternally optimistic star of stage and screen as one could get.

Singing was a part of her past. So was Kyle and everyone else connected with her career. She had spent a few days with her agent, Vance Hasslewood, after the scene with Kyle, but he wanted to be more to her than a sounding board. So she returned to Uncle Max and Aunt Lena; they took her in with open arms and helped her secure a few moments of peace. But she realized she wouldn't be able to remain with them: One day Kyle would wander in, and she didn't want to be around when he did.

If only it weren't Christmas, she kept telling herself. If only it were summer, if only everyone else didn't seem so *happy* and complacent, if only...

She stretched her hand out to collect some snow, and as the flakes melted against her warm skin, she thought about Rick. Where was he now? Would he even be willing to talk to her after what had happened in the restaurant? He was probably off having a wonderful Christmas Eve dinner with someone—that girl Lisa, perhaps. *Everyone had somebody they could turn to.*

Suddenly someone was calling her name. She looked up and saw three men running toward her from the boulevard entrance to the park. One of them, the shortest of the three, was pushing some sort of cart in front of him; the other two were carrying enormous backpacks and bedrolls. All three had on baseball caps and orange jackets, and there was something familiar about them...

"Minmei!" one of them shouted again.

And then she knew. Disguise or no disguise, new Minmei or old, these three would *always* recognize her!

She jumped up from the swing seat and began to run for the street.

Rico, Konda, and Bron gave chase, but encumbered by the toy sacks, backpacks, and such, they couldn't keep up with her.

"Minmei!" Rico called again, out of breath.

Aggressive sales tactics had gotten them thrown out of

the mall—they'd actually been grabbing kids and forcing toys upon them—and so they had wandered over to the park in search of fresh quarry.

"Maybe she didn't hear us," Konda suggested mildly.

"Maybe it wasn't her," said Bron.

Rico nodded. "Couldn't've been. We're her best fans."

Rick was in the kitchen of his quarters, waiting for water to boil, when he heard the television announcement.

"Last night we reported that famed singer and movie star Lynn-Minmei had been taken ill. But we have since learned that she is listed as officially missing, following her hasty departure from Monument City three weeks ago. Official sources believe that this has something to do with the disappearance of Miss Minmei's longtime friend and manager, Lynn-Kyle. There has, however, been no mention of foul play..."

Rick listened for a moment more. He was certain that the two of them had wandered off somewhere together. After what he had witnessed in Chez Mann, it was obvious that Minmei was completely under Kyle's spell. Rick didn't dwell on it, though; people made their own choices in life. Besides, he had problems of his own to dwell on: Lisa would talk to him only over the com net, and even then her tone left no doubt about how she felt toward him. She refused to talk about it, wouldn't so much as have a cup of coffee with him.

The newscaster was saying something about a discovery in the Amazon region when Rick heard the doorbell ring. He threw off his work apron and went to answer it.

It was Minmei, although he almost didn't recognize her. She had a forlorn and downcast look about her, snowflakes like a network of disappearing stars in her dark hair. She asked to come in, not wanting to impose, apologizing for not having called first.

"My friends don't have to call," Rick said, offsetting his initial stammering.

She began to cry, and he held her.

Inside, he put his wool officer's jacket over her shoulders and made some coffee. She sat on the edge of his bed and sipped at her cup, happier by the moment.

"I feel so tired of everything," she told him after explaining her fight with Kyle and her flight from Monument. "I'm sick of being fussed over all the time . . . Now, when I think about my life, I remember the things that I've lost instead of being grateful for what I have. I just don't have anyone to turn to for support anymore."

She was standing by the window now, her back to him, staring out at the snowfall. Rick, on the other hand, was staring at her long bare legs; even while he tried to listen to her complaints, he wondered if she was going to spend the night.

"You've still got your music," he said after a moment, not sure what he meant.

"If that's all I've got, then I don't want to sing anymore."

"Your songs are your life, Minmei."

"My *life* is a song," she demanded, lower lip trembling.

Rick made a face. "You can't be serious."

"I can't perform anymore, Rick."

"It's Kyle, isn't it?"

She frowned at him. "That's not it! I don't care if I ever see him again! We spent all our time together, whether we were working or not. He smothered me with his stupid attempts at affection, then yelled at me when he couldn't control me." Minmei looked hard at Rick. "I have nobody who understands, nobody who'll take the time to listen to me."

Rick resisted a sudden impulse to run. He was aware of what she was leading him into, and even though he'd played this scene through a hundred times before, he didn't want to win her from weakness. As much as he desired her, he didn't want to get her on the rebound from Kyle.

At about the same time Minmei showed up at Rick's door, Lisa was enjoying a holiday eggnog with Claudia, Max, and Miriya at the Setup, a health spa–pub on the boulevard. Later, she cabbed over to Rick's place, told the driver not to wait, and headed for his quarters, leaving footprints in the thin layer of snow.

She had a present for him—a shirt she had shopped long

and hard for, yet another peace offering in the seemingly constant war they waged with each other. She had considered drenching it in her own favorite scent ("SDF No. 5,"Claudia called it) but thought Rick wouldn't appreciate the joke. He had been calling her every other day with one suggestion or another—coffee, a movie, a *picnic*!—and she had turned him down each time. But with some distance from the battleground (her hours at the outdoor table forgotten), and this being holiday time, she decided that the time was right for forgiveness. Rick had been inconsiderate and all, but it probably wouldn't be the last time; and if she was going to make this thing work, she would have to learn not to hold on to her anger.

As she approached the house, she noticed that the front door was ajar. She neared it just as Minmei was saying: "I have nobody who understands, nobody who'll take the time to listen to me." The voice was as recognizable as the perfume.

"None of my friends in the business really know who I *am*," Minmei continued. "You see, Rick, you're the only one who cares. That's why I came: I was wondering if I could stay here for a while."

Lisa sucked in her breath and almost shoved her fist into her mouth. She *knew* she had no right to eavesdrop, but her legs refused to put her in motion.

Minmei was pleading with Rick: "I don't have anyone else to turn to!"

Lisa's life seemed to be hanging in the balance. Then she heard Rick give his okay and felt herself going over the edge. Silently she pulled the door closed and began to run, crying harder with each step. A short distance down the block a man stopped to inquire if she was all right. She turned on him like a harridan, telling him to mind his own business.

Claudia, meanwhile, had been hopping from bar to bar, party to party. Her brother, Vince, and his wife, Dr. Jean Grant, had invited her over for Christmas drinks, but she had declined. Likewise, she had no desire to return to her quarters and confront the intense loneliness that plagued her on each holiday. For all his bravado Roy had had a traditional side that revealed itself on holidays, and they had passed many wonderful moments together: quiet dinners, walks through the snow on moonlit evenings, midnight exchanges of gifts and affection. She saw this same shared magic in the eyes of each couple that passed her on the street, and it wasn't long before she found herself back at the Setup, hoping she would run into a friendly face or two.

The last person she expected to find there was Lisa, but there she was, draped over the bar, an almost empty wine bottle in front of her. She was singing—trying at any rate—one of Minmei's songs, "Stagefright," by the sound of it. Claudia's face dropped, then she gave a small shrug and took the adjacent stool.

"Misery loves company," Lisa slurred, and smiled.

Several hours and countless drinks later, after toasting everyone they knew or had known and solving all the world's problems, they kissed each other good-bye just as the sun was coming up over Lake Gloval. Claudia had the day off, but Lisa had put in for the morning shift. A young staff officer who had been a frequent visitor to their private party ran Lisa over to the SDF-2 in his open-air jeep.

Surprised at how sober she was—figuring she had somehow pierced the hangover envelope—she tried to let herself enjoy the ride, the cold air rushing at her face. But all that seemed to do was sober her to the point where last night's problems had little trouble creeping into her consciousness once again. It was time to give up, she told herself, give up and let Minmei have Rick once and for all.

As Lisa was approaching the command center, she heard Kim and Sammie discussing her—a common enough occurrence these days—so she waited outside the door until they were finished, wondering how much more of this she could stand.

Apparently, word of her all-nighter in the Setup had spread fast. Sammie was saying: "Well, you shouldn't believe everything you hear."

"You'd do the same thing if you wanted to forget him," said Kim, making Lisa think back on the evening to ascertain if she had really done something to be ashamed of. If only she had come into this a little sooner . . .

"Lisa's too nice a person to do something like that!"

"Of course—she's not as perfect as you," Kim teased.

That seemed to take the conversation in a different direction entirely, and a minute or so later Lisa felt safe to enter. Kim, Sammie, and Vanessa were, of course, all smiles by now, but Lisa didn't hold anything against them. Vanessa mentioned a Christmas party, the first Lisa had heard about it.

"You mean no one told you? It's for the bridge. Why don't you invite Rick—I'm sure he'd love to come."

Was Vanessa goading her? Lisa asked herself. "Ah, I don't think he'd be able to make it."

"But he's off today."

"Yeah, but he's at home with a miserable little . . ."

"Oh," said Vanessa. "Sick, huh? Too bad."

Just then the bridge PA came alive. A female voice said:

"This is ground base security! Zentraedi forces are attacking the industrial section! Emergency communiqué to all sectors!"

Khyron's Officer's Pod ran through the streets of New Macross, five tactical pods alongside it. They had entered the city before dawn, submerging themselves in the cold waters of the lake before the early-morning surprise attack. Grel's Battlepod had taken the point, but something was wrong: He had led them past the same storage tanks three times now.

"What are you doing?!" Khyron screamed into his communicator. "You're leading us around in circles!"

"The Protoculture has got to be here somewhere," Grel returned. "My agents—"

"Your agents are idiots! Now listen to me: Your incompetence may end up costing you your life! Now, find it!"

Jeeps and CD vehicles sped through the city announcing the attack and instructing the early-morning crowds to seek shelter immediately. Thus far the Zentraedi were restricting themselves to the storage facilities and factories across the lake, but there was no telling where their blood lust and thirst for destruction would lead.

Max and Miriya were opening presents for Dana when

the alert sounded. They left the baby with their neighbors, the Emersons, and headed for the base, awaiting further instructions from Admiral Gloval's headquarters. It was like old times, after all.

Gloval had been roused from sleep and was now putting in a rare appearance on the SDF-2 bridge. Exedore, recently returned from the Robotech satellite to continue his study of Micronian customs, was by the admiral's side. Surveillance cameras located throughout the industrial sector had captured the Zentraedis' curious movements. Both Gloval and Exedore were in agreement that the Officer's Pod was manned by Khyron.

"They seem to be looking for something," Gloval commented. "There has been very little destruction. Several sentries were killed when the pods made their first appearance, but nothing since."

The micronized Zentraedi adviser nodded his head solemnly. "Correct, Admiral. If this were an attack, he would be concentrating on military targets. Or whatever suits his fancy, as you say. It would be my guess that he is here to obtain the Protoculture he needs for his battlecruiser."

"We'll concentrate our defense in the industrial sector, then."

Exedore concurred. He then glanced about and added in a conspiratorial tone: "May I be permitted to make a suggestion, Admiral?"

Gloval's brow furrowed. "Of course, Exedore."

The Zentraedi said: "Let him find what he's looking for."

Frustrated by Grel's failure to zero in on the storage facility, Khyron left his mecha behind and went into the streets on foot to reconnoiter. He was armed with a single autocannon and his own brand of reckless abandon. He held his ground calmly as Veritechs dove in for strafing runs, picking them from the skies with hardly a lost step.

Across the lake Azonia headed up a diversionary force consisting of powered armor units and Quadrono Battalion Invid scout ships. Someday Earth would see many more of these in the skies . . .

She directed her squadrons against the city proper, successfully drawing off the Veritech teams that were going in after Khyron. The opposing forces met above the lake, filling the chilled air with furious exchanges of heat, harnessed lightning, and swift death. Max was at the center of the sudden hell storm, his blue Veritech reconfigured to Battloid mode, juking and dodging volleys of enemy missiles while his gatling cannon retaliated, spewing transuranic slugs against the invaders. Miriya went wing to wing with him, dropping one, two, then three scout ships and wondering which of the remaining mecha might hold her former commander, Azonia, now Khyron's consort!

Rick, ever the gentleman, had taken the couch. He was aware that Minmei had stood over him in the middle of the night while he pretended to sleep; she had fixed his blankets and smiled at him in the dark. But he hadn't slept well at all; his neck was cramped, his left arm was tingling, and some sort of fireworks had roused him much earlier than he wanted to rise—always the case on a day off.

He went to the window and saw thick columns of smoke in the clear skies above the lake. Quickly he switched on the television, conscious of Minmei's rustling around in the kitchen. Rick was already pulling on his clothes when he heard the announcement from the MBS newscaster, Van Fortespiel, "the Boogieman":

"This special bulletin just in: The Zentaedi attack force is believed to be concentrated in the industrial section of the city. Casualty reports are expected in at any minute now..."

Rick was stunned. "Why wasn't I notified?!" he shouted to the screen, pulling off his V-neck sweater and reaching for his uniform. "Lisa's on command watch—she knew where to find me!"

Minmei waited nervously by the front door. Rick saw her troubled look and tried to reassure her.

"Don't worry—this is routine."

Her eyes were wide with a sudden fear. "If something happened to you, I don't know what I'd do!" She held him. "Please don't let me lose you now that I've finally found you!"

Rick took her face between his hands and kissed her lightly.

"I'll be back soon," was all that he said.

Khyron's years-long familiarity with the Invid Flower of Life had imbued him with senses above and beyond the ordinary, especially when it came to homing in on the Flower itself, or in this case its repressed matrix—Protoculture.

He ripped away the metal chamber's tarpaulin cover and smiled to himself, his heart pounding and blood rushing through his system. "The storage matrix," he murmured aloud.

The cylinder was easily half his height and perhaps twice his weight, but he lifted it easily onto his back nevertheless. Returning to his mecha, he attached servoclamps to the chamber and winched it tight against the underside of the pod.

A savage battle was raging throughout the sector between Battloids and giants, but he put an end to it now by issuing a recall order to his troops. They regrouped and headed out in formation to the southwest.

Airborne in Skull One, Rick received an update from Max and signaled his team of Veritechs to follow his lead.

"Prepare to block their escape route in sector November! We can't let them get away with that Protoculture!"

Max broke off to join Skull, leaving the rest of the scout ships to Miriya and her fighter team.

"It's getting bad back there," he was telling her. But just then his eyes fixed on the Veritech's topographic display. Something massive was putting down in sector N... "A Zentraedi escort ship," he yelled.

Rick saw it land, the escort's four polelike legs spearing through the roofs of buildings and settling deep into tarmac roads. A bizarre-looking ship, shaped like the body of a bloated walrus, with legs that could have been an architect's compass and an enormous rear thruster like some outsize megaphone. Khyron's Battlepods and attack mecha were ascending into its open steel-trap belly, while Battloids and Excaliburs poured ineffectual fire against its armored hull.

"Attention, Micronians!" Khyron's voice suddenly blurted out as the ship began to lift off. "Khyron the Destroyer wants to wish you a merry Christmas, and I send you a special greeting from Santa Claus. May all your foolish hollow-days be as bright as this one! . . ."

New Macross didn't know what had hit it, only that the entire city seemed to go up in flames. Later, piecing together what passed for facts—Khyron's cryptic remarks and the observations of people in the street—evidence would point to a certain sidewalk Santa, an uncommon Santa with empty eyes and skin like polluted clay, a Zentraedi who might had been in radio contact with "the Destroyer" and set off the myriad bombs his agents had planted throughout the city . . .

The Veritechs abandoned their pursuit of the escort ship and returned to Macross to battle the blaze, diving into the citywide inferno again and again with fire-retardant bombs.

By the end of the day, the fires were brought under control and the city began to count its dead. The hospitals were filled to overcrowding, and whatever Christmas spirit remained was more funereal than festive. Still, by nightfall, most families had been reunited and a strange postholocaust calm prevailed. So often destroyed, so often reborn, the people of Macross were hardened survivors, nothing if not adaptable, and well accustomed to death. Church bells sang to one another from distant sectors, carolers took to the streets, and the SDF-2 crew went ahead with its preplanned surprise, lighting the ship with garlands of light, a sacred tree grown from the navel of the world . . .

Rick met briefly with Lisa afterward. He was angry in spite of the exhaustion he felt.

"I talked to Vanessa," he said sharply. "She told me you said I was sick in bed! And you know that's a lie! I should have been notified at the very first scramble alert!"

"I didn't say you were sick," she answered, averting his gaze for a moment. "Anyway, I didn't think you'd want to be disturbed . . ." She waited for his puzzled look, then added: "You should be more discreet when you have people coming over—or at least learn to close your front door . . . I came by last night to say merry Christmas. I know all about Minmei staying with you."

He let it go at that and returned home, entering the house like he was returning from a day at the office, with a cheery "Hi there!" for Minmei, who was visibly overjoyed to see him.

"Thank goodness!" she gushed, wiping tears away.

"I told you I'd come back." He smiled.

She ran off to fix her face. Rick noticed that she had prepared an entire dinner for the two of them—even a white-frosted cake with a candle and a small Santa.

"I made it for you," she said softly, hugging him from behind. "My sweet Rick . . . I was so worried."

Rick was speechless, feeling her pressed up against him like that, too good to be true.

"Do you think you could ever give up your commission with the Defense Force?" she asked him. "Please think about it because I never want to lose you, Rick—never again . . ."

She lit the candle after dinner and wished him a merry Christmas.

"May we have a million more like it," said Rick, the dog fights and fireworks suddenly forgotten.

Minmei sighed and leaned forward, closing her eyes. Rick followed her lead until their lips met . . .

CHAPTER EIGHTEEN

I believe Khyron suspected that Gloval's allowing him to leave Macross with the Protoculture matrix was a form of peace offering. It was Gloval's judgment for deportation as opposed to incarceration; Gloval's way of saying: You have what you need to get home—now leave! *But it remains unfathomable to me that Gloval and Exedore could so misread Khyron at this late stage.* Home—with the imperative unfilled? *Unthinkable. And yet, could the war have ended in any other fashion? . . . I have asked myself over and over again how events might have reshaped themselves had Khyron simply left.*

Rawlins, *Zentraedi Triumvirate: Dolza, Breetai, Khyron*

Vengeance, SNARLED KHYRON.

If there had been doubts regarding Khyron's leadership, the raid on New Macross not only erased them but instilled within his rank and file a sense of loyalty hitherto unknown, even among the Zentraedi. He was "the Destroyer" now, no longer the Backstabber who had sacrificed thousands along his own vainglorious campaign trail. By capturing the Protoculture matrix, he had effected a rescue; he had provided them with the means to take leave of the miserable world that had held them captive these two long years—a way to return home. His troops would have followed him into hell itself . . . And that was precisely where he meant to lead them . . .

"All energy inputs building to operative levels, sir," an engine room tech reported to the observation bubble command center.

"Check the reflex furnaces," Grel shouted into the communicator. He sat rigidly at his duty station, grateful to be alive after the way things had turned out in Macross. Had Khyron failed to find the matrix, Grel wouldn't have survived the day.

The Destroyer himself was pacing the deck, his hands clasped behind his back, the olive-drab campaign cloak swirling as he turned.

"Stable," relayed the engine room tech.

"We have full power," Azonia updated. Seated at the duty station adjacent to Grel's, she too was in full-dress uniform.

Khyron clenched his fists and approached the curved console of the command center. His eyes held a look that went beyond anger. "Excellent!" he hissed. "We will leave immediately to rejoin the Robotech Masters!"

Grel and Azonia were raising their hands in salute when he suddenly added: "But before I leave Earth, *I want to destroy the SDF-1*!"

His subordinates stared at him in disbelief, their protests ignored. The Earth Forces weren't foolish enough to permit a second sneak attack; they would be lying in wait, the guns of their newly constructed fortress primed and aimed! Surely Khyron recognized this, surely he wouldn't allow freedom to slip from their grasp now!

"I will have my final revenge on these Micronians," Grel and Azonia heard him mutter under his breath. Then he turned on them and ordered lift-off. They glanced at each other wordlessly and initiated the launch sequence.

The cruiser shuddered, vibrating to a bone-shaking bass rumble that was more feeling than sound. Protoculture surged through the ship's atrophied systems, empowering the massive reflex furnaces in its holds. Thrusters erupted with nearly volcanic force, inverted against the tangled tenacious growth that was partly of the ship's own creating. The Earth itself sensed the force of the cruiser's withdrawal, replying in kind with tectonic movements created and relayed from deep within its core, the last gasp of some opposing telluric intelligence bent on holding fast its dangerous captive.

But ultimately the powers of evil proved superior and the Destroyer's dreadnought tore loose, taking great hunks of earth and forest with it as it climbed toward freedom and headed north for its rendezvous with vengeance and death.

The end of the world, Lisa cried to herself.

Two weeks had passed since Khyron's Christmas morning attack, and Macross had yet to recover. Initially the residents of that often devastated place had rallied, once again prepared to pick up the pieces of their lives and rebuild the symbol of their dreams. But then a sort of delayed shock set in, sapping even the strongest of the will to prevail. People remained in their homes, leaving the streets deserted, the recent damage untouched; some had even taken up what amounted to residency in the shelters themselves. And yet others fled to other cities or wandered off into the wastes, a new breed of pioneer, abandoning the one thing that had brought salvation and devastation alike—the SDF-1.

Lisa Hayes was on the lookout bridge of the fortress now, her inner world as overturned as that one she glimpsed along the curve of the lake. Rick was lost to her, and his leave-taking had emptied her, much as the city itself. She contemplated the single decision that would free her, sobbing for all that might have been.

"Lisa!" Claudia yelled from behind her.

She wiped her eyes and turned around.

"Admiral Gloval sent me to look for you," her friend told her. "Why aren't you on the bridge?"

"I needed to be alone," she answered, the cold wind mussing her hair. "I'm thinking about resigning."

Claudia had sensed this coming for weeks now but found herself surprised nonetheless. "You've got to be joking," she said plainly.

"No, I'm serious, Claudia." Lisa's voice cracked. "I just can't take it anymore. The army . . . Rick . . . I'm giving up—I'm just not as tough as everybody seems to think I am."

Claudia sized her up for a moment, deciding to get

tough herself. "Come off it, Lisa—you're not fooling anybody but yourself!"

So much for the sympathy, Lisa thought, startled by Claudia's reaction. Maybe she just wasn't explaining all this properly—Claudia wasn't *seeing* it through her eyes.

"You're talking like some silly, simpering, weak sister schoolgirl!" Claudia stepped in to confront her further. "You're a military woman, born, bred, and trained, and you're too much of a scrapper to give in like this without a fight!"

But Lisa held her ground. "There's no use fighting—it all comes down to a battle with myself, Claudia. And I'm losing. If Rick prefers Minmei, that's just the way it is, and there's nothing I can do about it.

"Except *get over it and move on*!" Claudia emphasized. "The military is your *life*, girl. You give up and resign your commission, you might as well throw everything else away."

Lisa's lips narrowed to a thin line. "I have to get away."

"You mean *run* away."

Lisa turned her back to Claudia. "Call it what you want. I can't work with Rick and then watch him go home to *her* every day. If you can't understand that . . ."

He shouldn't have the power over you, Claudia wanted to tell her. *You shouldn't* permit *him that power!* But her heart understood only too clearly. "I do understand," she said quietly.

The loneliness of command, Gloval said to himself for the third time that morning. He wished Exedore hadn't chosen to return to the Robotech factory satellite so soon; he missed him, finding in the gnomish Zentraedi a keen mind unencumbered by emotional restraints. And yet far from being pure intellect, cool and remote like Lang, the man—and Gloval would always refer to him thus—the man had a loyal and unbiased nature, along with a compassion rarely encountered among Humans or aliens alike. The two had forged a unique friendship, built on shared interest, mutual trust, and nothing less than awe for the events that had shaped their histories, both racial and individual.

Gloval was in his favorite chair, the command seat on the SDF-1 bridge, staring out at Macross through the wraparound permaglass bays. Everyone knew to look for him here, more than anything his place of retirement. And indeed, the issue of retirement weighed heavily on his mind; he wanted the untaxed freedom to think back through the past two decades and make personal order out of the chaos he had so often seen there in moments of reflection. He needed to take a hard look at his successes and failures and evaluate his performance record, if for no other reason than to *justify* the decisions that had affected so many lives . . . countless lives.

He recalled saying once that he was allowed to make more mistakes than the rest of the crew, and indeed he had. He only prayed that his latest decisions wouldn't fall into the same category.

When Lisa finally reported to him, he stood and walked to the forward portion of the bridge, his hands behind his back.

"I have called you here to brief you on your new assignment, Captain."

"I'm . . . sorry, sir, but I can't take a new assignment," Lisa told him directly.

Gloval pivoted through his rehearsed turn, raising his voice a notch. "And why not?!"

Lisa's head was bowed. "Sir, I've decided to resign. In my state of mind I'm no good to myself or the service."

"And what state of mind would that be?" Gloval wanted to know.

"I . . . I need to get away for a while, Admiral—for personal reasons."

Gloval beamed. "Well, that's perfect, then, because this assignment calls for a certain amount of travel."

"No, sir." Lisa shook her head. "I'm sorry, sir."

Another tack, Gloval said to himself. "Nonsense. You can't disregard your duty just because of some unrequited romance—you're just going to have to get over it because I need you now more than ever before."

Lisa was staring at him wide-eyed. "You mean, y-you *know*?!"

The admiral made a dismissive gesture. "Good grief, I

have eyes, don't I?! I've probably known about you and Commander Hunter longer than *you* have known!"

Lisa brightened somewhat and smiled. "I'll bet you have, sir . . . This new assignment, then—is it in the way of a favor?"

"Nonsense," Gloval snorted. "You're the most capable and experienced officer in the entire command. The choice was an obvious one."

"Sir . . ."

Gloval cleared his throat. "As you know, construction of the new fortress has just been completed. I want you to command it."

Lisa put her hands to her breast. That she was to command the SDF-2 had been hinted at but never actually stated. "What?! My own command?"

"It's a long-term commitment," he cautioned her.

"I accept—whatever it is."

"Good," he said, asking her to step over to the forward bay. She did so and began to follow his gaze.

Stratified layers of blue sky and crystalline white arced across the eastern horizon. Above this was a darker, more menacing ceiling of swiftly moving storm clouds pierced by brilliant rays of winter sunlight. It was a majestic morning sight, breathtaking.

"Yes," Gloval was saying, "our Earth is a beautiful planet. And we must preserve its glories. That's why I must ask you to leave our world behind for a time."

Lisa experienced a fleeting moment of fear.

"The time has come for humankind to grow up and leave its cradle behind," the admiral explained. "To go forth and claim its place in the universe . . . Your assignment is to lead a diplomatic mission to the homeworld of the Robotech Masters."

"To Tirol, sir?!" Lisa said in disbelief. "But how?"

"That is the new purpose of the SDF-2. Commander Breetai and Exedore will accompany you, although it might be easier to follow Khyron's lead."

Lisa's brow furrowed.

"We let him have that Protoculture matrix for a reason, Captain. I'm only sorry we hadn't anticipated the explosions."

"Khyron's ticket home," Lisa mused. "But why Tirol, Admiral?"

"Because the Human race couldn't possibly survive another holocaust like the last one. Our defense system has been vastly improved, but even that would prove useless against the sophisticated technology of the Masters—or worse yet, to hear Exedore tell it, the Invid. It's essential that we make peace with the Masters, perhaps for the sake of both our races."

"Peace," Lisa said, as though hearing the word for the first time. "And we have to travel clear across the galaxy to secure it."

The downside of getting your wish, thought Rick.

From the picture window of his suburban quarters, he watched a formation of Veritechs streak overhead. He hadn't been airborne in more than a week, having taken the leave to spend time with his new roommate/partner/significant other . . . and that didn't begin to tell the tale of his confusion. As pleasant as it was with Minmei, Rick felt unfulfilled; without flying, without a mission, without something to strive for, it was just the two of them playing house. They would sleep late, cook together, watch the screen, and suddenly there would be nothing to talk about. She had stopped writing love songs, and he had stopped telling tales.

Minmei entered the room just then and seemed to pick up on his distance. Was he tired of her already?

"Rick, why not just quit the service? We could move somewhere else if you want. I mean, could you be happy if we settled down to a normal life?"

"Normal?!" he said, more harshly than he had to. "Take a look outside, Minmei. There isn't any more *normal*!" He shook his head. "I don't think we could even if there was."

"But why not? There's so much more to life than this, and we're missing it."

Rick held his breath, then exhaled slowly through clenched jaws. "People are depending on us. They look to people like me for protection, and to you for inspiration. How can we just walk away from that?"

She put her hand on his shoulder. "Life is funny, isn't it? Nothing turns out the way you think it will . . . When we first met, I was totally caught up in romantic dreams, and some of those actually came true. But not the dream I had for you and me, Rick."

"What *dream*?"

She tried to hold his eyes with hers. "Let's get married."

Rick reacted as if he'd been punched. *Wasn't she listening to anything he said?* . . . But even as he thought this, he knew that it was more black and white than he was making it out to be: Somehow the war and their separate careers weren't the real issues at all. It was something else . . .

When the doorbell rang, both of them jumped up to answer it, thankful for the intrusion. Lisa was standing there demurely, her uniform as bright as the patches of snow on the front lawn.

"I came to say . . . good-bye, Rick. I've received new orders, and I'll be going back into space soon." She pushed on through Rick's surprised reaction, fighting to maintain her even tone. "It's true. I can't believe it, but Admiral Gloval has given me command of the SDF-2." She grew almost cheerful now. "It's like a dream come true. Aren't you happy for me, Rick?"

"When are you leaving?" he asked her anxiously.

"Transfer of the reflex engines from SDF-1 will begin tomorrow. But we're bound for deep space soon afterward. To Tirol, the homeworld of the Robotech Masters. It's going to be a diplomatic mission—a mission of peace."

That could take years! Rick thought.

"So I just wanted to say good-bye and . . . see you in a few years." Lisa smiled at Minmei. "It's been a pleasure, Minmei. Your music has been a great inspiration to all of us."

Minmei thanked her, warily at first but more sincerely when Lisa wished Rick and her happiness in the future.

"I just have one more thing to say," Lisa stammered, her voice failing her all of a sudden. "I love you, Rick! I always have! And I always will!"

Rick was speechless. Minmei had latched on to his arm with a tourniquetlike grip. Lisa was apologizing, holding back tears.

"I may never see him again," she was explaining herself to Minmei. "And I had to tell him... Take care of him for me."

She saluted Rick, turned, and began to run.

Rick stood in the doorway a moment, then shook himself out of his stupor and called for her to wait. He took off down the walk, but Minmei was there in front of him, her arms stretched out to stop him.

"You can't go!" she said in a frightened rush. "What about me?! You've already done *more* than your share! How could you even *think* of going back into space again?!"

"Because . . . they *need* me," Rick lied.

And all at once the sky fell . . .

CHAPTER NINETEEN

Entropy—your belief that systems, biophysical and otherwise, are predestined to move from a state of order to disorder —is the one concept that continues to fascinate me; and I do believe that it has indeed shaped your thinking as a race as powerfully as Protoculture has shaped mine. This dissolution, this winding down... how typical of your thinkers to conjure up such a poetic *ending.*

Exedore, as quoted in Dr. Lăslo Zand, *On Earth as It Is in Hell: Recollections of the Robotech War,*

Good-bye, blue sky, good-bye...

Twentieth-century song lyric

A HAIL OF MISSILES FELL ON UNPREPARED MAcross, turning the sky a radiant yellow and leveling the heart of the city. Rick and Minmei were thrown to the ground by the concussion of a thousand blasts that filled the air with suffocating heat and fiery debris.

When Rick saw that Minmei was unhurt, he began a frantic search along what was left of the street in the direction Lisa had run. The sky was an orange fireball now, much of the city a memory. High-rise towers had crumbled like sand castles; houses imploded. Park Street and Macross Boulevard were buckled and heaved like roller-coaster courses.

Rick heard the high-pitched whine of secondary assaults above the howling of an alien wind; then that deadly thunder returned as explosions continued to punish the city and the surrounding hills.

He found Lisa lying in the street, miraculously alive though the buildings on the block had been utterly destroyed.

"What happened?" she yelled above the firestorm.

"We're under attack!" he returned, helping her to her feet. "The Zentraedi! One ship!"

Khyron! she said to herself. "We've got to get back to the SDF-2!"

Lisa took a step forward and would have collapsed, but Rick held her, his hands under her arms. "You're too weak," he spoke into her ear. "Let me take care of you . . . *I love you!*"

She turned in his arms and took his face between her scorched hands. "Am I dreaming this?" she said weakly.

Minmei was suddenly alongside them, urging them to get to the shelters and pleading with Rick to stay with her.

Projectiles shrieked like banshees in that chrome sky.

"Get yourself to safety!" Lisa told her. "Rick and I have our duty to perform!"

Minmei took a faltering step forward, confused.

"If you really love him," Lisa continued, "let go of him! He's a *pilot*—that's his *life*!"

"Life?" Minmei screamed, hysterical, her arms flailing about. "You call this a *life*?! War! Devastation! Battle after battle until everything is destroyed!"

Rick took her by the arms and tried to calm her, urging her to leave. "We're trying to put an end to all this. We hate it as much as you do, but the future of our race has to be preserved!"

Missiles exploded nearby, raining vengeful lightning on them and erasing words and thoughts. The three of them huddled together, showered by cinders and unheavenly tongues of airborne fire.

Minmei looked at Lisa and Rick, angry now. "There *is* no future!"

Rick turned to leave, and she grabbed hold of him, begging him to remain by her side. *If he loved her, he would stay with her.*

But he shook himself free.

"Someday you'll understand!" he shouted.

"I'll *never* understand!" she screamed to his back.

Lisa entered the bridge of the SDF-2 at a run, making straight for her station. Vanessa was already at her console, the threat screen in front of her flashing with display information.

"Give me a status report!" Lisa ordered.

"A single battlecruiser—ten degrees southwest. Present position twenty-seven miles but closing very fast."

"Right," said Lisa, and reached for the air com net switch . . .

The projecbeam field on the bridge of Khyron's cruiser showed the Micronians' new battle fortress, sitting in its circular puddle back to back with its crippled cousin, the SDF-1—Zor's ship, cause of so much *undoing*.

The Destroyer stood proudly in the observation bubble command center, his facial features distorted by intense hatred.

"The dimensional fortress now coming into range, sir," Grel reported from his station.

"Main gun at full power and standing by," said Azonia.

"My revenge was well worth waiting for! Admiral Gloval is going to wish he'd never heard of me!"

Azonia straightened in her seat. "Awaiting your orders, m'lord."

"Take out the new ship first," he commanded. "Then we'll finish them off. Zor's ship will soon be little more than a footnote in Zentraedi history!"

"Enemy ship still closing!" Sammie told Lisa from her station below the balcony area of the SDF-2 bridge.

Kim suddenly swung from her console screen. "I'm getting high-level radiation readings!"

"Vanessa?" Lisa said, asking for confirmation.

"They're firing on us, Captain!"

Glyphs of unharnessed lightning began to take shape along the blunt bow of Khyron's leviathanlike cruiser, leaping pole to pole across what could almost have been a full-lipped mouth, crowned and underscored with twin-muzzled spiked cannons like tusks on its armored hull. The energy danced and stretched, animated by the Protoculture charges enlivening the dreadnought's weapons systems.

Localized storms were unleashed as the ship tore through the winter clouds above Macross, orange thrusters aft propelling it swiftly toward the lake and the immobile fortresses.

The bolts crackled and hissed in the thin air as the bow began to open, revealing a network of blazing vertical shafts of power, fangs and incisors filed to gleaming points in the mouth of the beast. Ultimately, from somewhere deep within its black heart a cone of blinding light burst forth, spewing from the cruiser and fanning out to encompass the Earth itself, then narrowing and collapsing upon itself as it found its focus. It surged forward across the rooftops of the city, buildings collapsing in its wake, and struck the heart of the fortress, rending the fabric of spacetime on impact and opening gaps into antiworlds.

Colors reversed themselves; what had been light was now darkness, and what had been blackness glowed with an infernal radiance. The heavens rolled and gyrated as though the very stars had been thrown into chaos by the force of the explosion.

"SDF-2 has taken a direct hit!" a hurried and frightened male voice informed Rick over the tac net. "We've lost communications!"

Rick looked over his shoulder, dropping the Veritech's left wing as he turned. Below him Lake Gloval was a caldron of fire and smoke, less a reservoir of water than a volcanic cone. The new fortress was in ruins, holed through and through by the annihilation ray.

"They're listing!" the voice updated. "They're sinking, Captain!"

"Come in, SDF-2," Rick shouted into his helmet mike. "Lisa, do you read me?! Captain Hayes?!" His commo screen was a grid of black and white static, then a vertical column of blue and white bands. "Answer me!" he shouted once again.

Approaching Skull Team from twelve o'clock came an angry flock of Zentraedi mecha, pursuit ships, tri-thrusters, and Battlepods.

Rick locked onto his targets and pulled home the Hotas.

"You'll pay for this!" he snarled through bared teeth.

The rain was harsh but blessedly cool against her raw skin. Why hadn't she thought to include sunscreen in the beach basket? And was Rick as burned as she? . . . The wailing of tortured seabirds was taking her rapidly to the surface of the world, the roughhouse voices of beachgoers at play. . .

Lisa opened her eyes to a close-up view of her console keyboard and touch pads, water cascading between the tabs and puddling on the floor. Her hands were under her face, and the screen in front of her was blank and silent. She raised her head, pushed wet hair from her face, then struggled to her feet to ascertain the extent of the damage to the bridge.

On the floor below the flyout balcony, Sammie and Kim lay sprawled near their duty stations, seemingly dazed but uninjured. Klaxons were sounding throughout the ship, and the overhead fire control system had drenched everyone and everything in the hold. Lisa turned to check on Vanessa before opening the comlink to request assistance.

"Fire control teams needed on levels four through twenty," she managed.

Back at her station, Kim put in a call for medics.

"All section commanders file status reports as soon as possible," Lisa heard Vanessa say.

"Tell 'em we need more help on the flight deck!" a paramedic shouted from the floor.

Kim was working frantically at her controls. "Computer's dead!" she told Lisa. "No manual override. We have no control whatsoever!"

"Losing power, Captain," Vanessa said behind her. "Recommend we abandon ship!"

Lisa's mouth dropped open as she felt the impact of those words and understood what it meant to lose a ship.

She swept her eyes across the bridge: The fortress had taken a direct hit some floors below the control center, but secondary missiles had razed the bridge as well. There were huge holes in the bulkheads behind her, acrid smoke was coiling from the ventilation systems, and for the first time Lisa was aware that the ship was listing hard to starboard.

Think! she screamed to herself, as if to chase the demons of defeat from her mind. *What would Admiral Gloval do in a situation like this?*

She pictured him sitting in the command chair on the SDF-1 bridge, his white cap pulled low on his brow, the tobacco-stained fingers of his right hand gently tugging at the ends of his thick mustache . . . She could almost hear him:

"Lisa, you know that you'll always be able to find me right here."

And suddenly she understood why he had told her this; she understood why he had been absent so often these past months while the SDF-2 was nearing completion, why he had given her command of the fortress . . .

"Of course!" she yelled. She beckoned her bridge crew to follow her and hurried from the control room.

A winding service corridor still connected the two fortresses, a dark and spooky place now, but the four of them barely took notice of its sinister elements as they ran toward the mother ship, Lisa in the lead. Barely breaking stride, she hit the control switch for the bridge hatch, and they rushed in, surprised to find the overhead lights on and the display boards lit. They were equally surprised to find Claudia standing at her forward station, already initiating the lift-off sequence.

"Welcome aboard, ladies," she said calmly and with a hint of humor. "What took you so long?' "

"Don't just stand there," Gloval barked from the command chair. "We have a job to do. Battle stations—everyone!"

Lisa smiled to herself while she and the others hastened to their consoles and screens. So it was true: Gloval had half expected an attack of some sort. He had sworn to Khyron (and the entire crew, for that matter) that the

SDF-1 was nonoperational, when in fact it was not only spaceworthy but armed to the teeth. Robotech crews had to have carried out the top-secret reconstruction months ago, purposely leaving the battered exterior of the fortress untouched.

"What about the main gun, sir?" she asked Gloval.

"Enough power for one firing. We'll have to make sure it's effective."

"Computer countdown is already programmed, sir," Claudia reported.

Gloval called for maximum power on all thrusters.

"Antigrav power levels at optimum capacity," Sammie updated.

"All systems go," said Kim. "Ready for immediate lift-off on commander's mark!"

Claudia tapped commands into her overhead control board.

"Drive system is operational, and the chronometer is running. Four seconds to ignition. Three! Two! One! . . ."

"Take her up!" shouted Gloval, almost rising from his chair . . .

Minmei, her aunt and uncle, Mayor Tommy Luan, and thousands of others were pressed together in Macross's main shelter, an enormous aboveground structure of steel and reinforced concrete that also housed the city's communications system and data storage networks. Minmei had been entertaining everyone with songs and stories. They were all maintaining, despite the despair they felt when word of the destruction of the SDF-2 had reached them. Recent arrivals to the shelter described how that Zentraedi dragon had belched a flow of irresistible force and how the new fortress had slipped like a corpse beneath the frothing surface of Lake Gloval. The crowds in the shelter had keened and offered up their prayers.

But now incredible news had arrived: The SDF-1 was lifting out of the lake! And people all over the city were beginning to leave their shelters, heedless of the burning buildings and ravaged land, the death wind that blew like a gust from hell through the deserted streets. Their guardian was resurrected, and this was all that mattered. Even annihilation itself held no sway.

Minmei, too, left the shelter in time to see the fortress liftoff, parting the water as it rose from the lake, still a gleaming techno-knight despite its sorry appearance. The supercarriers that were its arms were held out in that characteristic gesture of supplication, and already the main guns were elevating into position above the knight's visored helmet . . .

Khyron's cruiser was continuing its deadly descent, disgorging blast after blast of white light from its unholy gullet. Streaks of blue lightning shot from pinpoint gun turrets, while power-armored Zentraedi troops steadfast along the warship's rusted hull loosed cannon fire against the Earth Forces mecha.

Rick skimmed Skull One along the cruiser's organic-looking surface, offing missiles as he broke and climbed across its bow. When the recipients of those Stilletos and Hammerheads exploded beneath him, he threw the fighter into another dive, reconfiguring to Guardian mode as he dropped. The skies were alive with tracer rounds, hell flowers, and annihilation disks. Veritechs and Zentraedi pursuit ships were locked in crazed dogfights amid it all, adding their own slugs and rounds to the chaos, their own deaths to the escalating body count.

In Battloid mode now, legs splayed on the sickly-colored hull and the autocannon at the ready, Rick's mecha emptied his rage at barbed turrets and solitary troops alike. Explosions encircled him, filling the air with white-hot shrapnel. But the great ship held to its course, hurtling toward the lake undeterred.

All at once there was a voice on the com net.

"Rick! Rick Hunter—is that you?!"

"Lisa!" Rick cried. "I must be hearing things!"

"You're not," she told him. "I'm aboard the SDF-1, and we're preparing to fire the main guns. So I strongly suggest you get yourself out of there!"

He was already reaching for his mode selector stick. "You don't have to tell me twice!" he exclaimed, running his mecha along the deck and lifting off.

Rick raised Max and Miriya on the tac net. Wing to wing the three fighters peeled away from the targeted cruiser . . .

"Main gun is in ready position," Claudia announced. "Energy reading at present . . . niner-five-zero."

Lisa ran calculations at the adjacent station, reporting the results. "The admiral was right—that's only enough energy for one shot, so make it a good one!"

Vanessa gave the word: The cruiser was centered in the computer reticle.

"Now, fire!" yelled Gloval . . .

The two columnar towers of the main gun were set in position side by side, a continuous cat's cradle of scintillescent energy uniting them running fore to aft. As Gloval issued the command to fire, the power web seemed to solidify itself for an instant; then the twin-boomed gun blowtorched.

A near hemisphere of incandescence erupted from the fortress, dematerializing the winter clouds and igniting the sky like a second sun. The collective force of an infinity of hyperexcited subatomic particles tore through Khyron's approaching cruiser like a radiant stake driven into its icy heart.

But the cruiser's forward motion was not yet arrested. Flayed of armor and superstructure and trailing a dense pillar of swirling black smoke, it continued to fall . . .

Khyron tasted blood in his mouth. In the dim illumination in the observation bubble provided by the cruiser's auxiliary power system, he traced the blood's course to a deep gash over his left eye. The eye itself was closed, swollen and hemorrhaging in its fractured socket. Azonia was in the command chair beside him, unscathed though the rest of the bridge was in ruin.

"All right," he said, as though taken in by a minor trick, "they've had their fun, and now it's our turn! I'll show them!"

Behind him, both Grel and Gerao had met their deaths. Weapons systems and communications were out;

likewise the computers and projecbeam screens. But the ship's navigationals were alive—the ship itself could be used as a final weapon.

"Now what?" Azonia asked eagerly.

Khyron took the second chair. "They can't erect a defense barrier without any power, correct?!"

"Right! They're helpless! Get them!"

He turned to her and smiled. "We both will," he rasped. "But it requires a sacrifice . . . are you willing to face it with me, Azonia?"

She reached out for his hand. "It will be glorious."

"Yes . . . glorious. Locking on guidance systems, now."

Its power systems depleted, the SDF-1 had dropped back in the lake, helpless.

Vanessa glanced up at the schematics on the threat board. The enemy hadn't altered its course. "It looks like he plans to ram us, sir!"

Gloval turned to Sammie: "Do we have *any* power left?!"

"Not enough to activate the main gun again, sir."

"Kim?" said Gloval.

"Same story here . . . I have no helm control!"

Claudia turned from her station: "Reserves and backups are out."

Gloval stood up. "Ready the ejection modules," he started to say. But Sammie was shaking her head, tears rolling down her freckled face.

"Only module C is operational. The rest are . . ."

Lisa felt her heart begin to race. Everyone looked at each other, saying more with their eyes than would have been possible through words alone. Sammie and Kim were crying, holding each other. Vanessa was tight-lipped, stoic, almost angry.

Lisa saw Claudia and the admiral exchange glances, then suddenly felt her friend's graceful hand on her shoulder.

"Lisa . . ."

Lisa stepped aside and clutched at herself, feeling a wave of hysteria mount inside her. "No!" she screamed.

"Lisa, *yes*!" someone said—it could have been Sammie, or Kim, or Vanessa.

Claudia and Gloval took a step toward her.

She began to shake her head wildly . . .

Max and Miriya, Rick and what remained of the Skull Team, had put several miles between themselves and Khyron's warship. Circling out over the lake, they regrouped and headed home, the SDF-1 at twelve o'clock, now resettled in the choppy waters.

Rick had witnessed the counterstrike leveled against Khyron's vessel and had naturally anticipated its complete destruction. But the cruiser had survived and was locked on a collision course with the dimensional fortress.

The Veritechs began to pour everything they had toward it: missiles, armor-piercing depleted transuranic rounds, heat-seekers, and the rest. Phalanx guns of the SDF-1's close-in weapons system were similarly engaged, challenging the gods with their volleys of thunder and blinding light.

All at once Rick knew in his gut that all the firepower in the world wasn't going to slow that skeletal ship's suicide descent . . .

The cruiser was a fiery javelin in a ballistic fall, called by the Earth's own inherent powers to deadly rendezvous with its techno-savior.

On the bridge of the Zentraedi ship, Khyron and Azonia stood hand in hand facing that *divine wind* in a way only warriors could, victorious in their final moments as much for destroying the object of their years-long pursuit as for the strength of their extraordinary bond, their marriage in death.

Gloval, in his place, hugged his crew to him, stretching his long arms around them all, courageous and loving father, while the Destoyer's warship eclipsed the sky.

The mile-long cruiser rammed into the main guns of the fortress, splintering the twin booms as it continued its dive. Metal shrieked against metal, shafts, connectors, and joints snapping and roaring in protest.

The bow of the leviathan ship forced the booms apart

and impacted against the main body of the SDF-1, shearing off the head and going on to crash and explode once, twice, and again. The fortress took the full power of these against its back and itself exploded, blowing the supercarriers from their mountings and ripping away the battle-scarred armor that had seen so much violence.

The lake boiled, releasing massive clouds of steam into the cold air, and lightning storms appeared spontaneously in the skies overhead.

A fireball rose and mushroomed there, announcing the event to the rest of the world . . .

When the smoke cleared, three ruins stood in the much shallower lake: the burned-out hull of Khyron's cruiser, the remains of the ill-fated SDF-2, and the blackened, headless torso of the original dimensional fortress—monuments to madness.

Most of the city along the lakeshore had been obliterated.

Veritech teams swept the littered waters and frontage lands for survivors but found none.

Rick made a pass over the leveled suburbs where his quarters had once stood—where Lisa and Claudia, Sammie, Vanessa, and Kim had lived; then he flew over the heart of downtown, where survivors were already leaving the shelters.

But there would be no rebuilding this time—not here at any rate. Rick guessed that the area would remain hot for decades to come. Evacuation and relocation of the thousands who had lived through the day would have to commence immediately. No simple task given the extent of the destruction, but there were nearby cities that would lend a hand, and the Earth would prevail, rid of its enemies at last.

He tried not to think about Gloval and the others; this was what waited for all of them at the end of the rainbow.

He piloted his fighter past the lake hulks, circled, and put down in Guardian mode at an intact landing zone not far from the shore. People were beginning to gather, many in shock, others staring at the fortress in stunned silence. He raised the cockpit canopy and climbed out, only to hear a ghost call him by name.

Lisa was walking toward his ship.

Rick approached her cautiously, more than willing to settle for hallucination but worried that real emotion might frighten it off. But the quaking shoulders he touched with his equally anxious hands were flesh and blood, and the feel of her brought him close to fainting.

"At the last moment," Lisa was saying, "Admiral Gloval and . . . Claudia forced me into the ejection module." She regarded the fortress for a moment, silent while tears flowed freely down her cheeks. "They wanted *me* to live . . ." She turned Rick and studied him intensely. "They said that *I* was the only one who still had something to live for!"

Rick held her while she cried, her body convulsing in his arms.

"I thought I'd lost you," he whispered. "Just when I realized how much you mean to me." He tightened his embrace. "You *do* have something to live for—we both do now."

Neither of them heard Minmei approach. Reflexively, they separated when she spoke; but Rick, in a rush, began to stammer an explanation.

Minmei spared him that.

"You're in love with Lisa," she said quietly. "I knew that."

"I would have told you sooner, but . . . I don't think I knew until today." Rick reached for Lisa's hand. "Forgive me, Minmei."

Now Minmei faltered. "Well, uh, only if you can forgive me, Rick. For trying to make you into something you're not. And, uh, for pretending to be something *I'm* not." Rick and Lisa looked confused, so she continued. "You see, I wasn't really that eager to get married. I realized that my music means as much to me as the service does to you."

Lisa seemed to stiffen, somehow able to locate just a hint of anger through her heavy sadness. "Oh, really?" she said flatly.

"My life is music," Minmei said innocently.

Lisa smiled to herself and gave Rick's hand a squeeze. Minmei couldn't bear to admit that she had lost Rick; and why bother to think that when it was so much easier to rearrange the facts? Looking around, Lisa wondered if she could do the same: just pretend all this hadn't happened, see blue skies instead of storms ahead.

"Good luck on your mission, Lisa," Minmei said straight-faced.

As though all this hadn't happened!

"I know you'll be a bigger star than ever by the time we return," Lisa told her, willing to give Minmei's blinder game a try.

Rick, too, wore a slightly puzzled look. But this began to fade when Minmei turned to him, wishing him well and kissing him lightly on the cheek.

"Don't forget me, Rick—you have to promise me you won't!"

"I'll never forget you," he said, meaning it.

She spun on her heel in an almost weightless turn and walked away, stopping once to wave to him before rejoining the crowds of survivors, already welcoming her with open arms.

Snow was beginning to fall. Lisa put her arm through Rick's elbow and snuggled up against him.

"What about our mission, Rick? Is there a chance—even without the SDF-1?"

Rick nodded slowly. He had already given it some thought.

"There's still the factory satellite and Breetai's ship. With his help, and Lang's and Exedore's, we'll make good Admiral Gloval's assignment. We'll reach the Robotech Masters' homeworld before it's too late. This time *peace* comes first."

Mesmerized, Lisa watched the snow begin to blanket the devastated city, the ruined warships that were to be its massive grave markers.

Perhaps Max and Miriya would sign on, she said to herself. Even *Minmei*! What did she care now? It was going to be a diplomatic mission, a proper meeting of two cultures bound to each other by a mysterious past and separated by nearly the breadth of a galaxy.

She looked over at Rick and managed a smile, which he returned though tears filled his eyes.

And if their plan failed for some reason, if it wasn't possible for Breetai's ship to undertake the journey... then other solutions would present themselves. Earth *would* rebuild itself and prevail. Perhaps, she speculated, the Robotech Masters would come here instead...

And as it turned out, new solutions would present themselves. Earth would rebuild and prevail. And as for the Robotech Masters... *come they would!*

The following chapter is a sneak preview of SOUTHERN CROSS—Book VII in the continuing saga of ROBOTECH.

CHAPTER ONE

Those who were surprised at Dana Sterling's choice of a career in the military displayed not only a lack of understanding about Dana, but also a failure to comprehend the nature of Protoculture, and how it shaped destiny.

After all, as a mere babe in arms Dana had played a pivotal part in a vital battle in the First Robotech War, the attack to take the Zentraedi's orbital mecha factory; with two of the greatest fighters in history as parents, is it any surprise that she would follow the warrior's trade?

But more importantly, Dana is the only offspring of a Human/Zentraedi mating on Earth, and the Protoculture was working strongly through her. She is to be a centerpiece of the ongoing conflict the Protoculture has shaped, and that means being a Robotech soldier in excelsis.

Dr. Lazlo Zand, notes for *Event Horizon: Perspectives on Dana Sterling and the Second Robotech War*

IT WAS A DATE THAT EVERY SCHOOLCHILD KNEW, though for some its significance had become a bit blurred.

But not for the people gathered in the auditorium at the Southern Cross Military Academy. Many of the veterans on the speakers' platform and among the academy teaching staff and cadre knew the meaning of the date because they had lived through it. Everyone in the graduating class revered it and the tradition of self-sacrifice and courage it represented—a tradition being passed along to them today.

"Today we celebrate not only your achievements as the first graduating class of the academy," Supreme Commander Leonard was saying, glowering down at the young men and women seated in rows before him. "We also celebrate the memory of the brave people who have served in our planet's defense before you."

Leonard continued, summarizing the last great clash of the Robotech War. If he had stopped in mid-syllable, pointed at any one of the graduating cadets, and asked him or her to take the story from there, the graduate would have done it, with even more detail and accuracy.

They all knew it by heart: how Admiral Henry Gloval had taken the rusting, all-but-decommissioned SDF-1 into the air for a final confrontation with the psychopathic Zentraedi warlord Khyron, and died in the inferno of that battle.

They also knew the high honor roll of the women of the bridge watch who had died with him: Kim Young; Sammie Porter; Vanessa Leeds—all enlisted rating techs scarcely older than any of the cadets—and Lieutenant Commander Claudia Grant.

Sitting at the end of her squad's row, Cadet Major Dana Sterling looked down the line of faces beside her. One, with skin the color of dark honey, stared up into the light from the stage. Dana could see that Bowie Grant—nephew of that same Commander Claudia Grant and Dana's close friend since childhood—betrayed no emotion.

Dana didn't know whether to be content or worried. Carrying the name of a certified UEG hero could be a tough burden to bear, as Dana well knew.

Leonard went on about unselfish acts of heroism and passing the torch to a roomful of cadets, none of whom had yet reached twenty. They had had it all drilled into them for years, and were squirming in their seats, anxious to get moving, to get to their first real assignments.

Or at any rate, *most* felt that way; looking down the line, Dana could see a withdrawn look on Bowie's face.

Leonard, with his bullet-shaped shaved head, massive as a bear and dripping with medals and ribbons, droned on to the end without saying anything new. It was almost silly for him to tell them that the Earth, slowly rebuilding in the seventeen years since the end of the Robotech War—fifteen since Khryon the Backstabber had launched his suicide attack—was a regrettably feudal place. Who would know that better than the young people who had grown up in it?

Or that there must be a devotion to the common good and a commitment to a brighter human future? Who had more commitment than the young men and women sitting there, who had sworn to serve that cause and proved their determination by enduring years of merciless testing and training?

At last, thankfully Leonard was done, and it was time to be sworn in. Dana came to attention with her squad, a unit that had started out company-size three years before.

Dana stood straight and proud, a young woman with a globe of swirling blond hair, medium height for a female cadet, curvaceous in a long-legged way. She was blue-eyed, freckled and pug-nosed, and very tired of being called "cute." Fixed in the yellow mane over her left ear was a fashion accessory appropriate to her time—a hair stay shaped to look like a curve of instrumentation suggesting a half-headset, like a crescent of Robotechnology sculpted from polished onyx.

The first graduating class received their assignments as they went up to the stage to accept their diplomas. Dana found herself holding her breath, hoping, hoping.

Then the Supreme Commander was before her, an overly beefy man whose neck spilled out in rolls above his tight collar. He had flaring brows and a hand that engulfed hers. But despite what the UEG public relations people said about him, she found herself disliking him. Leonard talked a good fight, but had very little real combat experience; he was better at political wheeling and dealing.

Dana was trying to hide her quick, shallow breathing as she went from Leonard's too-moist handshake to the aide whose duty it was to tell the new graduates their first assignments.

The aide frowned at a computer printout. Then he glanced down his nose at Dana, looking her over disapprovingly. "Congratulations. You go the 15th squad, Alpha Tactical Armored Corps," he said with a sniff.

Dana had learned how to hide emotions and reactions

at the academy; she was an old hand at it. So, she didn't squeal with delight or throw her diploma into the air in exultation.

She was in a daze as she filed back to her seat, her squad following behind. The ATACs! The 15th squad! *Hovertanks!*

Let others try for the soft, safe rear-echelon jobs, or the glamorous fighter outfits; nowadays the armored units were the cutting edge of Robotechnology, and the teeth and claws of the United Earth Government's military—the Army of the Southern Cross.

And the 15th had the reputation of being one of the best, if not *the* best. Under their daredevil leader, First Lieutenant Sean Phillips, they had become not only one of the most decorated but also one of the most court-martial-prone outfits around—a real black sheep squad.

Dana figured that was right up her alley. She would have been graduating at the top of her class, with her marks and honors succeeding generations would have found hard to beat, if not for certain pecadillos, disciplinary lapses and scrapes with the MPs. She knew most of it wasn't really her fault, though. The way some people saw it, she had entered the academy with several strikes against her, and she had had to fight against that the whole way.

Cadets who called her "halfbreed" usually found themselves flat on their faces, bleeding, with Dana kneeling on them. Instructors or cadre who treated her like just one more trainee found that they had a bright if impulsive pupil; those who gave any hint of contempt for her parentage found that their rank and station were no protection.

Cadet officers awakened to find themselves hoisted from flagpoles... a cadre sergeant's quarters were mysteriously walled in, sealing him inside... The debutante cotillion of the daughter of a certain colonel was enlivened by a visit from a dozen or so chimps, baboons, and orangutans from the academy's Primate Research Center ... and so on.

Dana reckoned she would fit into the 15th just fine.

She realized with a start that she didn't know where

Bowie was going. She felt a bit ashamed that she had reveled in her own good fortune and forgotten about him.

But when she turned, Bowie was looking up the row at her. He flashed his handsome smile, but there was a resigned look to it. He held his hand up to flash five outspread fingers—once, twice, three times.

Dana caught her breath. *He's pulled assignment to the 15th too!*

Bowie didn't seem to be too elated about it, though. He closed the other fingers of his hand and drew his forefinger across his throat in a silent gesture of doom, watching her sadly.

The rest of the ceremonies seemed to go on forever, but at last the graduates were dismissed for a few brief hours of leave before reporting to their new units.

Somehow Dana lost Bowie in the crush of people. He had no family or friends among the watching crowd; but neither did she. All the blood relatives they had were years-gone on the SDF-3's all-important mission to seek out the Robotech Masters somewhere in the far reaches of the galaxy.

The only adult to whom Dana and Bowie were close, General Rolf Emerson, was conducting an inspection of the orbital defense forces and unable to attend the ceremony. For a time in her childhood, Dana had had three very strange but dear self-appointed godfathers, but they had passed away.

Dana felt a spasm of envy for the ex-cadets who were surrounded by parents and siblings and neighbors. Then she shrugged it off, irritated at herself for the moment's self-pity; Bowie was all the family she had now. She went off to find him.

Even after three years in the academy, Bowie was a cadet private, something he considered a kind of personal mark of pride.

Even so, as an upperclassman he had spacious quarters to himself; there was no shortage of space in the barracks, the size of the class having shrunk drastically since induction day. Of the more than twelve hundred young people who had started in Bowie's class, fewer than two hundred remained. The rest had either flunked out completely and gone home, or turned in an unsatisfactory performance and been reassigned outside the academy.

Many of the latter had been sent either to regional militias, or "retroed" to assorted support and rear echelon jobs. Others had become part of the colossal effort to rebuild and revivify the war-ravaged Earth, a struggle that had lasted for a decade and a half and would no doubt continue for years to come.

But beginning with today's class, academy graduates would begin filling the ranks of the Cosmic Units, Tactical Air Force, Alpha Tactical Armored Corps, and the other components of the Southern Cross. Enrollment would be expanded, and eventually all officers and many of the enlisted and NCO ranks would be people who had attended the academy or another like it.

Robotechnology, especially the second generation brand currently being phased into use, required intense training and practice on the part of human operator-warriors. It was another era in human history when the citizen-soldier had to take a back seat to the professional.

And somehow Bowie—who had never wanted to be a soldier at all—was a member of this new military elite, entrusted with the responsibility of serving and guarding humanity.

Only, I'd be a lot happier playing piano and singing for my supper in some little dive!

Sunk in despair, Bowie found that even his treasured Minmei records couldn't lift his spirits. Hearing her sing "We Will Win" wasn't much help to a young man who didn't want anything to do with battle.

How can I possibly live this life they're forcing on me?

He plucked halfheartedly at his guitar once or twice, but it was no use. He stared out the window at the parade ground, remembering how many disagreeable hours he had spent out there, when the door signal toned. He turned the sound system down, slouched over and hit the door release.

Dana stood there in a parody of a glamour pose, up on the balls of her feet with her hands clasped together behind her blond, puffball hairdo. She batted her lashes at him.

"Well, it's about time, Bowie. How ya doing?" She walked past him into his room, hands still behind her head.

He grunted, adding "Fine," and closing the door.

She laughed as she stood looking out at the parade ground. "Su-ure! Private Grant, who d'you think you're kidding?"

"Okay! So I'm depressed!"

She turned and gave him a little inclination of the head, to acknowledge his honesty. "Thank you! And *why* are you depressed?"

He slumped into a chair, his feet up on a table. "Graduation, I guess."

They both wore form-fitting white uniforms with black boots and black piping reminiscent of a riding outfit. But their cadet unit patches were gone, and Dana's torso harness—a crisscross, flare-shouldered affair of burnt orange leather—carried only the insignia of her brevette rank, second lieutenant, and standard Southern Cross crests. Dark bands above their biceps supported big, dark military brassards that carried the academy's device; those would soon be traded in for ATAC arm brassards.

Dana sat on his bed, ankles crossed, holding the guitar idly. "It's natural to feel a let-down, Bowie; I do, too." She strummed a gentle cord.

"You're just saying that to make me feel better."

"It's the truth! Graduation blues are as old as education." She struck another cord. "Don't feel like smiling? Maybe I should sing for you?"

No!" Dana's playing was passable, but her voice just wasn't right for singing.

He had blurted it out so fast that they both laughed. "Maybe I should tell you a story," she said. "But then, you know all my stories, Bowie." *And all the secrets I've ever been able to tell a full-breed human.*

He nodded; he knew. Most people on Earth knew at least something of Dana's origins—the only known offspring of a Zentraedi-Human mating. Then her parents had gone, as his had, on the SDF-3 expedition.

Bowie smiled at Dana and she smiled back. They were two eighteen-year-olds about to take up the trade of war.

"Bowie," she said gently, "there's more to military life than just maneuvers. You can *make* it more. I'll help you; you'll see!" She sometimes thought secretly that Bowie must wish he had inherited the great size and strength of his father, Vince Grant, rather than the compact grace and good looks of his mother, Jean. Bowic was slightly shorter than Dana, though he was fierce when he had to be.

Bowie let out a long breath, then met her gaze and nodded slowly. Just then, the alert whoopers began sounding.

It sent a cold chill through them both. They knew that not even a martinet like Supreme Commander Leonard would pick this afternoon for a practice drill. The UEG had too much riding on the occasion to end it so abruptly.

But the alternative—it was so grim that Dana didn't even want to think about it. Still, she and Bowie were sworn members of the armed forces, and the call to battle had been sounded.

Dana looked at Bowie; his face registered his dismay. "Red alert! That's us, Bowie! C'mon; follow me!"

He had been through so many drills and practices over the years that it was second nature to him. They dashed for the door, knowing exactly where they must go, what they must do, and superlativel able to do it.

But now, for the first time, they felt a real, icy fear that was not for their own safety or an abstract like their performance in some test. Out in the corridor, Dana and Bowie merged with other graduates dashing along. Duffel bags and B-4 bags were scattered around the various rooms they ran past, clothing and gear strewn everywhere; most of the graduates had been packing to go home for awhile.

Dana and Bowie were sprinting along with a dozen other graduates, then fifty, then more than half of the class. Underclassmen and women streamed from other barracks, racing to their appointed places. Just like a drill.

But Dana could feel it, smell it in the air, and pick it

up through her skin's receptors: there was suddenly something out there to be feared. The cadet days of pretend-war were over forever.

Suddenly, emphatically, Dana felt a deep fear as something she didn't understand stirred inside her. And without warning, she understood exactly how Bowie felt.

The young Robotech fighters—none older than nineteen, some as young as sixteen—poured out of their barracks and formed up to do their duty.

ABOUT THE AUTHOR

Jack McKinney has been a psychiatric aide, fusionrock guitarist and session man, worldwide wilderness guide, and "consultant" to the U.S. Military in Southeast Asia (although they had to draft him for that).

His numerous other works of mainstream and science fiction—novels, radio and television scripts—have been written under various pseudonyms.

He has no fixed address.